FOR THE FATHERLAND

Walter S. Zapotoczny Jr.

ISBN: 1-4392-3592-9
ISBN-13: 9781439235928

Visit www.booksurge.com to order additional copies.

Dedicated to

My parents, Walter and Bertha, whose contributions
and sacrifices during World War II sparked
my interest in History

Acknowledgements

I am grateful to Peter Hewitt in Naples, Florida for his thought-provoking ideas. Special thanks to Ernie Spencer in Walnut Creek, California for his counsel and guidance throughout the process of writing this book.

I have to especially recognize my wife Bonnie. This book would not have been written if it wasn't for her inspiration, story ideas, and candor. To her, I am forever thankful. She was willing to share me with my other love, writing.

Preface

Over the years many national leaders have given lip service to the suggestion that the future of a nation lies with its youth. While they gave lip service, Adolf Hitler passionately believed this and acted on it with greater success than perhaps anyone. His vision of an entire generation of obedient SS officers extending the domination of the Third Reich to the farthest reaches of the world was almost realized.

While Jewish communities existed continuously in Europe for over 2,000 years, their social and religious uniqueness made them constant targets for persecution. The emergence of Christianity as the central religion in Europe intensified their persecution. Since both the religious and political life of Europe became organized around the Christian faith, Jews were seen as outcasts, the deniers and killers of Christ. For over 1,600 years the hatred and persecution of Jews was religiously sanctioned by millions of European Christians. Anti-Semitism increased during the 19th and 20th century industrialization of Europe as Jews participated more directly in the European economic and social life. By the time the Nazis came to power in Germany, the patterns of economic, social, and personal persecution of European Jews were well established. The use of Jews as scapegoats for all of the economic and social problems in Germany eventually resulted in genocide.

The fact of that genocide began not in the camps or in the gas chambers but with four small groups known as the

Einsatzgruppen or Special Action Group. Formed by Heinrich Himmler, *Reichsführer -SS*, and Reinhard Heydrich, head of the Reich Security Main Office, they operated in the territories captured by the German armies with the cooperation of German army units and local militias.

By the spring of 1943, when the Germans began their retreat from Soviet territory, this organization of about 3,000 men had murdered 1.25 million Jews and hundreds of thousands of Polish, Lithuanian, Latvian, Estonian and Soviet nationals, including prisoners of war and Gypsies. Their massacres preceded the invention of the death camps and significantly influenced their development. Their story offers insight into a fundamental Holocaust question of what made it possible for men to kill so many people so ruthlessly.

The culture that was created by the Nazis in Germany permeated all aspects of life. It contributed to the special motivation and actions of a generation who began with camping and singing songs and, for many, ended with mass murder.

This book is an historical fiction novel devoted to the story of a young boy and his friends who grew up in pre-World War II Nazi Germany. The central character became a member of the *Einsatzgruppen*, the purpose of which was simple – eliminate Jews and partisans from the eastern territories and make room for German settlers. They were, for the most part, SS soldiers who believed in their mission and carried out their assignments with vigor and resolve. They were to be Hitler's "makers of a new world."

While this story is set in historical fact, the main characters are fictional. However, they could have been any of the many German youths who grew up during this time. Any resemblance to living or deceased individuals is purely coincidental.

When we look at the horrific actions of the *Einsatzgruppen*, we cannot help but ask how they could have done what they did? This book attempts to explain how it was possible for average youths to be so captured by the Nazi ideals and goals that they could commit cold-blooded murder in the name of a new Germany. This book is not intended to condone or glorify the actions of any of the characters or organizations. Its only purpose is to tell a story and in this way help to us understand how such actions were possible.

As I was conducting the research for this book, I could not help but wonder if what happened in Germany could happen again and if it did, would we recognize it? I kept thinking about Hitler's words:

"I am beginning with the young. We older ones are used up...are rotten to the marrow. We have no unrestrained instincts left. We are cowardly and sentimental. We are bearing the burden of a humiliating past...my magnificent youngsters! Are there finer ones anywhere in the world? Look at these young men and boys! What material! With them, I can make a new world."

– Adolf Hitler, 1939

Chapter One
The Encounter

"Grandpa, how could you have done that?" She shouted. "All these years, I never knew. You never said a word! Mom and Dad never said a word!"

"I had to find out from one of my classmates that you are a mass murderer!"

"Is it true, did you kill all of those women and children? How could you do that?"

Stunned, all I could do was stare at her.

Finally, I managed to speak, "Leni let me explain! You must try to understand! At the time, we thought we were protecting Germany from its enemies...."

She would not listen.

She just kept shouting, "How could you have done those things? You should have been hanged for your crimes! I never want to see you again!"

She stormed out of the apartment slamming the screen door, breaking one of the hinges.

I sat at the table staring at the broken hinge.

The sunlight filled the kitchen from the window behind the sink. It was cold outside and the light warmed the room. The sun warmed the metal kitchen table as I opened a bottle of scotch that was hidden underneath the sink.

Filling a water glass I kept staring at it, as if waiting for some unknown voice to tell me it was okay to drink. Maybe I was waiting for Rolf to tell me that it was okay.

I drank the scotch without stopping and re-filled the glass. My hands were shaking as I kept thinking about Leni. I was devastated by her words that morning. When she walked into the apartment, I could sense that something was wrong. She was not her usual, cheerful self. Her green piercing eyes demanded an explanation.

How had she found out that I was a member of the *Einsatzgruppen*? I guess it was bound to come out. I should have explained everything to her before now. She is seventeen years old and by the time I was that age, I thought I knew what was right for Germany.

The light inside the kitchen was different then when I started drinking. It was changing, getting thinner with the shadows, and becoming longer as the day went on. I hoped that she would come back. I turned on the small lamp with a rose-colored shade. It provided more light as the sunlight faded. The lamp gave the room a reddish glow.

The apartment was becoming cold and the scotch warmed me. It was the first drink I had taken in thirty years. I had worked hard to forget. The memories of the past came rushing back when I drank. I took another drink of scotch and my hands were no longer shaking.

Hours went by and the outside light was almost gone. I could not get Leni's words out of my mind. I walked into the bedroom and found the Luger that I had given Anna so many years ago. I clicked off the safety and walked to the kitchen table. Taking a deep breath, I placed the pistol to my temple.

Then, like waking from a sleep, I thought *what am I doing?*

I had done what was right for my country at the time, hadn't I?

I had paid for what I did, didn't I?

If only Leni knew the whole story!

She could not possibly understand. No one could, unless they were there. Lowering the pistol to the metal kitchen table, I took another drink.

My granddaughter Leni made me forget about all of the killing and suffering of so many years ago. In a way, I was able to make up for all of the pain that I had been part of. I tried to teach her to be compassionate and caring. I taught her tolerance of other people's beliefs and religions. I don't know if I would have been able to live with myself if she hadn't come into my life.

Over the years I often thought *we were Hitler's chosen ones and we had done what he asked. It seemed so clear then.*

Maybe we were all wrong!

I looked forward to Leni's visits and to our walks through the old city of Rothenburg. My son Rolf would bring her to the main gate of the old city where we would meet. He wouldn't stay long. Our relationship had been strained ever since he married. His wife never came to visit. We never talked. She was a product of the new thinking in Germany. She, like many, believed that we who had caused so much suffering should be punished and swept aside and the past was never to be discussed. I guess I had been hiding from the new world and mostly myself here in Rothenburg all these years.

This was a good place to hide.

The tourists were interested in the landmarks, not in old Nazi shopkeepers. I was able to blend in and no one asked any questions. I often wondered how many more like me were living in similar villages all over Germany, just trying to blend in and be forgotten. One didn't talk about these things in the new Germany.

Our apartment was behind the shop and close to the north wall with a small garden off to the side. When Anna was alive, we would grow our own herbs, tomatoes, and lettuce. The garden provided all the vegetables we needed. We kept to ourselves and I ran the business, selling all of the traditional German hats and clothes. Our shop was a very popular shop in Rothenburg and tourists looking for souvenirs made it possible for me to make a good living for us.

I guess Uncle Frederick knew what he was doing when he bought the shop so many years ago.

I had watched Leni grow up. She had grown into a beautiful girl, with long flowing blond hair and sparkling green eyes. I looked forward to her visits and this was Christmas, always a special visit. We would go the Striffler bakery to buy plum cake. They made the best plum cake. It tasted like the cake Mother used to make in Berlin when I was a child. After the bakery, we were off to Kathe Wohlfahrt's Christmas Shop and the Christmas Museum. Then, it was back to the apartment where Anna would have a big meal ready.

Leni liked to climb the old weathered steps inside the city wall and walk around the city on the medieval walkways. She would run through the passage ways, up and down the steps and in and out of the towers. Rothenburg was the perfect playground for a child. Everyone who lived inside the walls knew each other and looked after each other's children. Outside the wall was a new Germany but inside, it was as if time stood still. The cobble stone streets and the old buildings had not changed in eight hundred years. Politics had no meaning in this tourist city. It was a city of the old past and the shops were geared to the rich history of the city.

Located about 70 miles east of Heidelberg, the town's full name is *Rothenburg ob der Tauber*, meaning Red Castle on the Tauber River. Its roots started in the year 970 A.D. when the first castle was built. The last castle was destroyed in the 14th century, and now the town has a garden in its place.

After its heydays ended around 1400, Rothenburg landed in a long slump which actually helped to save its medieval buildings and fortifications. The town has a legend which began in 1631, while the Thirty Years war was raging between Catholics and Protestants.

As the legend goes, Rothenburg, a Protestant town, was about to be overrun by a Catholic army. Just before the carnage was to begin, the Catholic general offered a deal. If anyone could drink a three-liter tankard of wine in one gulp, the town would be spared. Rothenburg's mayor rushed forward to take the challenge. Mayor Nusch grabbed the tankard, gulped down the wine in one gulp, and passed out for three days while the town rejoiced over his extraordinary commitment to civic duty.

This magic moment is immortalized in the clock on the Councilors' Tavern on the *Marktplatz*. At certain hours during the day, the clock's figures reenact Mayor Nusch's sacrificial gulp for his people while the Catholic general eggs him on. Tourists come from all over Europe to see the reenactment. Leni loved to watch the clock figures go through their motions. They were life-like in their movements, twisting and turning as the story unfolded.

The outside light was all gone now and the apartment was chilly. I started a fire in the wood stove and sat back to watch the flames. Father would tell me that the future and the past could be seen in the fire. When I was young, I never understood what he meant. As I got older, the fire became hypnotic and I began to see.

I stared at the dancing yellow and orange fingers, captivated by their movements. The past was in the flames. All one has to do is look for it. For me the flames were a mix of death and destruction and of camp fires and singing. The scenes blended, in and out of each other as if one story was laid over another. I couldn't see the future in the flames, only images of the past.

Anna was gone and now Leni too!

I picked up the pistol again, turning it, looking at it, reading the serial number.

I kept thinking about how nice it was growing up in Berlin, singing, camping, marching, collecting, and attending rallies.

I thought about my friends Rolf, Guenther, and of us going to *Jungvolk* (German Youth) meetings and collecting scrap metal and paper for Hitler.

I was ten years old then.

How wonderful the days of my youth had been.

Guenther, Rolf, and I had fun together. We did everything together. There were the many camping trips, the courage tests, marches, and rallies. They were both dead now. Father, Mother and Anna were dead too.

Everyone was dead!

My son Rolf had his life and wanted nothing to do with me. I began to think that maybe I didn't deserve to live either. I had belonged to an organization that killed thousands of people.

Maybe Leni was right!

Maybe I should have been hanged!

I looked at the pistol lying on the table, trying to decide whether to shoot myself. I took another drink moving to the over-stuffed chair beside the stove. I leaned my head back on a cushion listening to the crackling of the wood and watching the fire. It made ghost-like shadows on the wall. They danced and shifted like the figures in a ballet. My thoughts went back to the Hitler Youth.

I thought about the ideals of our youth.

We were the chosen ones and the future of the Third Reich. Our commitment was to be complete. We would become the master race. The German people would become great in the eyes of the whole world through our achievements. Germans of the future, as they grow up as little boys and Hitler Youth or as young girls and members of the German Girls' League would be educated to recognize German cultural values. We would learn our duties to uphold those values and make Germany great. We would represent the new German order. It was our destiny to show the way.

This is what we believed!

Chapter Two
In the Beginning

Among the many post-World War I political organizations hoping to lead Germany into the future was the German Workers' Party, founded in 1919 in Bavaria and led by young Adolf Hitler. In 1920, he renamed it the National Socialist German Workers' Party commonly called the NSDAP or Nazi Party.

It was cold that morning in Berlin on February 21, 1920 when I was born Kurt Schultheiss. Three days later, in Munich the National Socialist German Workers Party published its first program, officially called the Twenty Five Point Program. Point number four stated, "Only a German can have the right of citizenship. A *Volksgenosse* (Ethnic German) can only be a person who has German parents, irrespective of religion. Therefore, no Jew or Negro can be considered to be a *Volksgenosse*."

In that same year, Adolf Hitler authorized the formation of the Youth League of the Nazi Party. The new Nazi Youth League attracted very few members at first, competing against many other well-established groups.

That year the Paris Peace Conference meetings were held at various locations in and around Paris. Leaders of 32 countries representing about 75 percent of the world's population, attended. The Treaty of Versailles, quickly labeled "the edict" by the German public, galvanized the resentment that had accumulated during The First World War, much of which was turned back on the Weimar Republic itself. People began to blame the hated treaty on the Republic's socialist and democratic creators, whom they accused of having undermined Germany's efforts in the final stages of World War I.

The treaty held Germany solely responsible for World War I. A new map of Europe was carved out of Germany and the German military was non-existent. To the German people the treaty punished them for a war they were not responsible for, but had to fight. Many people asked whether the German army might not have been stabbed in the back by traitors on the home front.

The main terms of the Versailles Treaty were published on the front page of all the newspapers:

1. The surrender of all German colonies as League of Nations mandates.
2. The return of Alsace-Lorraine to France.
3. Cession of Eupen-Malmedy to Belgium, Memel to Lithuania, the Hultschin district to Czechoslovakia, Poznania, parts of East Prussia and Upper Silesia to Poland.
4. Danzig to become a free city.
5. Plebiscites to be held in northern Schleswig to settle the Danish-German frontier.
6. Occupation and special status for the Saar under French control.
7. Demilitarization and a fifteen-year occupation of the Rhineland.
8. German reparations of 20 billion gold marks to be paid on account up to May 1921.
9. A ban on the union of Germany and Austria.
10. An acceptance of Germany's guilt in causing the war.
11. Provision for the trial of the former Kaiser and other war leaders.

12. Limitation of Germany's army to 100,000 men with no conscription, no tanks, no heavy artillery, no poison-gas supplies, no aircraft and no airships.
13. The limitation of the German Navy to vessels under 100,000 tons, with no submarines.

Germany signed the Versailles Treaty under protest. The United States Congress refused to ratify the treaty and many people in France and Britain were angry that there was no trial of the Kaiser or the other war leaders.

Many took seriously the *Protocols of the Learned Elders of Zion*, which suggested that all of recent history, including World War I, resulted from a conspiracy of Jews seeking to control the world. Many people including Henry Ford, the American auto maker, believed the document was factual, as did Adolf Hitler.

For a majority of the middle class living in Germany during the early 1920's they lost all they had worked for and saved. They were resentful but were not exactly sure who to blame.

This was Father's view too.

Before the war, he had been a member of the first German youth movement, founded in 1901 in Stieglitz, a middle-class suburb of Berlin. Calling themselves *Wandervögel*, or hiking birds, they became wary and bored of materialism and the Industrial Revolution. They stressed individualism and wanted to lead their own lives away from homes, parents, and teachers.

Father told how they roamed the countryside, following their own rules of simplicity and honor. They dressed in makeshift clothing, singing rediscovered folksongs, eating simple food by the campfire, and championed a sexually clean life. They were in search of what they called the Blue Flower, a sort of romantic absolute. They were enthralled by mysticism, whose sources they found in the Cossacks of the Russian steppes or in Buddhist priests. Most of this was alien to their parents. When war came, Father and his friends did not hesitate to wholeheartedly embrace Germany's entry into it.

Father explained, "War was viewed by us as highly romanticized combat, and struggle in combat as natural. War was seen as the way to prove ones manhood."

He often talked respectfully of the battle near the Belgian village of Langemarck where, on November 19, 1914, thousands of *Wandervögel* youth, who had voluntarily enlisted, threw themselves against the British. They ran into concentrated machine gun fire and were literally mowed down. The official report said they met a hero's death in the attack, singing the German anthem as they charged forward.

"They were regarded by us as symbols of a tremendous sacrifice for the nation," Father would say proudly.

Father served with distinction and was awarded the Iron Cross in World War I for his bravery at the Battle of Verdun. He wouldn't talk about his actions but instead told us how the men in the trenches lived a life on primitive instincts. They lived constantly with fear, hunger, and thirst. The physical extremes of deafening noises, sudden flashes, and extreme cold and agonizing pain were the way of life.

On almost every day at least some shells would fall on the trenches, killing, maiming or burying a few unfortunate soldiers. I remember Father telling stories about the bravery of his comrades and how the most innocent of natural events, like relieving oneself, could be the cause of intense hardship.

He would tell us how contamination of food, water, tobacco, and equipment by chemical agents emerged as a significant problem for the troops. The scarcity of water often compelled men to risk drinking from a suspicious source. Driven by thirst, Father and a few from his squad ignored the warnings and drank stagnant water from a shell hole. Of all the weapons he talked about, probably the most feared by the soldiers was poison gas. It had a major effect on everyone who participated and had a lasting effect on society.

The use of poison gas deeply effected Father. He would become upset when the topic came up in conversation. He later suffered chest pains from the gas-contaminated water. After being evacuated he eventually returned to his unit after twenty-three days in a base hospital. That is where he met Mother.

Mother was a Red Cross volunteer at the base hospital. She met Father there as he was recuperating from gas exposure. She had seen many like him, and worse, in the hospital. They came in, half blind or their skin eaten away from the gas. Many were shell-shocked. I think her experience deeply affected her attitude about war. Something about him interested her. He seemed kind, almost out of place with the rest of the soldiers. They fell in love and wrote to each other for the rest of the war. They were married not long after Father's discharge from the army.

After I was born, the doctors told Mother that she could not have any more children. I remember when I was older her telling me that my birth was traumatic enough and she didn't want anymore children. She never worked outside our home, choosing to stay home and care for Father and me.

Mother smoked cigarettes at home, a habit that was frowned upon for women at the time. She would not smoke out in public. Cigarette manufactures would include cards with poems, film stars and other novelty items in each pack of cigarettes. The idea was to purchase an album and paste the items in them. Mother collected poems. She had several albums full of poems and would often read the new ones to us at dinner. While she never finished gymnasium (secondary education), she read constantly and taught herself many things. She always had several books scattered throughout the house that she was reading. She knew more about politics then she would often admit.

Mother loved coffee and would grind her own beans, blending different varieties that she would buy at the coffee shop around the corner from our building. The shop had big sacks of raw beans on the floor and shelves behind the counter held cans and prepackaged blends. There was a big roasting machine in the window. The smell of freshly roasted coffee beans permeated not only the inside of the store but drifted outside, enticing people walking by.

Whenever someone would visit she would offer a new blend for the visitor to try. Coffee was always brewing at our house. Mother always wore an apron over a print dress, had a cup of coffee in her hand and a cigarette in her mouth. Her light brown hair was always pulled up in a bun. Whether cleaning, cooking or attending to laundry, the coffee and cigarettes were part of her.

I remember the first time I saw her with make up, her hair down and without the apron, I almost didn't recognize her. She was a different woman, transforming herself into a woman as beautiful as any in Berlin at the time with her long flowing hair and deep brown eyes highlighted by make up and bright red lipstick.

Father was tall and thin with blond hair and blue eyes. He could eat anything and not gain weight although he exercised several times a week, a habit gained from the Army. He didn't smoke but didn't seem to mind Mother's habit. I think he just put up with it and her other eccentricities.

I never heard him complain.

He would often say, "Happy wife, happy life." I don't remember them ever arguing. They would discuss and debate about politics but never argue. I would consider Father conservative and Mother to be liberal, as politics goes.

Father's brother Frederick was the General Manager and part owner of the Lentz Printing Company. He got Father a job as a press operator apprentice. Uncle Frederick had done well during the war. The printing company had most of the government contracts and after the war, the government continued to use them.

Uncle Frederick rented Father and Mother an apartment in a building he and his partners owned on Lehrter Street. The building was three blocks from Tiergarden Park and Unter den Linden, Berlin's most famous boulevard lined with linden trees, cafes and elegant stores. Our building was across the street from Geschichts Park. It was an expensive district of Berlin and a good place to raise a family. Uncle Frederick charged Father nominal rent and Father helped with maintenance of the building. We considered ourselves a middle class family and very lucky.

The apartment building was the typical brick apartment building of the time. There were four levels plus the basement. Neatly trimmed shrubs were planted around the front and side. Each building had a family who collected the rent, cleaned the common areas, and performed minor maintenance and management of the building for the owner. Herr Schmitz and his wife performed these duties for Uncle Frederick and his partners. They lived in the basement apartment. The basement had one apartment and a storage area for the tenants. Each apartment had storage bins in the basement, where tenants stored coal, wood, bicycles, and other miscellaneous items.

There were four apartments on the first, second and third floor. The fourth floor consisted of the laundry room and a room with clotheslines. The laundry room had a large washer and tubs. Behind the laundry tubs was a stairway leading to the roof. I spent a lot of time playing on the roof with friends when I was older. Our apartment was on the second floor. We had two bedrooms, a combined kitchen and dining room, a living room and a small parlor. The rooms were large with new wallpaper in each. The kitchen had a balcony with metal stairs that led down the side of the building. The balcony was large enough for a table and several chairs. It became a popular spot to cool-off on hot summer nights.

Mother raised herbs and had numerous flower pots arranged on small stands in the corners and on hangers over the balcony rails. She was always changing out the flowers. We lived fairly well but things were not easy for the German government in those days and our life was about to get harder. In October, Adolf Hitler formed the *Strum Abteilung* (SA), or Storm Troops, to protect him during speeches and rallies.

In April of 1921, the Allied powers presented their World War I reparation bill to Germany. It was an incredible sum of 132 billion gold marks. The mark, normally valued at four to the U.S. dollar, fell almost instantly to 75 percent of a dollar. It continued to fall until, by the end of the year, a single U.S. dollar was worth four billion German marks. German salaries and wages were almost worthless and purchasing power was almost non-existent. The life savings had vanished for most of the middle class and our family was no different. Unemployment passed one million. Hundreds of thousands stood in bread lines.

While unemployment was high, Father continued to have work at the printing company. When he would come home with his paycheck, mother would immediately rush with a laundry basket full of paper money to the grocery and the bakery because during the time it took Father to get home, the prices could rise while the money value and its buying power dropped even further. They barely made ends meet in those days.

I was baptized on June 15, 1921 in our local church. A small party for family and close friends followed the ceremony. Uncle Frederick brought food to help our family. Father had depleted our small savings on food items and necessities. Everyone had ideas on how to fix the problems.

Radical ideas on both the right and left floated through the wild and exciting streets of Berlin throughout 1922. There were open-clashes between the left-wing Communists and right-wing Fascists. An announcement published in March 1922 in the official Nazi newspaper *Völkischer Beobachter* (People's Observer) called for new members, declaring:

"We demand that the National Socialist Youth, and all other young Germans, irrespective of class

or occupation, between fourteen and eighteen years of age, whose hearts are affected by the suffering and hardships afflicting the Fatherland, and who later desire to join the ranks of the fighters against the Jewish enemy, the sole originator of our present shame and suffering, enter the Youth League of the NSDAP."

There were no membership fees and an emphasis of the organization was on love of one's country and people. Membership promised the enjoyment of honest open combat and of healthy physical activity, the respect of ethical and spiritual values, and the rejection of those values originating from Jewry. Weekly meetings were held featuring lectures and discussions. Every second Sunday was spent in mandatory hiking trips across the countryside. The League also established its own libraries for members excluding what it considered to be trashy literature. The first uniforms were copied from the brown shirted SA. The new Nazi Youth League attracted very few members at first, competing against numerous other well established groups. The Nazis held a meeting in May 1922 at the *Bürgerbräu Keller*, a large beer hall in Munich, to officially proclaim the foundation of the League. That meeting attracted only 17 youths. The Nazi Youth League was headed by Gustav Lenk who established small units in Nuremberg and other cities. As the organization continued its slow but steady growth, Hitler officially named Lenk as national youth leader. In May 1923, Lenk published the first Nazi youth magazine, *Nationale Jungsturm*, which proved to be a money loser and was then reduced to a supplement of the *Völkischer Beobachter*. Pearl Buck, the American writer who became famous for her novels of China, was in Germany in 1923. She wrote later:

"The cities were still there, the houses not yet bombed and in ruins, but the victims were millions of people. They had lost their fortunes, their savings; they were dazed and inflation-shocked and did not understand how it had happened to them nor who the foe was who had defeated them. Yet they had lost their self-assurance, their feeling that they themselves could be the masters of their own lives if only they worked hard enough; and lost, too, were the old values of morals, of ethics, of decency."

The economic crisis of 1923 led to rifts in the government. Several coalition governments struggled to agree to a suitable course of action and as a result the democratic process fell into decline. Parts of Germany were in a state of emergency and the opponents of the Weimar Republic used the situation to try and further destabilize the situation.

In 1923 there were many strikes, fuelling a fear of Communism among the middle classes. People looked to the right wing for solutions. This played into the hands of political groups such as the NSDAP.

On the evening of November 9, 1923, while Bavarian State Commissioner Gustav von Kahr was making a political speech in the Hofbrau House, a Munich beer hall, Hitler and 600 Nazis surrounded the hall. Hitler burst into the building and leaped onto a table, wielding a revolver and fired a shot into the ceiling.

"The National Revolution has begun!" he cried.

The attempted coup spilled out onto the streets with sixteen Nazis and three policemen dead among many wounded when the episode was over. Hitler was sentenced to Landsberg prison, about 45 kilometers west of Munich, and the government banned the National Socialist German Workers'

Party. While in prison he wrote his historic book titled *Mein Kampf* (My Struggle).

Lenk was arrested and briefly imprisoned. After his release he founded another group, the Greater German Youth Movement. He was arrested again and sent to Landsberg Prison where Hitler was confined. Lenk wound up being released from prison about the same time as Hitler in December of 1924.

After his release, Hitler announced he would reestablish the Nazi Party and invited all German nationalists to join the rejuvenated Nazi Party with him as its undisputed leader. However, Lenk doubted Hitler could maintain his position as absolute leader. Lenk then founded a new nationalist youth group independent of the NSDAP. Hitler retaliated by discrediting Lenk by the use of trumped up charges that he was a traitor and petty thief. This resulted in Lenk's downfall and complete removal from the entire German youth movement scene.

Lenk was replaced by Kurt Gruber, a 21-year-old law student who had joined the Nazi Party in 1923. Gruber had served as a group leader under Lenk and was a skilled organizer. Hitler was impressed by Gruber's enthusiasm and organizational talent. The Greater German Youth Movement under Gruber became the sole official youth organization of the Nazi Party and was even allowed to retain a degree of independence from the NSDAP leadership.

For Hitler, 1925 was a year spent successfully rebuilding the Nazi Party and consolidating his position as its absolute leader. Amid this success, Hitler called for his first mass rally since his release from prison. He chose the city of Weimar, located in the German state of Thuringia, which was one of the few states where he could legally speak in public.

Following his experiences at Landsberg Prison, Hitler decided that what he did at a political level would be legal and above board. He reasoned that if he wanted to sell the Nazi dream to the people of Weimar Germany, then he had to be seen as being a legitimate party leader and not one associated with violence and wrong-doing. Hitler's approach was to highlight the failings of the other political parties in Weimar Germany.

In 1925, I entered kindergarten. The kindergarten building was on the way to the Lentz Printing Company so Father would drop me off and Mother would pick me up at 3:00p.m. We sang songs, played games and colored. I was one of only three boys at the school, along with Rudi who moved to Frankfurt after kindergarten and Guenther who was three-months younger than me. We boys played together while the girls stayed in their group. I was out-going while Guenther was somewhat shy and quiet, a trait that he became known for.

Guenther and his parents lived in our apartment building, on the third floor. His parents were both teachers at the Reisdorf Elementary School. His father taught Mathematics and his mother Literature. They had a Yorkshire terrier dog named Wally who would spin around in counter-clockwise circles and bark for no reason. I often thought the dog was neurotic.

Guenther and I, and later Rolf, would spend many evenings on the roof of our apartment building, playing and, later, dreaming of what we would become. Over the next year Guenther and I became friends and did everything together. Our parents became acquainted and would visit each other's apartment.

New guidelines stipulated that all Hitler Youth members over age 18 had to be Nazi Party members, must obey all commands issued by any Nazi Party leader, pay a membership fee of four *Pfennigs* per month, and wear standardized uniforms designed to avoid confusion with SA uniforms.

On January 6, 1926, the German airline Lufthansa was created. That same year, the Nazi Party held its first party congress since its reorganization and Joseph Goebbels was appointed head of the Berlin Nazi Party. On July 3, 1926, a two-day Nazi rally began and was attended by the youth group members.

Kurt Gruber was officially proclaimed as the Hitler Youth's first leader. With new branches in twenty different German districts, the Hitler Youth organization faced financial problems associated with its expansion. Paid dues and Party funds only covered a portion of the costs. Hitler Youth members began the practice of collecting money during propaganda marches. Those marches always included the attention getting, rousing singing of Hitler Youth boys.

On Sunday, July 4th, at the suggestion of Julius Streicher, Gruber's Greater German Youth Movement was renamed as the Hitler *Jugend; Bund der Deutschen Arbeiterjugend* and the Hitler *Jugend* or Hitler Youth was born. Kurt Gruber was then officially proclaimed as its first leader. All other independent National Socialist youth associations, including groups in Austria, were now absorbed into the Hitler Youth organization. Gruber next established various departments and procedures. Among the fourteen separate departments were ones for sports, propaganda and education.

Their songs, borrowed mainly from the pre-war German youth movement, were based on traditional German folklore and old ballads. They also borrowed tunes from other groups and other political organizations, even the Communists, and simply changed the lyrics.

In July of that year, *Mein Kampf* was published and become a best seller. Hitler formed the *Schutzstaffel* (SS), or Protective Squadron, to protect him from rival political parties. Many Germans could see nothing wrong in the SS claim to be elite. Many believed every period in history had its elite and no democracy or dictatorship could do without it.

"Liberation of our people from the rule of second-raters is a prize worth considerable sacrifice," announced the newspapers, echoing the thoughts of practically every German.

On November 14, 1926 three hundred and twenty SA men marched through the Berlin Borough of Neukoelln, one of the communist strongholds. The brown shirted SA men served as bodyguards to party leaders, distributed leaflets, collected donations, and solicited votes for Hitler.

The Lentz Printing Company was located in the Neu-koelln district of Berlin. When Father finished work that day, he walked out the door of the printing building and into the group of SA men. They handed him literature that he stuck in his pocket. When he arrived home, he placed the litera-ture on the kitchen table. Mother spotted it and asked him where he got it. He told her about the SA men.

She looked at the material and commented, "These ideas sound ridiculous!"

I recall Father saying, "Margaret, they do say some things that are worth thinking about."

After church on Sundays, our family would often picnic in the Tiergarden Park and stroll along Unter den Linden Street window-shopping and admiring the many fine clothes dis-played in the shop windows. Sometimes, Guenther would come along. We didn't have a lot of money but were bet-ter off than many in Germany at the time because Father was still working, as were Guenther's parents.

That same year I was six years old and entered first grade along with Guenther. The two of us had become very good friends. On my first day, I had a new leather school bag con-taining a pencil box with slate, pencils and chalk. I was very proud of that leather bag. I met Guenther as he was com-ing down the steps from his apartment and off we marched to school. The school we attended was seven blocks north from our apartment, just off Lehrter Street.

Our elementary school was a typical design of the time. It consisted of two L-shaped buildings bordering a school-yard. The "Ls" were identical with the short part of the "Ls" facing Lehrter Street. In the space between the ends of the buildings were gates and adjoining was a building housing the gym. One L building was the boy's school, the other the girl's school. The inside of the school was plain. The floors in the hallways and the stairs were tiles and the classroom floors were oiled wood. Classrooms had two large windows with the walls painted light green. Along the walls opposite the windows and at the back end were hooks for coats and hats.

On the top floor of the building were the auditorium, an art instruction room, and a chemistry lab. Physical exercise took place in the gym and, weather permitting, in the yard. Guenther and I sat beside each other on benches. Our school bags sat on a shelf under an attached table.

The first day of school was exciting and fun. Some other older students directed us to our classroom where our teacher, Frau Meyer, was waiting. After a roll call, she demonstrated on the blackboard how to draw a tree. The class copied this on our slates and colored it with chalk. After the class period, the bell rang. All the first graders went upstairs to the auditorium.

To mark this day as a special event for the first graders, the boys from higher grades put on a short play. After the play, Guenther and I went to the schoolyard for a recess. There we met Rolf who was standing with a group of other boys. Rolf was in second grade. His father was a postal worker and an Auxiliary member of the SA.

Guenther, Rolf, and I soon became friends. Boys kept to their half of the yard and the girls to theirs, ignoring each other. Our school did not have a cafeteria so we stood around and ate our sandwiches. Our parents began to get more acquainted with each other. Rolf, like me, had blond hair and blue eyes. Guenther had a darker complexion with dark brown hair and dark brown eyes.

For the next year, things didn't change much in our lives. We studied reading, writing, and arithmetic, played football in the neighborhood park or on the roof of our apartment building, which became our favorite spot. From there we had a clear view of the Tiergarden Park and the city center. Berlin was a hustling city in those years. We would watch the horse-drawn carriages carry the tourists in and out of the park.

A black rhinoceros caught by Lutz Heck between Lake Manyara and Lake Eyazi in northern Tanzania arrived at the Berlin Zoo on May 20, 1928. It captivated the entire city and when Father finally took Guenther and me to see it I remember expecting a dark black animal. Instead, the black rhinoceros was grey.

I was disappointed!

The 1920s, were a vibrant period in the history of Berlin. The culture was generally considered as decadent and socially disruptive by conservatives. Art, music, film, and other art-forms flourished throughout the country, but were firmly rooted in Berlin. Berlin was the centerpiece of European culture from about 1923-1932 and radical ideas on both the right and left floated through the wild and exciting streets of Berlin.

Above the streets was our haven!

Hardly anyone ever came up to the roof. Guenther, Rolf and I came to think of it as our own. Rolf was able to scrounge some wooden planks and we turned them into a lean-to that became our clubhouse. Heir Schmitz provided some straw and Mother provided some blankets. We slept in the clubhouse on many warm nights.

The roof was a perfect place to dream and to watch the stars. Our parents didn't have to worry about us because access to the roof could only be obtained through the laundry room and only the tenants of the building had a key. A fire escape that leads from the roof was folded and could only be straightened by walking down the ladder and releasing a catch allowing the ladder to unfold.

After he joined the *Jungvolk*, Rolf would bring magazines to our roof sanctuary. We would marvel at the pictures of the strong SS and SA soldiers. I think we all liked the SS uniforms the best. When we got older, we liked the pictures of the *Bund Deutscher Mädel* or BDM (League of German Girls). The *Jungvolk* magazine articles told of the many struggles Germans had made and how our country's enemies, the Jews and the Bolsheviks, were plotting to keep our nation poor. The magazines also had stories of the adventures of various *Jungvolk Heims* (Youth Home) as they camped overnight and hiked throughout the countryside singing songs. Rolf always had stories to tell about his experiences and Guenther and I could scarcely contain our enthusiasm. The *Jungvolk* seemed like an exciting life. It was not weighted down by tradition and seemed to offer an exciting opportunity for young people to be respected. It was free from parental supervision and filled with duties that seemed sheer pleasure.

The magazines told of precision marching, hiking, camping, war games, and many sports activities. More and more of our classmates were joining and Guenther and I began to feel left out. The many evenings we spent on our roof were some of the most memorable and happiest thoughts I can remember from my childhood.

In addition to the Hitler Youth, the youth groups that emerged at this time included the Catholic Youth Organization, the Boy Scouts, and many others. These youth groups were soon to be greatly changed forever in Germany. In Hitler's mind, young Germans were the key to the success of the nation. The youth organizations that developed reflected his views.

The collapse of the American stock market in 1929 had a disastrous effect on Germany. By February, the number of unemployed in Germany reached 3.2 million. The depression resulting from the crash provided the spark that allowed the Nazi's to gain support.

All of a sudden the support of the Americans and the aid plans were withdrawn, Germany was again isolated and the economy was in crisis. The rise in unemployment and a renewed fear of a Communist uprising gave Hitler's messages a new importance. People were again interested in the views of his party. Any alternative that appeared to be willing and able to combat the problems, through whatever means, was seen in a very positive light.

I was in fourth grade at the time. There wasn't a day that went by where Communists and Nazis didn't clash in the streets of Berlin. Men were standing around and sitting on the pavement begging or selling pencils or greeting cards. Most of them were World War I veterans. Some were amputees who were confined to a wheel chair or who were blind from gas exposure during the war.

These scenes really affected Father.

I think his attitude about politics started to change about that time. Up to then, I think he was indifferent to national politics. He began to read more about the Nazi Party. I think Rolf's parents were beginning to have an influence on him. They would come over to the apartment occasionally on a Saturday night. While we played on the roof, the parents would discuss world events.

Rolf's father and mother were avid supporters of Hitler. At first Father would listen but not offer much in the way of support. As the economic situation in Germany got worse, Father was beginning to see the Nazis as a viable option.

Mother, on the other hand, wanted nothing to do with the Nazis and made her views known.

To her credit, she never changed her convictions about the Nazis even up to the very end. Father convinced her to keep her thoughts to herself because after a while in Germany, it was dangerous to be considered anti-Nazi.

As the depression deepened, many families joined the breadline. Those who could no longer pay their rent were evicted from their apartments. There were homeless people through out the streets of Berlin trying to find a place to spend the night.

I remember people sleeping on the steps of our apartment building. Mother took them blankets and gave them something to eat. This would upset Heir Schmitz as he was used to sweeping the steps early each morning. The people sleeping on the apartment building steps upset his routine. He would have to wake people and chase them away so he could do his work. Aside from the economy, the big political issue that year was the World War I reparations. Meetings took place at The Hague in an effort to adjust the amount of reparations due to the economic crisis.

Berlin was a socialist and communist stronghold in 1929 and it seemed as though everyone discussed politics. Many clubs and organizations were formed where men sat around playing cards and women sat in another room or on the balcony doing needlepoint. The topics of discussion were enviably the economy and politics. Many clubs met in a café or pub. It seemed as though everyone in Berlin belonged to a club. Father and Mother belonged to a card club and I was looking forward to joining the *Jungvolk*.

Guenther was in classes with me. Rolf was in fifth grade at the same school. The three of us played together during school. Rolf's parents formally joined the Nazi party that year and were active in rallies and events. Rolf would come to school or come over to our apartment in the evenings and tell Guenther and me all about what he had done the night before at the *Jungvolk* meetings.

"Kurt, you have to hear what our leaders told us about the Jews," he would begin.

"Father agrees they are wicked."

Rolf would give us a blow-by-blow description of what was discussed at the meeting.

Our apartment balcony became a gathering spot and a place for us to discuss and debate. Rolf would bring copies of *Hitler Jugend Zeitung* (Hitler Youth Journal) for us. The pictures and stories captivated Guenther and I. Guenther's parents did not approve of the literature that he brought home with him.

He soon learned not to say too much to his parents about Hitler.

Many parents tried in vain at that time to discourage their children from associating with Hitler Youth organizations. The Roman Catholic Church, which had its own extensive youth organization, restricted young parish members from joining. To keep boys from defecting, Catholic youth groups copied some of the practices of the Hitler Youth such as target shooting with small caliber rifles. The Hitler Youth had less of a challenge in trying to incorporate the Protestant organizations. Many Protestant youths and their leadership had already declared their support on the Hitler Youth before 1933, as did their parents.

Many German Christians in the Protestant Church believed that the Jewish Jesus was a blond Aryan and Hitler had been sent directly by God in order to save Germany.

In April 1929, the Hitler Youth was declared the only official youth group of the Nazi Party. In September, Hitler Youth made a strong showing at the annual Nuremberg rally as about 2,000 members marched past Hitler amid great applause. Among them was a group of Berlin boys who had marched 400 miles all the way to Nuremberg.

I admired them for marching so far.

One day as we were walking home from school, I saw signs on the Jewish shop windows, "Germans Beware! Don't Buy From Jews!" and "The True German Does Not Buy In Jewish Shops!"

When I arrived home that day, Mother was cooking dinner. I told her about the signs I saw. As usual, she dismissed them as the work of a few radicals. However, I insisted on answers this time. I continued to ask questions about the Jews until Father came home from work. Father could see that Mother was beginning to get upset so he took me out on the balcony, presumably to get out of mother's way while she finished dinner. It became clear to Father that I had been following political events and was requiring answers. He was not prepared for the deluge of questions he got from me and told me that we had to have faith in the government and to do what they told us and not make a fuss. Father went back inside the apartment. It was time for dinner.

After playing with my food for a while, I said sheepishly, "Some members of the Hitler Youth were at school today."

"They gave a talk about the benefits of joining the *Jungvolk*. I want to join when I turn ten years old."

Mother, looking scornful said, "I am worried that the *Jungvolk* will have a bad influence on you Kurt."

I quickly responded, "It hasn't had a bad influence on Rolf."

Looking sternly, she said, "No, of course not, he has become the perfect little Nazi."

Father listened to the discussion and then said, "Mother and I will discuss this prospect later."

Mother gave him her exasperated look.

I finished my homework and went to bed. My thoughts were on the *Jungvolk*. I could not stop thinking about the things Rolf told Guenther and me.

Our parents just didn't understand!

The future of Germany belonged to our generation.

They didn't know that I had already been studying for the *Jungvolk* tests in our rooftop clubhouse. Mother didn't understand what the *Führer* was trying to do. Hitler said that parents were sentimental.

For many of us, the Hitler Youth represented the future of Germany. There were new ideas and new solutions to the national problems. Our parent's generation was part of the problem, not the solution. This is what we were told by the Hitler Youth speakers and we believed it. To many, Hitler appeared as the father or older brother they never had. The Nazi movement was coming across to many as a party made for youth. Members of the Nazi Party were visibly young, with the mean age of approximately thirty-one. Their numbers continued to grow and when the Great Depression hit Germany in October in 1929, their organization underwent enormous growth. The year was also full of turmoil in the streets.

Startled, I sat up in bed. The shots from down in the street woke me. After a few minutes, Mother came in my room and sat on the bed beside me. My room faced the street. My window was open and I could hear everything that took place out there. I asked Mother what was happening. She put her arm around me and said everything was all right.

After a few more minutes, Father came into the room. We all sat on my bed. Father told us that it looked as though the SA was chasing someone and it would be over soon.

I looked at Father confidently and said, "I know about the enemies of the German people. I know about the Bolsheviks and the Jews. I have read about them in *Hitler Jugend Zeitung*."

Father and Mother just looked at each other.

Taking a deep breath, Mother said, "So we have another little Nazi..."

Suddenly, we heard the sound of a car roaring around the corner. A large black car screeched to a stop in front of our apartment building. Brown shirted SA men got out. Someone shouted an order and the SA men began to scatter. One of the men was pounding on the front door of our apartment building. Heir Schmitz was a light sleeper so it did not take him long to answer the door. My window was open and we could hear everything that was being said.

One of the SA men shouted to Heir Schmitz that they were looking for a communist who had shot an SA member earlier. He wanted to know if anyone had entered the apartment building within the last thirty minutes. Heir Schmitz assured the SA man that no one had entered or left the building all night and he would very much appreciate it if the men would not make so much noise.

I didn't realize at the time how dangerous Heir Schmitz's comment was.

Apparently satisfied, the SA men gave Heir Schmitz a scowling look and left to begin pounding on the doors of other buildings in the neighborhood. Soon the commotion was over, the SA car drove off, and all was quiet again on the street.

I again asked what was going on.

Mother said, "Everything will be all right and we should now go to sleep."

After my parents left my room, I lay on my bed wide-awake. How could I go to sleep after all of the fuss? I kept thinking about how great it would be to chase criminals. I had read articles about chasing criminals in the *Hitler Jugend Zeitung*. I had been thinking about it for some time and it seemed to be the topic of conversation everywhere. Nevertheless, who were these criminals? I was to find out shortly.

The political situation in Berlin was not peaceful then. In one month alone, 99 men were killed and another 1,125 wounded in street brawls.

"The entire city," wrote an American journalist "lay under an epidemic of infectious fear. There were whispers of midnight arrests, of prisoners tortured in SA barracks, made to spit on Lenin's picture, swallow castor oil, and eat old socks."

At the end on 1929, the Nazi Party had a membership of about 178,000.

Chapter Three
The *Jungvolk*

By 1930, Germany's manufacturing had fallen seventeen percent from its 1927 level. Bankruptcies were increasing and farmers were having problems selling their crops. Some in the middleclass feared sliding into the lower class and some blamed the economic decline on unemployed people being unwilling to work.

Hunger was widespread.

The parliamentary coalition that governed Germany fell apart, and new elections were held. The biggest winner in these elections was Adolf Hitler's National Socialist Party.

From fourteen seats in parliament, they increased their seats to 107, becoming Germany's second largest political party.

On January 23rd, Wilhelm Frick, the first Nazi to take office in Germany, became the minister for the state of Thüringen in central Germany. Allied troops withdrew from the occupation of the Saar. No German troops were to be stationed on the left bank of the Rhine River. The area was to be a demilitarized zone.

Father was always against the stationing of foreign troops on German soil. Like most of the soldiers who had fought in World War I, he was bitter. They felt betrayed, and cheated from victory.

Three days after my birthday, Horst Wessel, a member of the SA, was shot when he opened his apartment door. He lay in the hospital for several days before he died. His funeral received extensive news coverage and became the catalyst of a violent clash between Nazis and Communists. I remember Father and Mother discussing the news each evening.

As the various factions fought each other, the Nazis tried very hard to make inroads into the strongly social democratic and communist Berlin.

This was a big year for Guenther and me. We were ten years old. We were old enough to join the *Jungvolk*. Our parents didn't know that we had already been studying with Rolf and preparing for the day when we could officially join. We were learning more about the Jew's role in our country's problems.

One day at school, it was Guenther and my turn to stay behind to straighten the classroom. Each day, the teacher would choose someone different. There was no rhyme or reason for the selection, at least that we could figure out. The rest of the class dismissed, they bolted out of the room as fast as they could afraid they may have to help. After erasing the chalkboard, straightening the chairs and tables, and arranging books on the shelf, the classroom was organized and presentable for the next day.

Heir Weimer came in and looked around announcing, as if the room was full of people, "The classroom is now ready for students!"

With the announcement, we were free to go. We thanked the teacher, put on our coats, and made our way out of the school, through the yard and to the street.

The sun was just beginning to go down, throwing shadows onto the street. The air was turning cooler as we walked down the street talking about the events in class that day.

Suddenly, we could hear shouting from across the street in the park.

Some of the older boys from school were in a circle with a boy in the middle.

They were chanting, "Dirty Jew! Dirty Jew!"

As we got closer, they could see that the boy in the circle was Joseph from Frau Apple's class. We had seen him around the school but he was in different classes. Joseph was bleeding. A couple of the boys were pelting the Jewish boy with stones.

They continued to shout, "Filthy Jew! Pig Jew!" Joseph just stood there taking the abuse and the stones. I wondered why he did not try to run or at least protect himself. He did not fight or try to escape from the center. Just then, an older man crossed the street in front of us and went directly into the center of the circle.

He put his arm around Joseph and told the boys, "You should be ashamed of yourselves. What could this boy have possibly done to you?"

Someone from the crowd shouted, "He is a filthy Jew!"

The man walked out of the circle with Joseph and down the street. The boys just stood there. Not one of them said a word for a while.

Finally, one boy said, "Lets go, there is no more to do here."

The boys dispersed. A couple of them crossed the street heading towards us. I recognized one of them. It was Rolf. He spotted us and came over to talk.

"Why did you two not join?"

I didn't have an answer.

I asked Rolf, "What had Joseph done?"

Rolf said confidently, "The pitiful Jew had to be taught a lesson. I will see you both in school tomorrow."

He continued the opposite way down the street.

I didn't know what to say.

I reasoned that since Rolf was older, old enough to belong to the *Jungvolk*, he must know something more about Jews then I did. I didn't know any Jews and there were none in our class. I only knew of Joseph in Frau Apple's class.

I could not wait to be a member of the *Jungvolk*.

Three more months until I could take the entrance tests!

Then I could learn the things that Rolf knew!

He seemed so much older than Guenther and I. It seemed as though he was many years wiser.

When I got home, I told Mother about the encounter. She listened carefully and shook her head.

She said, "Those boys should have been ashamed of themselves. I know Joseph's parents. They own the potato shop on Mink Street. They are very nice people. They would not hurt a flea and neither would their children. Those boys went too far! What are they teaching those boys?"

The next night at dinner I sat there playing with my food.

Mother asked, "Kurt, what is troubling you? Why are you playing with your food?

I said, "I am ten years old and Rolf invited Guenther and I to take the entrance tests to join the *Jungvolk*."

"We will march to a farm outside of Berlin and camp over night."

"It is going to be fun. If I pass, the *Heim* is only a couple of blocks from here and it won't interfere with home work or chores."

Father spoke up, "Kurt, your Mother and I have already discussed this and we have agreed to allow you to join."

I didn't know what to say.

I was expecting the exact opposite. I thought I would have to plead my case, but they agreed without any argument.

"Thank you so much."

"You don't know what this means to me. I will make you both very proud of me some day."

I couldn't wait to go to school the next day to find out how Guenther made out with his parents and to tell Rolf. I couldn't sleep that night. I kept thinking about how wonderful it was going to be to go camping and to be part of the *Jungvolk*. Rolf had made is sound so exciting.

When I met Guenther the next morning to walk to school he looked really down. I didn't have to ask. I knew that his parents had said no, to his joining.

"Guenther, they will change their minds, you will see."

"Just be patient!"

Guenther echoed our feelings at the time, "Parents just don't understand like Hitler does. We are the future and we have to be prepared."

When we arrived at school, Guenther went directly to the classroom and I looked for Rolf. I told him that my parents had agreed to allow me to join but Guenther's parents would not permit him to join.

"I will see what can be done. Don't worry. Guenther will be allowed to join."

A couple of days went by and then Guenther came out of his apartment one morning smiling from ear to ear.

He shouted, "I am allowed to join. My parents changed their minds."

I was happy for him. I didn't find out until years later that Rolf had gone home and told his parents that Guenther's parents would not allow him to join the *Jungvolk*. By then Rolf's father was an official in the Nazi party and called the principle of the school were Guenther's parents taught. The principle had apparently called them into the office and strongly suggested that Guenther be permitted to be part of the Hitler Youth. That was enough to convince Guenther's parents to relent.

The pressure on teachers was mounting. Many teachers who did not conform to the Nazi ideas were replaced.

Guenther and I began to attend *Jungvolk* meetings with Rolf. We were issued uniforms and participated in many events but were not permitted to wear badges or a shoulder strap. We all wanted to experience the outdoor adventures and camaraderie among friends that the organization had to offer. We would listen to the same lectures as the older boys and assist them with their chores.

The notion of German superiority over the rest of the masses was a central theme in our lectures. We were told that the German should be feared because he was a combination of the most superior beings in the world.

We learned that the German mass was best represented by the German army, encompassing all branches of the Nazi state including the *Jungvolk*, the Hitler Youth, the SS and the SA as well as the *Wehrmacht* (German army) itself, which was essentially the strongest, most masculine symbol of Germany.

The greatness of the German army was translated as the superiority of the German nation. Our leaders explained that the highest form of celebration of the German society was through war. Furthermore, the fighters of these wars were soldiers, the symbol of German culture and we would be soldiers. We were told that it was our destinies to some day become a German soldier.

I wasn't sure what all of this meant at the time but, the *Jungvolk* offered us an identity and a place to identify with other young people who shared the same ideals. We could not wait to become members. Soon, it was time to prove ourselves.

I was looking forward to Saturday. It was the day of the hike to a farm just outside of Berlin and staying overnight with the Hitler Youth. There would be a campfire and sausages cooked over the open fire. We would sing songs and stories would be told by the older leaders. Guenther and I were to complete our tests, after which, we would receive the coveted *Jungvolk* dagger and become official members of the *Jungvolk*.

I couldn't sleep Friday night.

I tossed and turned, wondering what it would be like. *Could I pass the tests?*

After looking at the alarm clock every hour, I finally got out of bed at 6:00 a.m., brushed my teeth, cleaned up and got dressed.

The smell of fresh baked bread was all through the house. It made me hungry. I made my way to the kitchen with my backpack to find Mother making sandwiches. I sat down at the table and began eating the fresh buttered bread with some strawberry jam. Strawberry jam was my favorite. While placing sandwiches and a loaf of bread in my backpack, Mother asked if I packed my toothbrush and clean underwear. This was the first time I would be away from my family overnight.

I told her not to worry.

"Rolf will be there and he had been camping before and knew what to do."

She responded sarcastically, "I'm sure the little Nazi knows exactly what to do."

"Mother, Rolf's father and mother are members of the Party. They know things about our enemies that we don't."

Another exasperated look from Mother!

Father came into the room for his coffee and sat down beside me. He told me how proud he was of me and not to worry about passing the tests.

I wondered how Father knew I was worried.

It was time to go and meet Guenther. I put on my backpack and hugged Mother and Father.

Mother cautioned, "Be careful and watch out for snakes."

I told her not to worry.

Proud of our smart uniforms, Guenther and I were off, bouncing down the street, to the *Heim*.

Father was standing in my room at the window watching us go down the street. Mother joined him. A tear came to his eyes.

Mother asked, "Fritz, what is wrong?"

Father looked at her and said, "I fear the boys are about to change, and I don't know if it is going to be for the good. Even so, what can we do? The nation and the world are changing."

Mother now had tears in her eyes as we turned the corner and were out of sight.

When we got to the *Heim*, we spotted Rolf who was talking with one of the older Hitler Youth leaders. He saw us and motioned us over. Rolf introduced Guenther and me to Hans Wolfe. Rolf told us that Hans was one of the Hitler Youth leaders who would be administering the tests. Hans greeted us and asked if we had been studying the assigned materials. We both nodded and said we were ready. Rolf left to talk with someone else, leaving Hans with us. Hans was tall and thin with the longest fingers I had ever seen. He seemed to like Guenther, placing his arm around him. As we talked, his hand moved to Guenther's back side and then to his crotch. He leaned close to Guenther and whispered into his ear. Guenther pulled away and Hans left to talk with some others.

When Rolf came back he said, "Hans likes boys, if you haven't already seen that."

Guenther replied, "Yeah, he grabbed me between the legs and whispered that we would have to get together later at the farm."

Rolf said, "There are many new things that you will experience. They are all part of being strong."

Guenther and I had been quizzing each other for weeks. We had learned how to recognize a Jew. We knew how dangerous the communists were. We learned the Horst Wiesel song backwards. We knew all about Hitler's struggles in the early days.

We were ready!

Our parents didn't know these things! Hans motioned to Rolf and the other Young Hitler Youth leaders to form up. Rolf called his squad to line up. We would march through the city, past other Heims where other chapters of Jungvolk would join us. Rolf told each member of his squad to tighten their shoestrings so our shoes did not rub. He inspected, pulled and tightened everyone's backpack and made everyone take a drink of water before starting. Rolf was our leader!

He was strong and tall! His backpack was heavy and pressed down on his shoulders. Rolf carried the cooking pot and food for his squad.

My backpack contained only sandwiches, a shirt, a pair of sneakers, clean underwear, a tooth brush, and a tarpaulin for rainy days, and a loaf of bread.

Off we went, winding through the city, with youthful enthusiasm. To show our patriotism we sang songs about sending all the Jews to Jerusalem, chopping off their legs making sure they could not come back.

People would salute us or wave as we went by. Each *Jungvolk* group carried the Hitler Youth flag with their own streamer attached, which led the group. As more and more groups joined the march, the banners looked like a sea of black and white. The flags had the ancient Germanic Sig-Rune "S" symbolic of victory in white against a background of black and white trim.

We were all so proud!

I enjoyed the respect we were getting from the citizens of Berlin. Our group looked sharp in our brown shirts, black shorts, and brown knee-high socks. Our hair was cut short in the military style. Guenther and I did not have any patches or the shoulder strap yet. The boys who passed their tests wore the patches, the shoulder strap and, of course, their dagger. Rolf marched beside his squad. I kept thinking how sharp he looked with the complete uniform plus a leader's patch. He watched over us like a mother hen, keeping us in step and lined-up.

We had been marching for two hours and were at the edge of the city. The leader ordered us to stop in front of a park where we would rest before moving to the farm, which was another two-hour march. We dropped our packs and started eating our mother's sandwiches. My feet were a little tired, but I did not feel any blisters developing.

I was glad that Rolf has made us tighten our shoes.

After a couple of minutes, about ten *Jungmäedel* (Young Girls) came around the corner. They were singing as they marched, carrying water jugs and pastries for us. They looked sharp in their dark-blue jumpers and white blouses. Their blond hair was long and braided. They marched up to the crowd and began passing out the food and water.

A young girl, about my age I thought, came over to Guenther and me and asked if we wanted any water. I looked up to see a cute blond-haired girl.

All of a sudden, I couldn't breathe!

All I could do was gaze at her.

It seemed as though that's all she could do too. We just kept looking at each other for what seemed like an eternity.

Finally, Guenther spoke up and said. "I will take some water."

The trance was broken.

She said, "My name is Anna. What are your names?"

I still could not speak. I was not sure what was wrong with me. Maybe it was the hot sun. I was really beginning to sweat. I kept looking at her. She was the most beautiful girl I had ever seen. Her body was perfect in every line, her face clear and bright and her blue eyes the most innocent eyes one could imagine. Her golden hair was braided.

Guenther told her his and my name.

Finally, I spoke up asking her were she lived. She told us she was from Burger Street and had come to help her cousin, who belongs to the local *Bund Deutscher Mädel* chapter.

The *BDM*'s purpose was to mold girls as closely as possible to conform to the Nazi ideal of womanhood. They were to learn to be obedient, dutiful, disciplined, and self-sacrificing. They were to prepare themselves to marry and have children with the Hitler Youth boys who would become soldiers of the *SS* and the future of Germany.

I said that I was from Lehrer Street, which was not far from where she lived. She was on the other side of the Tiergarden Park from me, not far, but another world, another school district, a neighborhood of more well to do families.

I wondered if we would see each other again.

Anna said that she goes to a *Jungmädel Heim* on Hufeland Street every Thursday night. I said I would try to see her there if I could.

With that she said, "I had better be getting around to the others."

She turned and said to me, "I will see you again, won't I?" All rested and ready to go, the groups reformed, we were ready to leave the city. By this time, the march had grown from the original forty from our *Heim* to about three hundred *Jungvolk* and Hitler Youth leaders. When we sang, we drowned out all other noise. I could not resist looking around to see the stream of blond hair and brown shirts flowing along the road. After we left the city streets, the march was less formal and more like a route step. There were ditches to cross and rocks to go around, all the time singing.

My thoughts kept coming back to Anna. I had questions.

What was she like?

What was her school like?

Did she like hiking and singing?

I had never felt like this before. It was a strange feeling. A feeling I could not explain. I felt different.

After about two hours, the procession arrived at the farm. Rolf got his squad together and told us we would be sleeping in the barn. Our squad would be responsible for building the campfires. Rolf instructed us to stow our packs in the barn and to report back when done.

Once back, we all gathered wood from the nearby forest and began making the fires. We all had studied the proper way to stack wood for a large fire. Once the fires were burning, some of the older boys began to prepare the food for cooking over the fire. They cut sausages into six-inch length. Other boys found sticks for holding the meat over the fire. Guenther and I selected suitable sticks and cooked our meat until the casing split and the meat was dark on the edges.

The entire campsite smelled of delicious sweet sausage and spices mixed with the wood smoke. The sausage, along with the bread that every boy was instructed to bring, made a wonderful supper.

Once everyone had eaten, Hitler Youth leaders organized us *Jungvolk* candidates into groups. Candidates had to go up to their Hitler Youth leader and sit in from of him on a log. The leader would then ask a series of questions to test their knowledge of Nazi doctrine, racial purity, and survival skills. The leader would mark the results of the tests in his book. Guenther went before me. Rolf looked at me and winked, as if to say that everything would be all right.

Then it was my turn.

I went up and sat down. The Hitler Youth leader was Hans Wolfe who we had met earlier. Without any acknowledgement, Hans started asking the questions. I answered with confidence and was sure that I had passed.

It was the courage test that worried me.

No one knew what the test would be. We had heard about rope climbing. There was rope in the barn and rafters to climb up to. We had heard about jumping onto a stretched canvass and leaping over campfires.

We waited patiently for everyone to be done. By this time, it was dark. After all were finished, the senior Hitler Youth leader announced what the courage test would be.

It was to be the campfire leap!

Guenther and I looked at each other and wondered why we had built the fires so large.

Gathering around one of the campfires, everyone watched as the candidates demonstrated their courage. The Hitler Youth leaders called out the name of the boy whose turn it was to leap over the flames. Allowed only four running steps, he could not land on any of the coals on the other side. Each boy had two tries. The first boy just made it. After landing, he almost fell back into the fire.

I was starting to worry!

I looked at Guenther and then at Rolf. It was Guenther's turn while I watched attentively. Guenther made it with about 12 inches to spare.

The leader announced, "Next will be Kurt Schultheiss!"

I took my position and readied myself. I ran and jumped but my left foot landed on some of the coals on the other side.

I kept thinking *boy was that hot!*

The leader announced, "The first jump did not count."

I was scared now.

I had to do it.

On the way back to the other side of the fire, I glanced over to Rolf. He nodded as if to say, *you can do it.*

Guenther had already made it and there were three hundred boys watching me.

Determined, I ran and jumped as I had never jumped before. This time, I cleared the fire by two feet. I took my place around the fire while the other candidates took their turn. Everyone passed the courage test but no one knew the results of the verbal questions.

Hans and the other leaders huddled off to the side while we waited for what seemed like hours. Then they came over to the fire with a box full of daggers. Of the forty-one candidates, thirty-five had made it. The others would have to study some more and try again.

Guenther and I had passed and were called to stand in front of the gathering with the others. I went to the front and received my Hitler Youth dagger. The inscription on the dagger read *"Blut und Ehre"* (Blood and Honor). Rolf looked on with obvious pride. All five candidates in his squad made it.

We sang songs the rest of the evening and played games. Guenther and I were sitting by the fire when Hans came over to Guenther and whispered something in his ear. Guenther stood up and said that he would be back. He and Hans went into the barn where Hans made Guenther take his clothes off while he masturbated. Guenther never said a word about the encounter when he came back. It wasn't until weeks later that he told me.

Sexual abuse was often involved in displays of manhood with younger boys being abused by the older, more masculine boys. Struggles for power through sexual oppression were a sort of rite of passage that we had to pass in order to be accepted by the group. We all had to take our turn masturbating in front of a group. In some cases, it went further.

The next morning we packed our things to get ready for the march back to our *Heim*. Everything had to be put back the way we found it. The ashes from the fire had to be spread and any trash packed up to be carried back. Nothing could be left to lie around. Our Leaders told us that we should always take everything we brought with us. They said our enemies are always looking for something to use against us. The hike back seemed easier then the hike out. Maybe it was the shinny new daggers hanging from our belt that made the trip easier. I couldn't wait to show Father and Mother and to see if I could find Anna. After arriving at the *Heim*, Hans took turns congratulating those of us who passed the tests. We were then dismissed. Guenther, Rolf, and I walked home together.

Rolf said, "I am very proud of you two. You are no longer little mama's boys."

We thanked him for all of his help.

I was tired but felt good.

Mother and Father were waiting when I got home. They both wanted to hear all about the weekend. Mother had made potato dumplings for dinner. I ate several helpings while I told them everything that had happened. They both listened attentively but Mother was particularity interested to hear about the girl I had encountered. I remember sleeping well that night. Camping was fun but it was nice to sleep in my own bed. My thoughts kept coming back to Anna. Guenther and I re-hashed our weekend experience on the way to school the next day.

For some reason, the *Jungvolk* leaders decided to change our meetings to Wednesday nights. I decided to try to locate Anna. I remembered that she said she went to the *Jungmädel Heim* on Hufeland Street every Thursday night. I was not sure were she lived.

I dressed in my *Jungvolk* uniform, with dagger, and made sure my shoes were highly polished. I walked to her *Heim* hoping to see her outside. There were several girls sitting on the front steps talking. I got up to nerve to ask one of them if they had seen Anna. They said she would be along soon and asked if I wanted to join them. The girls giggled then said I looked very nice in my uniform and proceeded to ask me many questions about our *Heim*. I was beginning to tell them about my courage test when Anna came along.

As soon as she spotted me she said, "Kurt, you remembered!"

I responded, "Yes, our meetings have been changed to Wednesday nights so I..."

She cut me off, "This is good that you came. You will come in and have something cold to drink and something to eat. You will wait in our reading room until my meeting is over. Then, you will walk me home and we will talk."

I leafed through the girl's magazines. They were a lot like our magazines but emphasized cooking, sewing and taking care of babies instead of military training. I sat in the reading room for what seemed like an eternity until the meeting was over.

Finally, Anna came in the room and announced, "The meeting is over. Now you will walk me home and we will talk."

We exchanged stories about what we both had done since our encounter at the edge of the city. Anna did most of the talking. I was to discover that she usually did. We arrived at her apartment building and agreed to meet the next Thursday.

Just before entering her building, she turned and said, "Kurt, you are pure Aryan aren't you? Our leaders caution us not to waste time with non-Aryans."

A little taken back by the question, I simply responded, "Yes."

Anna had become a fanatical member of the *Jung-mädel*. First as a nursing assistant, then later as a member of the BDM and a dairy helper during a summer on the farm, Anna excelled at everything she did.

Anna and I went on meeting on Thursday nights every week for a couple of years. Her parents and mine became acquainted and Guenther, Rolf, Anna, and I would often go to the park together and meet on my apartment roof. Rolf and she would engage in some interesting conversations about the future of Germany. Anna and I became very good friends over the years. We would often discuss what was being taught in school and at our respective Hitler Youth meetings. While courteous, Mother never warmed to Anna.

Chapter Four
A New Mood

On June 5, 1931, two years before the NSDAP came to power, German Chancellor Brüning gave authorization to create a national work service called the *Freiwilliger Arbeitsdienst,* or *Arbeitsdienst,* for short. Konstantin Hierl was appointed as the head of this new national voluntary labor service organization. Soon after its formation, Hierl began to absorb the many independent camps that had been formed earlier in a process of centralizing state control over the area of national labor work.

In October 1931, Hitler appointed Baldur von Schirach as chief of all the youth activities for the NSDAP. He had been the leader of the Nazi University Student League since 1928, as well as the Nazi Pupils' League. Schirach had proven himself a talented organizer and propagandist while he was a student leader. Although he was from an upper class background, he became a militant opponent of his own social class. He was also an anti-Semite as well as an opponent of Christianity. As one of the earliest members of the Nazi Party, he was among Hitler's inner circle and was personally well regarded by Hitler. Schirach was a self-styled poet who had admiration for Hitler.

He soon introduced a new structure to the Hitler Youth, based on age. Young boys aged 6 to 10 were allowed to hang around the older boys and participate informally. As in our case, this had been done informally in many *Heims.*

Boys 10 to 14 belonged to the *Jungvolk*, and then from 14 to 18 were in the actual HJ, the commonly used abbreviation for Hitler *Jugend*. Each boy was given a performance booklet recording his progress in athletics and Nazi indoctrination throughout all of his years in the HJ.

Girls 10 to 14 joined the *Jungmädelbund* (Young Girl's League) and from 14 to 18 belonged to the *Bund Deutcher Mädel*. The girls wore a schoolgirl-style uniform with skirts and blouses along with hiking boots. However, the Hitler Youth organization was primarily male oriented and would remain so throughout the duration of the Third Reich, although the HJ and BDM did share common traits including a very heavy emphasis on competition. Just about every task, no matter how big or small, was turned into an individual, team, or unit competition. This included boys and girl's sports, the quality of singing during propaganda marches, and Winter Aid collections. Boys and girls were kept constantly busy. The Nazis capitalized on the natural enthusiasm of young people, their craving for action and desire for peer approval, hoping, ultimately, each young person would come to regard his or her HJ or BDM unit as a home away from home, or perhaps as their real home.

Activities for boys included games of hide and seek called Trapper and Indian, and war games in which they formed platoons, put on red or blue armbands, and then were supposed to hunt down the enemy and rip off the other color arm bands. This often resulted in fistfights and outright brawls between platoons. Younger, weaker boys got pummeled while platoon leaders stood by or even encouraged the fighting. Ripped shirts, along with scrapes and bruises were common during these field exercises, which were intended to toughen them up.

Rolf, Guenther and I received our share of cuts and bruises.

Hitler Youth members also had to participate in the search for mushrooms and herbs, used for medicinal purposes, as well as helping out in towns in carious positions, such as tram conductor, coffee dispenser or letter carrier. It wasn't long before we began to see changes at school.

After winning about 30 percent of the seats in the Reichstag, the Nazis were able to influence the educational system.

One day, shortly after my eleventh birthday, we arrived at school and were directed into the auditorium. There wasn't a scheduled event so we all wondered what was happening. Once we were all settled in our seats the principle, Heir Steinbauer, addressed the assembly. Standing beside him on the stage was an adult Hitler Youth leader that we did not recognize.

Heir Steinbauer said, "Beginning today, your studies will be changing some. Based on a directive from the Reich Education Ministry, you will learn about your racial heritage and about the enemies of Germany and the racial purity of our nation. Additionally, there will be more time allotted during the day for physical training. Captain Schill here has been assigned to our school to oversee this training. Does anyone have any questions?

No one spoke.

"Then, go to your home rooms."

Guenther and I wondered what this new training was all about as we went to our classroom. The new physical training period was to begin the next day. We all looked forward to anything that got us out of class.

One of the new requirements was to learn the Twenty Five Point Program of National Socialism and to discuss each point. Many essay assignments required us to describe one or more of the points and explain what they meant to Germany. There were contests for the best essays. I remember having to read out loud the entire list on several occasions. We were all given a card listing the Twenty Five Points to carry with us:

1. We demand the union of all Aryans within the world into a greater transcontinental National-Socialist Empire on the basis of the principle of self-determination of all peoples.
2. We demand that the Aryan people have rights equal to those of other nations and by that our nations shall remain sovereign.
3. We demand the land of Europe, North America, South America, Australia, and parts of Asia and Africa for the maintenance of our people and the settlement of our surplus population.
4. Only those who are of our race can become citizens. Only those who have Aryan blood, regardless of creed, can be our countrymen. Hence no Jew or Negro can be a citizen.
5. Those who are not citizens must leave our lands or live as foreigners and must be subject to the law of aliens.
6. The right to choose the government and determine the laws of the State shall belong only to citizens. We therefore demand that no public office, of whatever nature, whether in the central government, the province, or the municipality, shall be held by anyone who is not a citizen. We wage war against the corrupt parliamentary administration whereby men are appointed to posts by favor of the party without regard to character and fitness.
7. We demand that the State shall above all undertake to ensure that every citizen shall have the possibility of living decently and earning a livelihood. If it should not be possible to feed the whole population, then aliens (non-citizens) must be expelled from the Realm.
8. Any further immigration of non-Aryans must be prevented. We demand that all non-Aryans who have entered our lands since August 2, 1914, shall be compelled to leave the Realm immediately.
9. All citizens must possess equal rights and duties.

10. The first duty of every citizen must be to work mentally or physically. No individual shall do any work that offends against the interest of the community to the benefit of all. Therefore we demand:
11. That all unearned income, and all income that does not arise from work, be abolished, breaking the bondage of interest and Jewish financial slavery.
12. Since every war imposes on the people fearful sacrifices in blood and treasure, all personal profit arising from the war must be regarded as treason to the people. We therefore demand the total confiscation of all war profits whether in assets or material.
13. We demand the nationalization of all trusts.
14. We demand profit-sharing in large industries.
15. We demand a generous increase in old-age pensions.
16. We demand the creation and maintenance of a sound middle-class, the immediate communalization of large stores which will be rented cheaply to small trades-people, and the strongest consideration must be given to ensure that small traders shall deliver the supplies needed by the State, the provinces and municipalities. 17. We demand an agrarian reform in accordance with our national requirements, and the enactment of a law to expropriate the owners without compensation of any land needed for the common purpose. The abolition of ground rents, and the prohibition of all speculation in land.
18. We demand that ruthless war be waged against those who work to the injury of the common welfare. Traitors, usurers, profiteers, etc., are to be punished with death, regardless of creed or race.
19. We demand that Roman law, which serves a materialist ordering of the world, be replaced by an Aryan common law.
20. In order to make it possible for every capable and industrious Aryan to obtain higher education, and thus the opportunity to reach into positions of leadership,

the State must assume the responsibility of organizing thoroughly the entire cultural system of the people. The curricula of all educational establishments shall be adapted to practical life. The conception of the State Idea (science of citizenship) must be taught in the Schools from the very beginning. We demand that Uniquely talented children of poor parents, whatever their station or occupation, be educated at the expense of the State.

21. The State has the duty to help raise the standard of national health by providing maternity welfare centers, by prohibiting juvenile labor, by increasing physical fitness through the introduction of compulsory games and gymnastics, and by the greatest possible encouragement of associations concerned with the physical education of the young.

22. We demand the abolition of the regular army and the creation of a national (folk) army. We also demand that all technological means be employed to maintain the most advanced army in the world.

23. We demand that there be a legal campaign against those who propagate deliberate political lies and disseminate them through the press. In order to make possible the creation of an Aryan press, we demand:

   (a) All editors and their assistants on newspapers published in Germanic, Romance, or Slavic languages shall be citizens within a sanctioned National-Socialist state.

   (b) Non-Aryan newspapers shall only be published with the express permission of the State. They must not be published in any European language.

   (c) All financial interests in or in any way affecting Aryan newspapers shall be forbidden to non-Aryans by law, and we demand that the punishment for transgressing this law be the immediate suppression of the newspaper and the expulsion of the non-Aryans from the Realm. Newspapers transgressing against

the common welfare shall be suppressed. We demand legal action against those tendencies in art
and literature that have a disruptive influence upon
the life of our folk, and that any organizations that
offend against the foregoing demands shall be dis-
solved.

24. We demand freedom for all religious faiths in the state,
insofar as they do not endanger its existence or offend
the moral and ethical sense of the Aryan race. The
party as such represents the point of view of a positive
Christianity without binding itself to any one particular
confession. It fights against the Jewish materialist spirit
within and without, and is convinced that a lasting recovery of our folk can only come about from within on
the principle.

25. In order to carry out this program we demand the creation of a strong central authority in the State, the unconditional authority by the political central parliament
of the whole State and all its organizations. The formation of professional committees and of committees
representing the several estates of the realm, to ensure
that the laws promulgated by the international central
authority shall be carried out by the Aryan states. The
leaders of the party undertake to promote the execution of the foregoing points at all costs, if necessary at
the sacrifice of their own lives.

From then on a portrait of Hitler hung in every classroom. Particular emphasis was paid to the subject of history,
which was rewritten to emphasize Nazi themes of racial
struggle and German pride. Hitler's struggle for power was
emphasized, glorifying events such as the Beer Hall Putsch
and offering hero-worship of Nazi figures such as Horst Wessel
along with Nazi mythology concerning Hitler's liberation
of Germany from the international Jewish/Bolshevik world
conspiracy.

Teaching included how to spot a Jew by describing the physical traits, which Nazis believed were associated with inferior peoples.

I heard that in some classrooms, where Jews were still present, a Jewish child would be brought to the front of the class as an example. The teachers would then use a pointer, highlighting certain facial characteristics.

A Nazi doctor came to the school one day and talked to us about the dangers of allowing Jewish doctors to touch German boys. When the doctor asked if any of the students had ever been touched by a Jewish doctor, Guenther responded that he had and gave his doctor's name. The next time Guenther went to the doctor there was someone new in the office.

Because of what we were taught in school and at *Jungvolk* meetings, we believed that goodness was determined by race. This conflict between two authority figures, our parents and the state, caused much turmoil within us at the time. Though we did not want to upset our parents, we also did not want to let down *our* Germany.

That year, a new department store named *Karstadt* was built at the *Hermannplatz*, at the center of Neukolln. The store took up the entire length of the square. The building had twin towers that were topped by columns that were lit up at night by purple fluorescent lights. The lights could be seen many blocks away. I remember being impressed by the purple glow.

In 1932, Hitler was nominated as the National Socialist candidate for president, although he failed to gain enough votes to win. The Reichstag elections took place with the Nazis winning 230 seats in the 608 seat Reichstag. The National Socialist Party became the largest party in Germany. Communists and Nazis rioted in Berlin and the Reich threatened the death penalty. Herman Goering was elected president of the Reichstag and unemployment reached over six million.

These were very unsettled and difficult times because of the political and economic situation. The Great Depression was as bad in Germany as it was elsewhere, if not worse. The economic situation in Germany was still deteriorating, as the number of unemployed people rose steadily. Many families had no money. To help underprivileged children, schools through the Quaker Food Relief for Needy Europeans, were able to provide a hot meal at the cost of a few *Pfennigs*. For many families, this was the only hot meal their children received. Workers from a central kitchen delivered the food to the school and served it in the basement on long tables covered with oilcloth. It was a very simple meal usually consisting of a bowl of oatmeal with milk or a bowl of soup. Boiled potatoes, gravy and meat were served once a week.

The Hitler Youth, along with the SA, took part in election campaigns for two Reichstag elections and two Presidential elections. However, the campaigns cost a lot of money and the Nazi Party ran into serious financial difficulties. The Hitler Youth organization essentially went broke. Although it continued to attract more members, new boys mostly came from unemployed families.

During overnight camping trips, we relaxed around the campfire and learned Nazi slogans while joining in sing-a-longs of Hitler Youth and Nazi anthems. Our main political instruction took place during weekly *Heimabends* (home evenings) in the houses of other members or at our *Heim*, a converted shop once owned by a Jewish family.

The agenda was usually set via special educational letters sent to local Hitler Youth leaders giving detailed instructions on how to conduct the meetings. During these meetings, propaganda activities for the following week were also planned. The economy was always on the agenda for discussion.

To the average German, their elected democratic leaders seemed unable to cope with the enormous daily sufferings brought on by the Great Depression. Throughout

Germany, thousands of businesses and banks had failed. People lost their life's savings. Millions were now unemployed, struggling to put food on the table to feed their children.

As the democratic government in Berlin slowly unraveled under this pressure, the Nazis and other rival political groups, especially the Communists, positioned themselves to seize power. The Communists were the Nazis main rivals and had their own storm trooper organization, the Red Front, whose members were always willing to fight Nazis in the streets. Violent street incidents also erupted between Hitler Youths and young Communists. Uniformed Hitler Youth, like the brown shirted SA, were a visible force in the streets campaigning for Hitler and conducting frequent propaganda marches. Street battles between Communist youths and Hitler Youths occurred regularly.

Rolf was involved in several confrontations on the streets.

They battled with fists and sticks but increasingly resorted to the use of firearms. Between 1931 and 1933, twenty-three Hitler Youths were killed in the streets.

The best-known case involved twelve-year-old Herbert Norkus. Early on the morning of Sunday, January 26, 1932, he went out with his local Hitler Youth troop posting notices of an upcoming anti-Red meeting. The boys were then attacked by a troop of Communists and scattered, but Norkus was caught and stabbed twice. He ran to a nearby house for help but the owner shut the door in his face. Norkus was then stabbed five more times and left a trail of bloody hand prints along the outside wall of the house as he tried to pull himself up.

The incident became the focus of the Nazi feature length propaganda movie *Hitler Junge Quex*. Rolf, Guenther and I were selected to be in the movie.

Hitler Youth Quex was about the sacrificial spirit of the German youth. In the movie, a German youth faces a conflict of ideals between his Communist father and his growing allegiance to the Hitler Youth movement, which eventually leads to his own death. The movie unfolds as a family drama, set against the chaotic political and economic crisis of the late Weimar years. Heini Völker, a printer's apprentice, joins a communist youth group at the prompting of his father, an unemployed worker and war veteran, and a chronic drinker who torments his mournful wife. During a weekend outing Heini quickly grows disenchanted with his unruly communist comrades and flees their alcoholic and sexual revelry. Retreating into the woods, he spies an idealized group of Hitler Youths and looks upon their nighttime ceremony with fascination, an interest undiminished even after the Nazis discover him and send him away.

Ten of us from our *Heim* were chosen to sit around the campfire during the filming of the movie.

Heini returns to Berlin talking about the order and discipline of the Hitler Youth, singing their anthem to his mother, and causing his father to scold and beat him. Despite this outburst and the promptings of the communist leader, Stoppel, Heini seeks out the young Nazis Fritz and Ulla. He refuses to participate in a communist raid on the new Hitler Youth dormitory, but cannot fully convince the Nazis of his good faith until he warns them that Stoppel and his group plan to bomb the new hostel. Mother Völker confronted by an enraged Stoppel after the communist plot backfires, fears for her son, but does not know how to protect him. In desperation, she turns on the gas to put an end to both herself and the sleeping boy.

After awakening in a hospital, Heini finds himself surrounded by a group of Hitler Youths who express their gratitude and present him with a uniform and a mirror. As a result of his mother's death and his father's submission to the special plea of Hitler Youth Brigade Leader Cass, Heini moves into a Nazi dormitory. Active and energetic (so much so that his enthusiasm gains him the nickname "Quex," or quicksilver), Heini works all night to print leaflets for the upcoming election and insists on distributing them in his old neighborhood, Beuselkitz. Members of Stoppel's group, headed by the vicious Wilde, learn of Heini's presence and chase him through the streets, cornering him in a fairground where Wilde bludgeons him with the knife once coveted by Heini. When his Nazi associates reach him, it is too late. With his last breath Heini gestures upward and utters the words, "Our flag flutters before us; it leads . . ." as the image segues into a close-up of a party banner over which marching figures parade in geometric configurations.

We were all so proud to be in the movie.

In April 1932, attempting to halt the widespread political violence, the German democratic government banned the SA and the Hitler Youth. However, for most of us German teenagers, the lure of joining this now-forbidden youth organization resulted in a surge of new recruits. I was twelve years old and was beginning to develop a mind of my own.

A few months later, due to behind-the-scenes political manipulations by Hitler, the ban on the SA and Hitler Youth was lifted. Hitler and the Nazis were now close to achieving power.

We were called upon to distribute literature about the Nazi Party on weekends. We would wear our uniforms and organize in teams of two. Guenther and I would always team up while Rolf generally organized the teams and insured everyone looked their best.

I remember one Sunday going to the *Monbijou* Park. It was a bright sunny day and many people were in the park enjoying the day. The street vendors were set-up, cooking sausage on a stick and serving beer. The aroma of the sweet sausage made us hungry.

Guenther and I arrived about 11:00am and began passing out pamphlets. We usually tried to get close to the food vendors. Everyone commented that we looked sharp in our uniforms.

People were very polite and returned the national salute saying, "Heil Hitler."

We had been handing out literature for about an hour when I noticed some commotion beside the bandstand.

Most of the larger parks had bandstands where bands played on the weekends. Father would often take us to hear the music.

Peter and Hentz, from our *Heim*, were being shoved by a man who was shouting derogatory comments about Hitler. Apparently, Peter and Hentz began shouting back and the atmosphere was getting tense.

Guenther and I ran over to lend assistance when a police officer came by and demanded to know what was going on. The man began shouting at the officer and wouldn't let Peter or Hentz say a word. The police officer had enough and began blowing his whistle. Soon other police officers came to the scene with two SS soldiers. As soon as the enraged man spotted the SS soldiers, he calmed down and became very apologetic to Peter and Hentz.

That experience made me realize how important the SS was.

I admired how they were given respect.

I think it was from that moment that I started thinking about becoming a member of the SS.

They were different than other soldiers and police we saw. They looked sharp in their black uniforms and exuded confidence. They were obviously special. Guenther and I talked about the SS for the rest of the day. We were much influenced by the way they carried themselves. They walked with a confident swagger and people respected them.

I didn't realize it at the time that the respect they received was largely out of fear.

When we got back to the Heim, we told Rolf about what we had seen. It was then he told us that he was going to be an SS officer some day and his father had made all the arrangements. He said his father had planned everything for him. He would go to a special school, study law, and serve the Fatherland in the SS. He would marry a woman who would bear many children and after his SS service, he would practice law.

In the parliamentary elections held on July 31, 1932, the Nazis became the largest political party in Germany, receiving 13.7 million votes granting them 230 seats in the Reichstag. The tireless propaganda activities of the Hitler Youth had helped enormously to achieve this. All over Germany, they had handed out millions of pamphlets and special editions of Nazi newspapers and conducted countless propaganda marches.

The leadership of the National Socialist SS stated their intention to enforce a previously proposed racial Nazi law within their own ranks. Initially, it was their intention to force this law onto all German people. An order, issued by the Reich leadership of the SS, made marriage approval by a racial authority compulsory for all SS members.

There were five elections that year. Placards, posters and flags were displayed everywhere on Election Day.

It was very colorful.

The main difference between the Nazi Party and those of the Communists and the Socialists was that the latter promised better living conditions at some future time while the Nazis stressed work and bread now. This gave hope to the unemployed. The Nazis constantly appealed to and played on people's emotions by condemning the Treaty of Versailles. This attracted many who were disillusioned because it promised to restore dignity and pride in Germany. On January 30, 1933 President Hindenberg appointed Hitler Chancellor in a coalition government. At the Hotel *Kaiserhof*, Berlin's most elegant hotel and Hitler's headquarters, Hermann Goering read the announcement just after noon. That night, Father took Mother and me to see the event. We stood along Under den Linden and watched thousands of SA men as they marched through the Brandenburg Gate along *Under den Linden* to the *Wilhelmstrasse* and the Chancery. Column after column of men, carrying torches passed by, singing the "Horst Wessel Song." The sound of boots hitting the pavement in unison was exciting. We discussed the events for several weeks at school.

I remember that on February 27, 1933 we were all astonished by the news of arson in the Reichstag. Fires were set in more than twenty places in the building. It was almost completely destroyed. The newspaper said the ringleader was the head of the Communist faction in the Reichstag, Representative Torgler.

The press brought another unsettling report. In the basement of the Karl Liebknecht Building, the Communist Party Headquarters, secret passages and hidden tunnels were discovered. Material that encouraged civil war was found. Detailed plans to murder both individuals and groups of Germans citizens were found. The bloody uprising was supposed to begin throughout Germany in the immediate future. There was to be murder and arson in cities and villages. These news items had a strong effect throughout Germany. The newspaper article read:

"The indifferent citizen who had not wanted to see the enormous danger of Bolshevism looked in horror toward Berlin. He too realized now that Germany faced a terrible threat. The burning Reichstag building was the signal that brought every German to his senses. The National Socialists, however, were not surprised. They saw it coming. They had long recognized the danger of Bolshevist world criminality. They had long predicted that what everyone now could see. They had warned the German people about it in a hundred thousand meetings; they had called them to battle against it in thousands of mass meetings. They organized a mass movement of millions against it. The German people have woken up. It has risen up. It wants to fight against Bolshevist criminality. It demands its destruction, its

defeat, and its extermination. However, the German people do not know who is guilty. They do not know the cause of this terrible uprising, this criminal murderous arson. The German people will fight in vain against this plague, against this poison, if they fail to recognize the scoundrels who mix the poison and spread the plague. It is not difficult to find the true cause of Marxist-Bolshevist world criminality. It is as clear as the light of day, and one need only open one's eyes to know the truth. The truth is that Jews founded both parties that want civil war, that hate the fatherland and that recognize only an "Internationale." The Jew Karl Marx, who gave his name to the movement, wrote the program. The Jews LaSalle (Wolfson), Kautsky, Bernstein, Dr. Hilferding, Dr. Moses, Rosa Luxemburg, Liebknecht, Münzenberg and others led and still lead the SPD [Socialist Party] and KPD [Communist Party]. The truth is that the leaders, rabble-rousers, and fomenters of the November Revolution of 1918 were a clique of Jews. Haase, Mühsam, Toller, Eisner, Levien, Neurath, etc., all belonged to the Jewish people. The truth is that the Marxist movement is in reality a Jewish movement. The goal of the movement is to make the confused, roused masses into an enormous army of Jewish slaves. This army would be used and exploited to reach the great goal of Jewry, Jewish world domination. Let anyone who doubts it read the "Zionist Protocols," the Jewish plan for world domination. There he will be enlightened. The scales will fall from his eyes. The events in Berlin will no longer be a secret; they will no longer be a surprise. He will have found the guilty party. The "Zionist Protocols" were agreed on by the Jews at the World Jewish Congress in 1897 in Basel. They were written and read by Achad Cham, the secret leader of Zionist world Jewry. They fell into the hands of the Russian government through bribery, and were translated and printed by Professor Nilus. A copy of this translation has been in the British National Library since 1906. This is what is written in the Third Protocol: "Hunger gives finance more secure power over the workers than the legal strength of the king. We will cause hunger by bringing to a halt all the stock exchanges and industries. The people will fall under the power of rich newcomers Barmat, Kutisker, Sklarek, Coal-Jew Petcheck, Industry Jew Silverberg, etc. They will lay a pitiless yoke on the workers. We will then arrive to save the workers from their slavery. We will urge them to join the ranks of our army of anarchists, socialists and communists. The masses today blindly believe the printed word and the false doctrines it contains. In their ignorance, they hate any class above them. We will intensify this hatred. With the help of the money that we completely control, we will bring about a general economic crisis. At the same time, we will throw armies of workers out on the streets throughout the world. The masses will then gladly shed the blood of those National Socialists we say are their enemies, and whose possessions they can then steal. This will all take place under the banner of "Freedom" which is the epitome of animalistic power. We will transform the masses into blood-thirsty beasts. They will fall asleep once they have shed blood. Then we can easily put them in chains. But if they do not have blood, they will fight rather than sleep." Thus the goals of Pan-Jewry and the secret of Marxism, which tears the world and the nations apart, are revealed. The Jews planned everything that is happening today in 1897. They stilled the industries, brought about economic crises, threw workers out on the streets and weakened them through hunger, and then led these desperate people against those who opposed the Jews, against the National Socialists. It all follows the Protocols sentence-by-sentence, word-by-word. It is all following plan. The plan of the "Zionist Protocols." The Marxist factory worker became a tool of the Jewish world criminals. The National Socialists, under their Führer Adolf Hitler, saw through this chicanery. They fought with all their strength for 14 years with unprecedented determination. On 30 January 1933, they took power. Adolf Hitler became the Reich Chancellor. Pan-Jewry was seized with terror, rage, and hatred. It made a last attempt to regain its power in Germany. The 9th Protocol of the "Zion-

ist Protocols" discusses its method: You might think that the non-Jews will attack us, weapons in hand, once they recognize that we are behind everything. In this event, we have a last terrible weapon in our hands that will bring dread even to the bravest heart. Soon underground subway tunnels will be under all the great cities of the world. We will use them, if necessary, to blow all the capital cities up. We will poison the water lines and send whole classes to death. We will burn down all public buildings."

I remember being very impressed by the newspaper article. We were told at our *Jungvolk* meeting the next evening that what the Jews planned in Basel in 1897 was to become reality in Berlin in 1933 and the Communist sub humans were to be the tools.

The burning of the Reichstag, we were told, was to be the signal for the attack. The Jews did not succeed in carrying out their treacherous plan. The National Socialist Minister Goring had put a halt to their plans however; the Jew will find new intrigues and crimes, we were told. We discussed how his Zionist program and his Jewish brain would help him. We were told that he will not rest until a new attack on Germany is ready.

I was convinced, like most of the youth of Germany, that the Jew was guilty. He was guilty of the arson in Berlin, of the crimes of Bolshevism, of the crimes of Marxist agitation. I came to believe that Germany would not be at peace until the last of these guilty ones is tried and convicted.

Soon, the Swastika and the Empire Banner side by side replaced the flag of the German Republic. The Reichstag gave Hitler the power to rule by decree and Jews were banned in business, professions, and from the schools.

After the Nationalist Socialists came to power in 1933, they were in a position to re-align the education and schooling programs to more optimally conform to the needs of the party. High on their priority list was to introduce all of Germany's students to a full and comprehensive physical fitness routine.

Also high on the list was to introduce more politically correct textbooks and curriculum into the education system. Strong emphasis was laid on the theory that from now on, everything that was learned in school would only do Germany good if the learned knowledge remained inside of Germany and was put to use for Germany. If a field of study or a particular view was not approved by the NSDAP, it was considered bad for Germany.

From the very smallest or rural schools to the most prestigious of German universities, German Nationalist Socialists ideology and party leaders removed all the teachers and professors who were adherents of the Jewish faith from their jobs and posts. In addition, they removed those who were declared by the state to be anti-German in their views. One's standing in the international community did not provide any layer of protection, though it shielded a few very high-profile individuals from persecution for a short while. Some teachers were sent to the re-education camp that was established at Dachau, located on the grounds of an abandoned munitions factory near the medieval town of Dachau, about 10 miles northwest of Munich.

Opened on March 22, 1933, the Dachau concentration camp was the first regular concentration camp established by the National Socialist government. Heinrich Himmler, in his capacity as police president of Munich, officially described the camp as the first concentration camp for political prisoners.

For example, in class we were now expected to submit politically appropriate materials to our teachers in our essays. Teachers were afraid to challenge or question the new curriculum for fear of being turned in to the Gestapo as being anti or un-German. Only the party's view was the correct educational view.

Our assignments, such as "How did Adolf Hitler save the Fatherland?" or "The German man," were now standards of education excellence in Germany.

For *Jungmäedel* and *Jungvolk* students, a new school plan was established. During the first school year, Germanic gods and Germanic mythological heroes were studied. In the second school year, Great Germans like Bismarck, Frederick the Great, Carl Peters, Widukind, etc. were studied. The Twenty years struggle, Battle of Upper Silesia in 1919, the Battle of Tannenberg in 1914, World War I, HJ in the *Kampfzeit*, the Battle for Berlin, were the focus. In the fourth school year Adolf Hitler and his political supporters including Baldur von Schirach, Horst Wessel, etc. were presented to students.

The inclusion of Nationalist Socialist philosophies was not only limited to writing essays in school. It was also worked into the sciences. I remember two problems from a school examination for mathematics.

The first problem compared the cost of an asylum to apartments. At the time, the construction of an asylum for the mentally challenged costs six million *Reichsmark*. The first problem asked how many apartments, each individual unit costing 15,000 Reichsmark could one have built in place of the asylum?

The second problem dealt with state subsidy. A mentally challenged person requires a daily state subsidy of 4 Reichsmark, a physically challenged person 5.50 Reichsmark daily and a common criminal 3.50 Reichsmark daily. It is estimated that there are about 300,000 people in Germany for whom the state must pay these costs. We had to answer how many state sponsored, 1,000 Reichsmark marriage loans, could be supported for the same amount of money?

In school and in the community we were expected to become obedient servants of the state. Strict discipline was to be maintained at all times in both home and school environments.

We all said "Heil Hitler," what seems like 100 to 150 times a day.

If you meet a friend on the way to school, you say it. Study periods are opened and closed with "Heil Hitler."

"Heil Hitler" says the postman, the street-car conductor, the girl who sells ice cream at the local store. We were told that if your parents' first words when you come home to lunch are not "Heil Hitler" they have been guilty of a punishable offense, and can be denounced.

"Heil Hitler" is shouted at the *Jungvolk* and Hitler Youth meetings. Officially, when you say hello to your superiors in school or in a group, the words are accompanied by the act of throwing the right arm high.

This Hitler greeting became a German greeting and was repeated countless times from morning to bedtime stamping the whole day.

All the way down the street, flags are waving, every window colored with red banners, and the black swastika in the middle of each.

We never stopped to ask why. It's bound to be some national event.

In addition to re-aligning the educational standards more in line with NSDAP philosophies, a new school system was also created in Germany, paralleling the existing public schools. This new system was supposed to be for the education and training of German future elite, its future SA and SS administrators, law enforcement forces and labor service leaders.

I remember coming home one day and telling Mother and Father about what was happening in school.

Mother kept shaking her head as if in disbelief.

Father said, "Margaret, there must be something to it or the Reich Ministry would not have changed the school curriculum."

Mother responded, "Oh, so the Nazis would not lie?"

Father gave her an exasperated look.

We talked about it more after dinner.

I said, "Captain Schill came into our classroom and told that we must be on the look out for adults who would talk against the new teachings. He said that these people might be working with the Jews and our other enemies to undermine Germany. He said that we should report anyone who is suspicious. He said that anyone who says anything bad about the government should be reported. This way, they can be checked out and cleared if innocent."

Mother spoke up, "Kurt, just because someone disagrees it doesn't mean they are a traitor."

Father interrupted, "Just the same Margaret, one must be careful what one says these days. We don't want to give the wrong impression."

From that day on, I never heard Mother or Father comment about the government or the Jews.

I do not know if they thought that I might repeat something they said inadvertently in school or that I might actually turn them in. Any time the topics would come up, they would change the subject.

Looking back at what was happening in Germany at that time, they must have been very frightened. If you were not a Nazi party member or at least enthusiastic about what the Nazis were doing you were looked upon with suspicion.

I guess for my parents to hear their son talk about turning people in must have been discomforting.

The changes that were taking place around the country were subtle, at least to me. First, there were the boycotts of Jewish businesses. Then, Jewish businesses were attacked. Windows were broken and shopkeepers were beaten. I heard about these things on the radio or at school but they remained distant activities since my family did not associate with any Jews.

After a while, officials fired Jewish teachers and replaced with ones who promoted the Nazi party doctrine. We did not realize it at the time but we, the children, were the targets of the party. As the months went by, more and more of the class time was spent on racial purity. I had not really understood the things we had to memorize in order to pass our test to join the *Jungvolk*. However, as we discussed these things increasingly in school, the aspects of racial purity were beginning to make sense.

Our education in the classroom was supported by the group readings that we did at the *Jungvolk* meetings. The stories reinforced what our teachers and the leaders were telling us. I eventually came to believe that if so many people were saying the same things about the Jews that at least most of it must be true.

Guenther was slower to come along to the realization about the Jews. Perhaps that was because of his parents influence. They had been admonished at school for not being as enthusiastic about racial purity as they should have been. I knew that they were not fans of Hitler or the Nazis but they were very nice people.

Rolf had come to the realization about the Jews before me. He was a year older and his parents were ardent members of the party. They were very nice people too. Mother and Father used to visit with Guenther's parents when we were younger. They stopped visiting all of a sudden and I wondered if someone had cautioned my parents that Guenther's parents were liberal.

Rolf's parents would come to our apartment on several occasions for dinner. The conversation always came around to the wonderful things that the party was doing. I knew my mother was uncomfortable. Father could carry on a conversation with anyone. He always seemed to know the right things to say.

It was not uncommon for me to go to the zoo with Guenther and his parents or for Rolf to go out to dinner with my parents and me. Although our parents were friendly with one another, Rolf, Guenther, and I, and later Anna, spent the most time together.

Chapter Five
Radio

The year 1933 saw the advent of radio as a method for the government to provide propaganda to a large number of people. On February 1, Hitler made his first radio address to the German people after becoming Chancellor.

He declared, "The members of the new government would preserve and defend those basic principles on which our nation has been built up. We regard Christianity as the foundation of our national morality and the family as the basis of our national life."

Political broadcasts were typically aired during work hours, and work was often paused in order for the workers to listen to Hitler on the radio.

The Nazis produced a new inexpensive radio called a *Volksempfanger* or people's radio, which could only pick up one channel. Over three million of them were sold. Radio wardens used to encourage people in blocks of houses and apartment buildings to buy a radio, and listen to the broadcast. The wardens also reported anyone failing to listen to Hitler's speeches and other important announcements. They were Nazi Party members who would act as discussion facilitators and to insure that the Marxist radio broadcasts did not influence the people.

The new media was proving itself, and it was winning the hearts of the people, with thousands of radio clubs springing up in Germany. In fifteen months, the number of listeners grew from 4.3 million to 5.5 million, an increase of 25 percent. Rolf's father became a radio warden and led discussions at the local club.

We did not have a radio in 1933 so Father and Mother joined the local club, which met at the Rolf's apartment. I remember going to Rolf's on April 20th, Hitler's birthday, to listen to a broadcast by Dr. Joseph Goebbels. It was the first time I heard him on the radio and I was very impressed. The following speech was called "Our Hitler."

"The newspapers today are filled with congratulations for Reich Chancellor Adolf Hitler. The nuances vary, depending on the tone, character, and attitude of the newspaper. All, however, agree on one thing: Hitler is a man of stature who has already accomplished historically important deeds and faces still greater challenges. He is the kind of statesman found only rarely in Germany. During his lifetime, he has the good fortune not only to be appreciated and loved by the overwhelming majority of the German people, but even more importantly to be understood by them. He is the only German politician of the post-war period who understood the situation and drew the necessary hard and firm conclusions. All the newspapers agree on this. It no longer needs to be said that he has taken up Bismarck's work and intends to complete it. There is enough proof of this even for those who do not believe, or who think ill of him. I therefore do not think it necessary for me to discuss the historical significance and still unknown impact of this man on the

eve of the day on which, far from the bustle of the Reich capital, Adolf Hitler completes his 44th year. I feel a much deeper need to personally express my esteem for him and in doing so I believe that I am speaking for many hundreds of thousands of National Socialists throughout the country."

At this point, Goebbels stopped speaking and another voice announced that there would be a fifteen minute intermission to allow the radio wardens an opportunity to discuss these important words. Rolf's father began the discussion recalling the many triumphs and deeds that Hitler had performed for the nation. We all agreed that Hitler's character was above reproach. Dr. Goebbels began again:

"We shall leave it to those who were our enemies only a few months ago and who slandered him. They came to praise him today with awkward words and embarrassing pathos. We know how little Adolf Hitler appreciates such attempts, and how much more the devoted loyalty and lasting support of his friends and fellow fighters correspond to his nature. The mysterious magic that he exerts on all who come in contact with him cannot alone explain his historic personality. There is more that makes us love and esteem him. Through all the ups and downs of Adolf Hitler's career, from the beginning of his political activity to the crowning of his career as he seized power, he has always remained the same: a person among people, a friend to his comrades, an eager supporter of every ability and

talent. He is a pathfinder for those who devoted themselves to his idea, a man who conquered the hearts of his comrades in the midst of battle and never released them. It seems to me that one thing has to be said in the midst of the profusion of feelings. Only a few know Hitler well. Most of the millions who look to him with faithful trust do so from a distance. He has become to them a symbol of their faith in the future. Normally the great men that we admire from a distance lose their magic when one knows them well. With Hitler the opposite is true. The longer one knows him, the more one admires him, and the more one is ready to give oneself fully to his cause. We will let others blow the trumpets. His friends and comrades gather round him to shake his hand and thank him for everything that he is to us, and that he has given to us. Let me say it once more: We love this man, and we know that he has earned all of our love and support. Never was a man more unjustly accused by the hate and slanders of his ill-wishers of other parties. Remember what they said about him! A mishmash of contradictory accusations! They did not miss accusing him of every sin, or denying him every virtue. When he nonetheless overcame in the end the flood of lies, triumphing over his enemies and raising the National Socialist flag over Germany, fate showed its favor toward him to the entire world. It raised him from the mass of people and put him in the place *he deserved because of his brilliant gifts and his pure and flawless humanity. I remember the years when — just released from prison — he began to rebuild his party. We passed a few wonderful vacation days with him on his beloved Obersalzberg high above Berchtesgaden. Below us was the quiet cemetery where his unforgettable friend Dietrich Eckart is buried. We walked through the mountains, discussed plans for the future, and talked about theories that today have long since become reality. He then sent me to Berlin. He gave me a difficult and challenging task, and I still thank him today that he gave me the job. A few months later we sat in a room in a small Berlin hotel. The party had just been banned by the Marxist-Jewish police department. Heavy blows were falling on it. The party was full of discouragement, bickering and quarreling. Everyone was complaining about everyone else. The whole organization seemed to have given up. Hitler, however, did not lose courage, but immediately began to organize a defense, and helped out where he was needed."*

There was another intermission and a discussion of how Hitler built the Nazi Party from scratch. This went on for the entire fifteen minutes with Rolf's father doing most of the talking. Dr. Goebbels began again:

"Although he had his own personal and political difficulties, he found the time and strength to

deal with the problems and support his friends in the Reich capital. One of his fine and noble traits is that he never gives up on someone who has won his confidence. The more his political opponents attack such a person, the more loyal is Adolf Hitler's support. He is not the kind of person who is afraid of strong associates. The harder and tougher a man is, the more Hitler likes him. If things fall apart, his capable hands put them together again. Who would have thought it possible that a mass organization that includes literally everything could be built in this nation of individualists? Doing that is Hitler's great accomplishment. His principles are firm and unshakable, but he is generous and understanding toward human weaknesses. He is a pitiless enemy of his opponents, but a good and warm-hearted friend to his comrades. That is Hitler. We saw him at the party's two large Nuremberg rallies, surrounded by the masses who saw in him Germany's hope. In the evenings, we sat with him in his hotel room. He was dressed in a simple brown shirt, the same as always, as if nothing had happened. Someone once said that the great is simple, and the simple is great. If that is true, it surely applies to Hitler. His nature and his whole philosophy is a brilliant simplification of the spiritual need and fragmentation that engulfed the German people after the war. He found the lowest common denominator. That is why his idea won: he modeled it, and through him *the average man in the street saw its depth and significance. One has to have seen him in defeat as well as victory to understand what sort of man he is. He never broke. He never lost courage or faith. Hundreds came to him seeking new hope, and no one left without receiving renewed strength. On the day before August 13, 1932, we met in a small farm house outside Potsdam. We talked deep into the night, but not about our prospects for the next day, but rather about music, philosophy, and worldview issues. Then came the experiences one can only have with him. He spoke of the difficult years of his youth in Vienna and Munich, of his war experiences, of first years of the party. Few know how hard and bitterly he had to fight. Today he is surrounded by praise and thanks. Only fifteen years ago he was a lonely individual among millions. The only difference between him and them was his burning faith and his fanatic resolve to transform that faith into action. Those who believed that Hitler was finished after the party's defeat in November 1932 failed to understand him. Only someone who did not know him at all could make such a mistake. Hitler is one of those persons who rise from his defeats. Friedrich Nietzsche's phrase fits him well: "That which does not destroy me only makes me stronger." This man, suffering under financial and party problems for years, assailed by the flood of lies from his enemies, wounded in the depths of his heart by the disloyalty of false friends, still found the limitless faith to lift his party from desperation to new victories. How many thousands of kilometers have I sat behind him in cars or airplanes on election campaigns. How often did I see the thankful look of a man on the street, or a mother lifting her child to show him, and how often have I seen joy and happiness when people recognized him. He kept his pockets filled with packages of cigarettes, each with a one or two mark coin. Every working lad he met got one. He had a friendly word for every mother and a warm handshake for every child. Not without reason does the German youth admire him. They know that this man is young at heart, and that their cause is in his good hands. Last Easter Monday we sat with him in his small house on the Obersalzberg. A group of young hikers from Braunau, where he was born, came by for a visit. How surprised these lads were when they got not only a friendly greeting, but all fifteen lads were invited in. They got a hurriedly prepared lunch, and had to tell him about his hometown of Braunau. The people have a fine sense for the truly great. Nothing impresses the people as deeply as when a person truly belongs to his people. Of whom but Hitler could this be true: As he returned from Berchtesgaden to Munich, people waved in every village. The children shouted Heil and threw bouquets of flowers into the car. The SA had closed the road in*

Traunstein. There was no moving either forward or back. Confidently and matter-of-factly, the SA Führer walked up to the car and said: "My Führer, an old party member is dying in the hospital, and his last wish is to see his Führer." Mountains of work were waiting in Munich. But Hitler ordered the car to turn around, and sat for half an hour in the hospital at the bedside of his dying party comrade. The Marxist press claimed he was a tyrant who dominated his satraps. What is he really? He is the best friend of his comrades. He has an open heart for every sorrow and every need, he has human understanding. He knows each of his associates thoroughly, and nothing happens in their public or private lives of which he is not aware. If misfortune happens, he helps them to bear it, and rejoices more than anyone else at their successes. Never have I seen his two sides in anyone else. We had dinner together on the night of the Reichstag fire. We talked and listened to music. Hitler was a person among people. Twenty minutes later he stood in the smoldering, smoking ruins of the Reichstag building and gave piercing orders that led to the destruction of communism. Later he sat in an editorial office and dictated an article. For those who do not know Hitler, it seems a miracle that millions of people love and support him. For those who know him, it is only natural. The secret of his success is in the indescribable magic of his personality. Those who know him the best love and honor him the most. One who has sworn allegiance to him is devoted to him body and soul. I thought it was necessary tonight to say that, and to have it said by someone who really knows him, and who could find the courage to break through the barriers of reserve and speak of Hitler the man. Today he has left the bustle of the capital. He left the wreaths and hymns of praise in Berlin. He is somewhere in his beloved Bavaria, far from the noise of the streets, to find peace and quiet. Perhaps in a nearby room someone will turn on a loudspeaker. If that should happen, then let me say to him, and to all of Germany: My Führer! Millions and millions of the best Germans send you their best wishes and give you their hearts. And we, your closest associates and friends, are gathered in honor and love. We know how little you like praise. But we must still say this: You have lifted Germany from its deepest disgrace to honor and dignity. You should know that behind you, and if necessary before you, a strong and determined group of fighters stands that is ready at any time to give its all for you and your idea. We wish both for your sake and ours that fate will preserve you for many decades, and that you may always remain our best friend and comrade. This is the wish of your fellow fighters and friends for your birthday. We offer you our hands and ask that you always remain for us what you are today. Our Hitler!"

Rolf's father summarized the speech, repeating key points, while we all listened attentively. The radio broadcasts usually followed clear lines in cultural and racial areas and the radio wardens were always there to guide the discussion. Guenther's parents did not belong to a radio club. This led some of the local clubs members to speculate whether they might be less than enthusiastic about National Socialism.

It was important to be seen as enthusiastic about the programs and ideas of the government after Hitler took office.

Mother would attend the radio club meetings but usually did not offer many opinions. She stopped going after we got our own radio. She would say that she preferred to listen to Hitler at home and enjoy the broadcasts in private although she rarely had the radio on when she was home alone. At the *Jungvolk* meetings, we discussed many of the same topics that were being broadcast. The topics included anti-Semitism, militarism, nationalism, supremacy of the Aryan race, cult of the *Führer*, anti-modernism, and traditional German culture.

Radio reception was not free. Telephone and radio came under the management of the post office. A *Geldbrieftraeger*, or money mailman, would come monthly and collect the two marks for the radio. Later, when we had our own radio, Rolf's father would come to collect and visit for a while. He and Father would talk over a glass of Schnapps.

Through radio, the Nazis encouraged the worship of Hitler by making him more accessible to the common man. Sentimentality was evoked in the German people through the use of stories detailing somewhat intimate details about Hitler, such as the fact that he enjoyed sweets. Hitler was portrayed as a god-like figure.

The story of Hitler's childhood was also told and retold over the radio and in school and turned into a sort of myth in order to create feelings of identification amongst rebellious youth. These stories and details about Hitler's life contributed to the magical hold that he possessed over his followers.

This identification with Hitler also provided him with much undying loyalty from his followers since many believed their actions would directly affect Hitler.

Eventually, directly or indirectly, the press was controlled by the Nazi publishing house. The Ministry for Enlightenment and Propaganda told editors where to place articles and the Nazi Press Agency supplied an estimated 50% of content.

From 1933 on, all editors and journalists had to be accredited by the Propaganda Ministry. Germany had a rich classical tradition, which suited the Nazi's cultural propaganda objectives. The Jewish composers Mahler and Mendelssohn were banned. New wave, modernist composers like Stravinsky and Schoenberg were ridiculed and new genres, such as jazz, labelled Negroid and degenerate.

In May, public announcements began in the newspapers. I remember Father and Mother discussing them at dinner. One of them described a conference of German ministers, Reich Minister of the Interior Frick said, "The idea of liberal education has completely undermined the meaning of education and our educational institutions."

Mother thought it was all, "hog-wash," in her words.

Father preferred to study the words before commenting.

A new law was being implemented in the schools that emphasized the political person, whose actions, service and sacrifice was rooted in service to the people. The people and the nation were to be the most important areas of education. History of our people was to take first priority. Next to the strong emphasis on history and German values ranked biology and race science.

One newspaper announcement spelled out regulations for Good Friday. Forbidden activities included races, sport and physical exercise events of a commercial nature and similar performances, as well as sporting and physical training events of a noncommercial nature in as far as they are offered to a large audience. Music featured in bars or pubs was prohibited. Permitted activities were theater and musical performances of a religious and solemn nature. Only serious music could be played and radio programs had to be of a solemn nature. During the hours of main church services, from 9 a.m. to 11:30 a.m., all performances were forbidden.

For many of us, the lure of the National Socialist religion was much more exciting than the Christian religion offered to us by our parents. We would often find excuses to avoid going to religious classes and services. We always found some excuse or pretext to cut classes.

Rolf, Guenther and I believed we were too busy with our Hitler Youth activities to be bothered by church. The fact that our leaders did not encourage church participation made it much easier for me to justify to myself and to Mother why I did not attend religious class.

Mother was not happy that I was distancing myself from the church but, after awhile, she resigned herself to it.

Nazi ideology taught youth to admire those who were willing to kill a person who opposed the Nazis. Our leaders asked how we could worship Jesus who was portrayed by Nazi propaganda to have died "whimpering on the Cross."

Though there was not an implicit demand that all youth adhere to the Nazi religion over the Church, the policies and propaganda concerning the Church caused most of us to pick the state over it. Due to the influence of Nazi philosophy, the reverence with which Christianity had been held was no longer present. We could not be expected to admire the "whimpering Christ" when the heroic Nazi was also held before us. We chose the more exciting hero, which were generally the Nazis.

The use of laws to discriminate against Jews began on March 24, 1933, when the Reichstag passed the Enabling Act giving the new Chancellor, Adolf Hitler, and the Nazi Party dictatorial powers. The Reichstag's action gave the government power to govern and legislate by decree, thereby providing the Nazis a cloak of legality with which to cover their official actions.

The biological premises of Nazi anti-Semitism prescribed a specific approach to anti-Jewish legislation. It would have been reasonable to predict in 1932 that the first anti-Jewish laws of a Nazi regime would be designed to halt the process of biological assimilation. It is not surprising, therefore, that the first concrete proposals for anti-Jewish legislation were aimed at de-assimilating the Jews from Germany.

However, the set of four laws publicized in April 1933 had little to do with what Nazi ideology proclaimed to be the heart of the Jewish question. They were directed against the Jewish professionals who had been the object of party intimidation. The first two laws, both decreed on April 7th, were aimed at the civil servants and legal profession. Two more laws, one affecting Jewish doctors practicing within the National Health Service, the other affecting Jewish teachers and students, went into effect on April 22nd and April 25th respectively.

The April Laws were followed on July 14th by a Denaturalization Law, which allowed the Reich government to revoke the citizenship of people it considered undesirable. Three further pieces of legislation affecting the Jews came into effect in 1933.

On September 29th, a Hereditary Farm Law excluded Jews from owning farmland or engaging in agriculture. The remaining pieces of legislation in 1933 dealt a major blow to Germany's Jews. The first law established Chambers of culture within the Propaganda Ministry, to regulate the film, theater, music, fine arts, literature, broadcasting, and the press. The law establishing the Chambers of Culture contained no Aryan clause. None was necessary. Goebbles, Minister of Propaganda, had been granted authority to refuse admission of undesirable to any of the chambers. The second, a more specific law dealing with journalists, was effected on October 4. Its provisions were similar to the ones that established the chambers of culture. None of these laws, though, were sufficient in defining the Jew. It wasn't until 1935 that the definition of a Jew was established.

One day when Guenther, Rolf and I were walking by the Potato Shop on Mink Street we discovered the door and windows to be boarded shut. Painted on the wood was the Star of David.

Joseph didn't come to school after that day.

He and his family just disappeared. We figured they moved away from Berlin.

A couple of days later, Mr. and Mrs. Weismann's neighborhood bakery was vacant. A German couple took over operation of the business. The Weismann's too must have decided to move from Berlin.

Chapter Six
Collecting

Rolf was the squad leader of our *Jungvolk* group. It only seemed right. He was fourteen years old and his Mother and Father were Nazi Party members. Rolf wore his hair in short military-style and seemed more grown-up then us. We all liked getting together on Thursday nights at the *Heim*. We read books aloud, sang songs, and played games.

On Sundays, we would participate in collections of scrap metal and newspaper or various other collections of money, food, or whatever the local Hitler Youth leader wanted us to collect. We would sell buttons to raise money for the Hitler Youth.

One Sunday we met at the *Heim* as usual. Rolf was already there with a stack of burlap sacks. The assignment was to come back with a full bag of scrap items. Rolf decided that we should begin at the Brandenburg Gate and go up and down the intersecting streets. Rolf and another boy would go to Lehrter Street while Guenther and I would start on in the opposite direction of the Brandenburg Gate. We would all meet back at the *Heim* at 5:00 p.m.

I wanted to work Lehrter Street. I was sure my neighbors would feel bad for me and contribute.

Rolf insisted, and we were off. As Guenther and I walked away, I could not help but wonder why Rolf had insisted that we go to another street. I was determined to ask him when we got back.

The first stop for Guenther and I was a neat looking brick apartment building with five doorbells. The shrubs in the front of the building were neatly trimmed. The dirt underneath was neatly raked in one direction. We reasoned that this place should yield a lot. We decided to try the top apartments first, figuring that it would be easier to drag full sacks down the steps rather then trying to carry it up four stories.

We were nervous!

We looked at each other; both of us were wearing black shorts, pressed brown shirts with the red swastika armbands on our left arm. We wore a belt buckle with the runic lighting bolt symbol. Our shoes polished to such a high shine that we could see our reflection in them. We wore caps with diamond shaped pins. We convinced ourselves that no one would ever turn us away. Guenther confidently pushed the doorbell to apartment number five. We waited a few seconds and pushed the button again.

Suddenly, a voice came over the intercom, "Who is there?"

We looked at each other. Who would speak?

Guenther spoke up, "We are *Jungvolk* collecting any scrap metal or paper. Do you have anything?"

The voice on the other end answered, "Go away. We barely have enough for ourselves!"

We looked at each other in disbelief.

We had not expected rejection.

Not knowing what to do next, we stood in from of the door, frozen. I suggested we try the next apartment. We looked each other's uniform over again.

We were ready!

This time I pushed the bell on apartment four. There was nothing, not a sound. Guenther pushed the bell with the same results. Guenther could see the curtain move at one of the windows out of the corner of his eye. He pushed the button again, the curtain closed but no response. We pushed the remaining buttons. Curtains moved, but still no response.

Frustrated, we decided to move on to another building. Still confident of our plan, we pushed the button for the top apartment. We saw more curtains move but there was still no response. It was common practice for tenants to peek around their curtains to decide if they wanted to respond or release the door lock. We knew this but could not understand why people would not respond or open the door. After all, we were *Jungvolk* and it was all over the newspapers that the *Jungvolk* would be collecting today. We could not understand why people were not anxious to help.

Finally, at the fourth apartment building, at apartment number four, the door lock released as soon as we pushed the button.

We did not expect it and looked at each other with amazement.

We slowly opened the front door and climbed the stairs to apartment number four.

Guenther knocked.

The door opened.

An old man with silver hair was standing at the door. Guenther explained why we were there.

The old man said, "Wait here," as he disappeared into the apartment.

After what seemed like an eternity, he appeared at the door with a tin box from chocolate. He deposited the tin in the burlap sack and proceeded to tell us that he was in the army during the war. He told us to keep up the good work, wished us luck, and closed the door.

Outside on the curb, we began to realize that we had little to show for our efforts. At this rate, it would take a week to fill our sacks and the *Führer* needed all of the scrap metal that we could get. It had been three hours since we left Rolf.

I wondered how Rolf was making out.

If only Rolf had given us Lehrter Street, the sacks would have been full.

Sitting on the curb, we concluded there must be a better way. I suggested we try a business. Guenther was reluctant though. Rolf was very explicit. We were to go from apart-ment building to apartment building and not miss one. We agreed that businesses were buildings too and if we did not miss any, we would have followed Rolf's instructions.

With a renewed enthusiasm, we set off to the first business we could find. The first shop we came to was a bookstore. Smiles filled both of us as soon as we spotted the shop. We reasoned that bookstores must have a lot of scrap paper. We just knew we would fill the sack. Then, we could go back to the *Heim* and wait for the others.

This collecting was hard work and we were getting hun-gry!

As we opened the door, our confidence soared. There was paper everywhere. It was as if we had discovered a se-cret. The proprietor was a middle-aged woman who could have passed for one of our teachers. She was behind the counter waiting on a young couple. The couple was the postcard images of the new Aryan race. Blond hair, blue eyes, fit, and neatly dressed.

As soon as they spotted us, they said, "Heil Hitler!" and saluted us.

Guenther and I felt proud. This was the first time anyone had actually saluted us. All of the salutes, so far, had been in groups or to the HJ Regional Leader, when he visited the *Heim*.

We snapped to attention and returned the salute to the couple. Still struck by the moment, our eyes fixed on the couple as the left the store.

The woman behind the counter cleared her voice and asked, "Can I help you boys?"

Confident, I explained our purpose and began opening up the sack. The woman listened patiently as I explained why it was important to collect paper and how the *Führer* needed help, and so on. The woman told us she had none to give and that a company collects her paper and uses it for pulp. She apologized for not being able to help and disappeared into the backroom.

We didn't know what to do now. We had spent another two hours with nothing to show for it but one chocolate tin and we were hungry. Our plans were shattered. Now what were we going to do? We left the bookstore and continued down the street, agreeing that collecting was not so easy and wondered how Rolf and the other boys were making out.

The next shop was a butcher shop. Again, we went into the shop, announced our mission, and received more rejection.

Another hour had passed.

It was now 1:00 p.m. and we were hungry.

Against the advice of Rolf, we hadn't brought anything to eat with us, convinced that we would be back at the *Heim* before lunch with an overflowing sack. There was no need to carry sandwiches. There were four hours left before we had to be back at the *Heim* and, we probably had a forty minute walk from were we had ventured to.

It was not looking good for us.

We decided to try one more shop before going back to the apartment buildings.

Our feet were getting tired and the hunger pains were setting in.

The next shop was a bakery. In our hungry state, this was probably the worst place to stop. We halted at the window and began admiring the baked goods and pastries displayed. The aroma of fresh baked goods flowed out onto the street. We couldn't take it any longer, we had to go in. I had thirty *Pfennigs* and Guenther had twenty *Pfennigs*. We wondered what we could buy with fifty *Pfennigs*, vowing to split whatever we could get in half.

Neither of us ever had to actually buy anything from a bakery. My mother used to send me to the bakery on Lehrter Street but since our family had an account there, the items were always charged and the bill paid when Father was paid. I never paid attention to prices. Guenther's older brothers were the ones who fetched the baked goods.

We walked into Eidleman's Bakery and forgetting that we were collecting, asked the man behind the counter what fifty *Pfennigs* would buy. We decided on two cream–filled pastries with chocolate icing, my favorite. Within seconds, we had devoured the pastries with the man behind the counter asking if we had eaten in a week.

Suddenly, we remembered collecting.

Guenther gave the speech while the man listened attentively. Although neither Guenther nor I held out much hope that a bakery would have any scrape metal or paper.

After Guenther finished, the man said, "I have some items in the back that I was saving for the collection. No one ever came in to ask. They must have assumed that a bakery did not have anything."

The man motioned us to follow him into the back room. Once there, we could not believe our eyes. There were empty sugar, flour, and yeast tins covering almost one-third of the room.

We had struck gold!

The man told us to take as many as could fit into our sack. We stacked the tins inside one another and filled the sack to overflowing. The man told us to come back every Sunday. He would have plenty of tins for us, and to bring another sack.

We looked at each other.

We both knew this was the way to get donations without any effort. After thanking the man and assuring him that we would take care of his tin problem we left the store and started back.

Back at the *Heim*, the other teams were coming in with their sacks. None were as full as our bags. The regional Hitler Youth leader came at 5:00 p.m. to collect the donations. This took a while since he had to count and weigh the items and record what had donated. He placed a tic marks beside our names. For the next several collections, we had the most tic marks.

Uncle Frederick was a frequent visitor to our apartment. He liked Mother's coffee. One day he came to our apartment and announced that he had sold his share of the printing business to his partners and purchased a hat shop in the old walled-city of Rothenburg.

Rothenburg, situated on the "Romantic Road" between Würzburg and Dinkelsbhuhl, was considered by many to be the most beautiful small town of Germany. Located 220 kilometers northwest of Munich, in Bavaria, the narrow cobblestone streets, and authenticity of the medieval architecture made it a popular tourist attraction.

He said he was retiring from the printing business and was going to move to Rothenburg and run the shop.

He also announced, "Kurt, I have no children and you are my only nephew so, the shop will belong to you when I die."

We were all rather shocked by the news although Uncle Frederick was known to be eccentric.

There was the time when the city cut down the large old linden trees on *Unter den Linden* Street and replaced them with new ones. Uncle Frederick was so upset that he demanded to see the *Führer*. He was so persistent that he finally got an appointment with Albert Spear who explained that the new growth represented a new beginning for Germany. Spear was so impressed with Uncle Frederick's enthusiasm that he appointed him to serve on the Berlin Beautification Council.

I began eighth grade in April 1933.

My friends, undoubtedly echoing their parents, were talking about how the Jews were ruining Germany.

Father and Mother rarely discussed politics in front of me but it was clear that Father was conservative and Mother was liberal. I didn't have any Jews in my class at school. Father was uncertain if the propaganda about the Jews was the reason the German economy was in dire straights. He had served in the Great War with Jews. They had distinguished themselves and even won the Iron Cross for Valor.

Mother often dismissed the propaganda as just that. Every time the topic would come up, she would point to the nice Mr. and Mrs. Weismann. She would ask how that nice couple could be responsible for anything bad. That would usually end the discussion.

The school system was authoritarian even before 1933. The students respected teachers. Parents instructed their children to be obedient and upheld the authority of the teacher. There were never discussions in my classes. I, like my fellow students, listened to the teachers. I would raise my hand if I knew the answer to questions. If picked to answer, I stood up and remained standing until instructed by the teacher to sit down. Although there were occasional parent/teacher conferences, parents had no influence on the system and parents where not permitted to question the content of the curriculum.

The Reich Minister of the Interior Wilhelm Frick made the following announcement, which appeared in all the newspapers:

"The idea of liberal education has completely undermined the meaning of education and our institutions. The national revolution issues a new law to German schools for their educational obligations: The German school must train the political person, whose reasoning and actions, service and sacrifice is rooted in his Volk (People) as well as completely, indivisibly and deeply in the history and the fate of his Fatherland (Nation). Volk and fatherland are the most important areas of education. The lure or exotic, foreign things from faraway places has at all times provided to be a great temptation for Germans, has enticed them into foreign countries

and made it easy for them to be absorbed unto foreign cultures. One of our noblest, most valuable assets, the care of which must be close to our hearts, is our mother tongue, pleasant to the ear, powerful and flexible. We can be proud of it. Unfortunately, its purity is still not being nurtured the way it should. Even official sources habitually use superfluous foreign words. We also want to think of German script, which should most definitely take precedence over Latinate script. History takes the first priority. Next to a strong emphasis on history and German culture, values rank biology and race science. Again and again, we realize that the character of a people and the fundamental strength of its historical development cannot be fathomed without sufficient knowledge of its utter uniqueness. Therefore, race science must be given sufficient time and attention in school so that the basic characteristics of the most important races become intimately known to the pupil and his/her continuous visual observation of race differences will be honed. These subjects must become second nature to the growing generation and influence their choice of a mate."

The year 1934 was labeled by Schirach as The Year of Training. Vocational training was also emphasized as Schirach and Nazi Labor leader Robert Ley initiated the Annual National Vocational Competition for Hitler Youth in which teens learning various trades were judged and rewarded. The winners in each category got to meet Hitler.

Father had steadily risen in the company and was a manager of presses. The improvement in our family income enabled us to do more than we had been able to, including purchasing new pots and pans for Mother, a new living room rug, and a radio.

The Government started a program called *Eintopf* (one pot), which meant that there was to be a meal in every restaurant in Germany that was in one pot. It was usually a stew. You would pay the usually three or four marks for a full meal, and stew would probably cost a mark and a half. The difference between the *Eintopf* and the menu price was collected at the restaurant. Collectors came around to the families too. They came around to our apartment building once a month and we had to give the difference between what the one pot meal cost and what our meal cost. It wasn't much but it showed solidarity and support. The collector would give Mother a little button to show that our family supported the program. She refused to wear it and complained every time they came.

The radio became a gathering point for us, especially after dinner. I was so happy to be able to tell Rolf that I had listened to one of Dr. Goebbels speeches. The speeches echoed what Rolf was telling Guenther and me. There was much information about the *Arbeitsdienst*.

The *Arbeitsdienst* was initially a party organization but on June 26, 1935, the Reichs Labor Service Law was passed in which service in the *Arbeitsdienst* for 6 months time was made compulsory and nation-wide. The *Arbeitsdienst* was no longer a party organization, and was made a Supreme Reich Authority and full-fledged state organization equal to the other Reich ministries. Before the Reich Labor Service Law, a law was passed in which military service was also made compulsory. Together, the two laws created a centralized, national and compulsory system in which all males between the ages 18 and 25 would first enter labor service for a period of 6 months, and upon completion, enter service for two years in one of the branches of the *Wehrmacht* -

the German Armed Forces. Although later in WWII they were even allowed to carry weapons, they were never actually a part of the official armed forces, a status reserved exclusively for the *Wehrmacht, Luftwaffe* (Air force) and *Kriegsmarine* (Submarine force), and tactically, the *Waffen-SS*.

The pre-war *Arbeitsdienst* was based at a specific camp location from which its members would train, drill, practice, and take part in the various labor projects their unit was assigned to. Each camp and its *Abteilung* (Detachment) were given a number designation listed along with its higher *Arbeitsgruppen* (Detachment group) number. These two numbers were often displayed together on an arm badge in the shape of a downward pointing shovel blade worn on the upper left shoulder of all uniforms and great coats worn by all personnel. An *Abteilungen* consisted of 214 men grouped together in a six man staff and four platoon-sized units called *Züge*, each of 69 men. Each *Züge* was in turn made up of three 17-man section-sized units known as *Trupps*. The "front-line" rank and file members who made up the bulk of the work force were armed with spades and transported by bicycles.

Before WWII began in 1939, the *Arbeitsdienst* took part in labor projects such as the reclamation of marshland for cultivation, the construction of dykes, drainage improvement work, vast tree removal operations, the reclamation of fallow or wasted land, and the construction of roads. When the Reich's Land Service was introduced it offered young city dwellers the opportunity to experience life on German farms. All HJ and BDM members were expected to participate in the *Arbeitsdienst* or the Land Service, helping to bring in the harvest, while learning the value of hard labor and the simple life.

A new development within the Hitler Youth also appeared that year. *HJ-Streifendienst* (Patrol Force) units were formed, functioning as internal political police, maintaining order at meetings, ferreting out disloyal members, and denouncing anyone who criticized Hitler or Nazism including, in a few cases, their own parents. Rolf was a *HJ-Streifendienst* in our chapter.

One case involved a teenaged HJ member named Walter Hess who turned in his father for calling Hitler a crazed Nazi maniac. His father was then hauled off to the concentration camp at Dachau under protective custody. For setting such an example, Hess was promoted to a higher rank within the HJ.

By now, about 60 percent of Germany's young people belonged to the Hitler Youth. Sports Competition Medals were awarded to youths who performed rigorous athletic drills and met strict physical fitness standards.

Every summer, a day would now be set aside as the "Day of the State Youth" for these events. Physical fitness, according to Hitler, was much more important for his young people than memorizing dead facts in the classroom. School schedules were adjusted to allow for at least one hour of physical training in the morning and one hour each evening. Prior to this, only two hours per week had been set aside.

Hitler also encouraged young boys to take up boxing to heighten their aggressiveness. Our activities began to change from singing folk songs around the campfires and hiking to pre-military training.

Local Hitler Youth and *Jungvolk* groups enthusiastically played war games against each other, during which we would be roughed up by older boys in order to steel ourselves for greater adventures.

Our group was no different.

Local camp events often took place in tents, with mandatory overnight stays. The game plan included many military features, such as roll calls during flag ceremonies, military trumpet fanfares, and rifle practice. Much more importance was given to the study of maps and the spotting of imaginary or designated enemies. Constant vigilance and discipline were practiced. This applied as well to regional and national hikes, which would take us on strenuous marches to historically important sites, preferably near borders of countries to be conquered later, such as Denmark and Poland.

Learning how to shoot was a key element in pre-military training and a regular part of the agenda early on for all boys, from ages ten to eighteen. Those up to fourteen years practiced with air guns, while the older boys were taught how to use small-caliber rifles.

In addition to the activities that we all participated in, there was the opportunity to specialize. Some of the specialized units were regarded as more elite than others, such as the glider unit. Many of the boys in that unit went on to be pilots in the *Luftwaffe*.

Guenther developed an interest in motorcycles. In addition to our meetings, he would attend additional meetings with the Motor Hitler Youth unit once a month. Some of the motorcycles were owned by senior leaders or by wealthy families who would donate them for use.

There were other specialty groups to include communications, equestrian, marine, medical, and the music divisions. Boys and girls who were artistically inclined flocked to the music division. They were generally attached to radio stations and performed live broadcasts from the studios.

In the North, the Marine Hitler Youth was sought after, since many youths in Hamburg, Bremen, or Kiel were already familiar with sailboats and kayaks. Their members would go to join the *Kriegsmarine*.

Like the motor branches, members of the Equestrian Hitler Youth and the Communications Hitler Youth, which trained with the telephone and Morse code, would merge with conventional ground troops of the *Wehrmacht* later.

I preferred to stay with the General organization, not specializing.

Chapter Seven
The Hitler Youth

The ceremony began on February 25, 1934, four days after my fourteenth birthday, with the flags being carried into the room by some of our members. The room was decorated with greenery and flowers. We sat at the front of the room. Our parents received a formal invitation from the Nazi party and were all seated in the rear.

This was the official 1934 Hitler Youth Induction Ceremony. At the same time about a million Nazi Party officials gathered at points around Germany to swear an oath to Adolf Hitler. Rudolf Hess gave a speech on the occasion, which was broadcast to the nation. We all sat motionless, spellbound by his words.

"German men, German women, German boys, German girls, over a million of you are gathered in many places in all of Germany! On this the anniversary of the proclamation of the party's program, you will together swear an oath of loyalty and obedience to Adolf Hitler. You will display to the world what has long been obvious to you, and what you have expressed in past years, often unconsciously. You are swearing your oath on a holiday that

Germany celebrates for the first time: Heroes' Memorial Day. We lower our flags in remembrance of those who lived as heroes, and who died as heroes. We lower the flags before the giants of our past, before those who fought for Germany, before the millions who fought in the World War, before those who died preparing the way for the new Reich. I name Horst Wessel because he has become a symbol for us, and remember through him all those "shot by the Red Front and Reaction." Woe to the people that fails to honor its heroes! It will cease producing them, cease knowing them. Heroes spring from the essence of their people. A people without heroes are a people without leaders, for only a heroic leader is a true leader able to withstand the challenge of difficult times. The rise or fall of a people can be determined by the presence or absence of a leader. We do not want to forget the mothers, women, and children who gave their dearest, often their provider, and bear their fate with quiet heroism. The battle-ready manly heroes and the quiet sacrifices of mothers and women are holy examples of loyalty for us Germans. The flags that we now raise once more are the symbols of this loyalty, which for Nordic mankind is closely bound to heroism! Loyalty not only in deed, but in character is demanded of you. Loyalty of character often demands no less heroic virtue than does loyalty in deed. Loyalty in character is unbreakable loyalty, a loyalty that knows no ifs or buts, that knows no weakening, Loyalty in character means absolute obedience that does not question the results of the order nor its reasons, but rather obeys for the sake of obedience itself. Such obedience is an expression of heroic character when following the order leads to personal disadvantage or seems even to contradict one's personal convictions. Adolf Hitler's strength as a leader is that he almost always works through the power of his persuasion; rarely does he command. He must know, however, that when he commands, or allows a command to be given, that it will be obeyed absolutely, down to the last block warden. The power and effectiveness of a good organization is even greater when discipline prevails. The greater its obedience even in small things, the more clearly it marches to the right or the left depending on the command of the leader, the more exactly the command to march in short or long steps is followed, the more surely the Führer can take the steps necessary to realize the National Socialist program. All we National Socialists work for the realization of this program, just as we once worked to gain control of the state. We fought for the souls of the farmers, for the souls of the workers, for the souls of the middle class, for the souls of men, for the souls of women, for the souls of the old, for the souls of the young — we the members of the main organization of the NSDAP as well as the men of the Labor Service, the leaders of the affiliated organizations of the party such as the National Socialist women. With the same will young men and women strive toward the same goal, to become those who will replace us as the masters of Germany's fate. Hitler Youths, you have given the same absolute loyalty to the Führer that Germany's young volunteers gave twenty years ago at Langemarck, which demanded their heroic deaths for our people and the Reich. You have made the youth of Langemarck your model. You have the good fortune to live in a Reich that the best warriors of 1914 could only dream of — a Reich that for all eternity will remain united if you do your duty. For you, doing your duty means: Obey the Führer's orders without question! You will be the best living memorial to the dead comrades of the first years of the war when you maintain discipline in your ranks. The more a Hitler Youth leader demands discipline from his boys, the more he must display it himself. He must demand discipline from them above all when his boys long for glorious freedom or wild behavior. It should be easier for the youth of today to accept discipline and subordination — combined with an appreciation of the accomplishments of the older generation — since the older generation is the generation of the World War. I know how you were persecuted, maligned, hated and mocked because of your faith in the Führer. I know how many of your comrades sacrificed their young lives! I know it well! But I also know that all the dangers and sorrows that a Hitler Youth suffered, even in the most Communist neighborhood in the years before the seizure of power, are not comparable to the dangers and sorrows that a front soldier experienced in a single day! Never forget that when your leader, who endured the battleground for us, demands self-discipline of you. I say to the political leaders what I said to your comrades in Gau Thuringia as they were sworn in last year: Be true to Hitler's spirit! Ask in all that you do: What would the Führer do. If you act accordingly, you will not go wrong! Being true to Hitler's spirit means knowing that a leader has not only rights, but above all duties. Being true to Hitler's spirit means always being a model. "To be a leader is to be an example," just as Hitler and his work are an example for you. Being true to Hitler's spirit means being modest and unassuming. Being true to Hitler's spirit means remaining a thorough National Socialist in good times and bad. Being a thorough National Socialist means to think ever and only on the whole National Socialist German people. It means that no matter what, always to be a servant of the total National Socialism of Adolf Hitler, to be a fully conscious, heartfelt follower of the Führer above all else. Be ever a servant of the whole, within the movement as well, and never forget that only the whole movement, not a part of it, can guarantee victory and the conquest of the future. Be ever aware that, wherever you are, you owe thanks to the Führer, for his leadership enabled every victory. Wherever you are, be it high or low, work for his movement, and therefore for Germany. Remember what Adolf Hitler says: it makes no difference if one is a street cleaner or a professor, as long as he works for the whole and does his duty. The reward for your labors is the feeling of having done one's duty for the movement, for Adolf Hitler, for Germany. All of you, whether political leader, SA, SS or Hitler Youth share a common pride: Being a member of Adolf Hitler's NSDAP! You are all the scouts and the defenders of the National Socialist army of the movement. You are each indispensable and equal. Each of you is as unique in history as National Socialism itself. You are typically National Socialist. SA, SS, and political leaders have a common tradition, embodied in the "Old Guard." It includes all who fought, sacrificed, suffered, risked or gave their lives for Germany's resurrection under National Socialism. It has the honor to have bled and sacrificed for our people's future. You have earned the thanks of all who enjoy the blessings of life in a new Reich. It is a Reich led by men who share a desire for national freedom, socialist community and peace in dignity and honor. Political leaders! Leaders of the Labor Service, the forces of labor! Women's leaders, HJ leaders! Leaders of the BDM! You will now take an oath to Adolf Hitler! Your oath is not a mere formality; you do not swear this oath to someone unknown to you. You do not swear in hope, but with certainty. Fate has made it easy for you to take this oath without condition or reservation. Never in history have a people taken an oath to a leader with such absolute confidence as the German people have in Adolf Hitler. You have the enormous joy of taking an oath to a man who is the embodiment of a leader. You take an oath to the fighter who demonstrated his leadership over a decade, who always acts correctly and who always chose the right way, even when at times the larger part of his movement failed to understand why. You take an oath to a man whom you know follows the laws of providence, which he obeys independently of the influence of earthly powers, who leads the German people rightly, and who will guide Germany's fate. Through your oath you bind yourselves to a man who — that is our faith — was sent to us by higher powers. Do not seek Adolf Hitler with your mind. You will find him through the strength of your hearts! Adolf Hitler is Germany and Germany is Adolf Hitler. He who takes an oath to Hitler takes an oath to Germany! Swear to great Germany, to whose sons and daughters throughout the world I send our best wishes. Throughout Germany people take the oath. This has been the greatest common taking of an oath in history! We greet the Führer!"

Hitler Youth and the League of German Girls sat in uniform behind us *Jungvolk* boys. The boys on the right and the young girls on the left. I sat in the second row in the second seat from the aisle. Rolf was in the aisle seat. The seats were made of oak and resembled church pews. The aisle seats were for the leaders. Guenther sat to the left of me. We looked forward as instructed. We did not dare move our heads around.

The ceremony began with the Hitler Youth Anthem and we all jumped to our feet and sang.

Then the Hitler Youth Leader began to speak, "This transition is an important moment for you. It marks the beginning of a new stage of life. It is true that the young person in not yet fully adult. Nevertheless, the body has completed the greater part of its growth. With this physical growth, the young person becomes increasingly able to determine his own life. This ceremony marks the point at which boys and girls increasingly become men and women. As you become mature, you must increasingly follow the laws and meet the duties of life. Young people, you stand here on the threshold of your lives."

Then there was a brief drum roll!

The Leader went on, "You enter joyfully through the open door. You face your fate courageously, for while fate defeats the cowardly, God helps the brave!"

Another drum roll!

"You the youth are the bridge from ancestors to grandchildren."

Then the Leader nodded and one of the boys rose and went up to the podium and recited, "We affirm: The German people have been created by the will of God. All those who fight for the life of our people, and those who died, carried out the will of God. Their deeds are to us holy obligation."

All of the boys and girls participated, "This we believe."

The speaker continued: "We affirm that God gave us all our strength, in order to maintain the life of our people and defend it. It is therefore our holiest duty to fight to our last breath anything that threatens or endangers the life of our people. God will decide whether we live or die."

"This we pledge!"

The speaker went on, "We want to be free from all selfishness. We want to be fighters for this Reich named Germany, our home. We will never forget that we are German."

Everyone chanted, "That is what we want!"

The band played and everyone sang the national anthem followed by *Die Fahne Hoch* the Horst Wessel Song. As the Horst Wessel Song began, we filed out of our seats alternating as we went up on the stage to receive a picture of the *Führer* and a copy of the book *Remember That You Are German* from the Hitler Youth Leader.

Once the presentations were made and we were back in our seats the signal was given to retire the flags. I had chills running up and down my spine the entire time. All of us in the room had been looking forward to this ceremony from the day we joined the *Jungvolk*. This ceremony was all the older boys talked about.

It defined us as Hitler Youth.

Until this time, we would do errands for the HJ boys. We would set-up tables and flags for the HJ meetings and would do whatever the older boys wanted us to do. Today, we were to become one of the older boys. This ceremony marked a huge step, for many, to the ultimate goal of one day being a member of the SS.

As the music played, and the speaker recited, I felt an immense sense of pride.

Father shared some of that pride with a lump in his throat. He watched his son grow up, starting with the *Jungvolk* and now, about to become a member of the Hitler Youth. Mother was proud too, although she did not want to have too much pride show.

The long shadows made by flags in the candlelight somehow made the room seem supernatural. A swastika was fashioned out of candles behind the podium and the reflections on the ceiling seemed to dance as the candles flickered. We all stood and sang the Hitler Youth Anthem:

Our banner flutters before us.

Our banner represents the new era.

And our banner leads us to eternity!

Yes, our banner means more to us than

death.

After the anthem, the Hitler Youth Leader concluded the ceremony with, "The pledge has been made. A new group of our people has joined our fighting and creative people's community. We are happy in the confidence this experience gave us in the eternal growth of our people. We conclude his pledge and this ceremony with a greeting to the *Führer*, Adolf Hitler, Sieg Heil! Sieg Heil! Sieg Heil!"

The ceremony was over and we congratulated each other. We found our relatives in the back of the hall where refreshments were served. Everyone mingled and talked with each other for a while then began to leave the hall.

Three days after the ceremony was our first Hitler Youth meeting. Rolf and Guenther where already seated. I made my way to the seat they had saved for me.

Rolf commented, "Kurt, you were almost late!"

Then the Hitler Youth Leader can into the room shouting, "Attention!"

We leaped to our feet!

The Hitler Youth Leader cleared his throat.

"Quite a lot will change for you in the Hitler Youth," he began without greeting.

"First, you are no longer *Pimpfs* (little boys), but Hitler Youths. You bear the name of our *Führer*.

"Second, this obliges you even more than before to demonstrate always and everywhere why the *Führer* has chosen you. All childish behavior stops forthwith."

"Third, I regard it as the mission of the Hitler Youth to prepare you for your upcoming military service. With the recovery of the Ostmark, the Sudentenland, the Memel district and the dissolution of Czechoslovakia, the creation of a greater German Reich and a reordering of Europe are no longer out of our reach."

"Fourth, In order that we may fulfill the mission given us, we need experienced leaders. Only trial in service will prove whether former leaders among you will prove yourselves further."

"Fifth, The Hitler Youth, consists as it does of young working men, apprentices, and schoolboys, requires different hours. Duty in the Hitler Youth, therefore, falls primarily on evenings and Sundays."

"Sixth, Sundays belong to the Hitler Youth, not to going to church. You are old enough now to discard bourgeois prejudices."

"Seventh, I expect absolute loyalty to the *Führer*. The enemies of the *Führer* are your enemies too, be they Jews, Bolsheviks, parsons, or whatever."

"Eighth, I demand from you unwavering dedication to the ideals of National Socialism. The *Führer's* word is both command and revelation."

"Ninth, I demand from you the readiness to sacrifice blood and life for *Führer, Volk*, and the Fatherland. To be a Hitler Youth is to be a hero."

"Tenth, I demand obedience, obedience, unconditional obedience."

"Up!" he shouted, "and now we will sing our song!"

Forward! Forward! With resounding fanfares,
Forward! Forward! Youth knows no peril.
Germany, you will stand resplendent although we might die.
Forward! Forward! With resounding fanfares.
Forward! Forward! Youth knows no peril.
Be the goal ever so high, youth will gain it.
Our banner precedes us, fluttering in the breeze,
As we march into the future, man after man.
We'll march for Hitler through night and through danger
With the flag of youth, for freedom and bread.

Our banner precedes us, fluttering in the breeze.
Our banner signals the new time.
Our banner leads us to eternity.
Yes, our banner is worth more than death.
My first Hitler Youth meeting was over.

On the way home I said to Guenther," I don't know if I'm going to like it in the Hitler Youth."

"I don't either," Guenther promptly agreed.

Rolf walked behind us without a word.

Finally, he said, "You will get used to it."

As time went on, we did get used to it and had fun. Eventually, I liked the comradeship of the Young Hitler Youth. I was full of enthusiasm and fired up to hear about comradeship, loyalty, and honor. Then too, there were the snappy uniforms, the impressive parades, and the solemn vows to the *Führer*. It was all heady stuff for a 14 year old. I was beginning to see the differences between us and the racially inferior Jews and Slavs.

It was Anna's birthday on April 19th, the day before Hitler's when Guenther, Rolf and I, along with everyone's parents, filled into the hall for Anna's induction ceremony into the *Bund Deutcher Mädel*.

We were dressed in our Hitler Youth uniforms, pressed to perfection with highly-shined shoes. The girls all wore long, straight black skirts, white short sleeved blouses; black kerchief's held in a leather knot at the front and black flat heeled shoes.

The hall was decorated with the BDM flags beside the Swastika on both sides of the room. Flowers were placed between the flags and in the front. There was a stage in front with a podium in the middle. Rolf's mother and Anna's mother had become acquainted and sat behind us.

"Anna looks like the perfect Aryan female, the holy tree of Germany," commented Rolf's mother. "You should be very proud. Look what Adolf Hitler has done for our youth."

Anna's mother replied, "Thank you, and you should be very proud of Rolf. He is growing up in the true Nazi tradition." Guenther, Rolf and I elbowed each other and giggled.

The BDM leader went to the podium, and began, "You are to be integrated into the *Bund Deutcher Mädel* today."

The girls replied," I swear to serve the *Führer* Adolf Hitler faithfully and selflessly in the Hitler Youth. I vow that I will, at all times, work for the unity and comradeship of the German Youth."

"I pledge obedience to the Reich Youth Leader and all leaders of the BDM."

"I vow by our sacred flag that I will always strive to be worthy of it, so help me God."

The leader continued, "In my capacity as a responsible BDM leader, I admit you into the ranks of the *Bund Deutcher Mädel*."

Everyone sang the Hitler Youth anthem ending the ceremony. We all gathered in the back for a reception congratulating the girls.

I was very proud of Anna!

The next spectacular public event in 1934 was the Annual Nazi Party Rally in Nuremberg. I was selected to carry a banner at the Rally.

This was quite an honor and I could not wait to get home from the Hitler Youth meeting to tell my parents. The rally began on September 4th and lasted two weeks. Schools had instructions from the Reich Minster of Education to excuse Any Hitler Youth participant from school.

Each day, every event was covered. Every minute detail was published in the press. The newspapers published the Führer's speeches verbatim. Live radio broadcasts allowed people to hear all the speeches, the singing, and the descriptions by enthusiastic commentators of the marching, the setting, and actions taking place. Radio stations played the Horst Wessel Song repeatedly. The radio remained on all day and in the evenings as Father would listen. Mother was less interested but would pause and listen to something that got her attention.

Other activities at the rally were sports demonstrations, ceremonies to honor those who died for the Nazi movement and vows of fidelity by the various factions. All of the rally events could be seen at length in the cinemas.

Father took Mother every time new footage was advertised, hoping to catch a glimpse of me.

The rally was most spectacular. Thousands of SA and SS men, Labor Service men with shouldered spades and Hitler Youths marched in impeccably straight columns through the city for hours. Ten thousands of cheering, flag-waving and flower throwing people lined the streets.

The city was full of houses decorated with flags and garlands. People leaned out of every window. Films of the gigantic assemblies in the specially built stadium showed a sea of fluttering flags and thousands of standards being carried and marched around the stadium by the SA and others to the sound of rousing march music.

The thousands of SA men marching in perfect columns were reminiscent of Roman legions. Each delegation's standard bore the name of their part of Germany.

One night, a seemingly endless torchlight parade wound its way through the ancient streets of Nuremburg, past the floodlit fifteenth and sixteenth century buildings of this beautiful old city, to the Zeppelin Meadow, a huge assembly place. Many people carried a sea of 21,000 flags, torches, and then posted them around the entire grounds.

Antiaircraft searchlights, placed close together around the upper edge of the field, aimed to meet at a central point above the field. A "cathedral of light" was the way the press described it.

It was an overwhelming and awesome sight!

Just before the *Führer* made his appearance, the music stopped. An expectant hush fell over the huge stadium.

It was as if the crowd held its breath.

Then the band struck up the Badenweiler March.

The *Führer* finally made his dramatic entrance.

The people in the movie theater acted as if they were there. They were in awe of the event. Father wondered how it must have felt to be there. He was proud that I was carrying a banner at this historic event. Mother, although more reserved, was very proud of me too. Their friends would come up to them at the cinema or in the market and tell them should they be very proud of their son and his accomplishments.

When I later viewed the film The Triumph of the Will by Leni Riefenstahl, chills would run up my spine for I had been there and witnessed the splendor.

1934 was a good year for the Schultheiss family. I was fourteen and the economy was turning around. Everyone was healthy and our family had some disposable income. After I returned from Nuremburg, Father decided to take the family out to dinner.

Berlin had a chain restaurant by the name of Aschinger. There was one located near the Tiergarden. Most Aschinger restaurants consisted of two parts. One was open to the street for fast food, with a few tall round tables where customers could stand and eat. The other was a dining room. The fast food side served Aschinger's famous yellow pea soup with or without hot dogs. A large bowl of this thick, hot, delicious soup cost only 50 pfennig.

Mother would sometimes stop for a bowl when shopping.

Baskets of fresh rolls stood on the tables and customers could eat as many as they liked. Students, in particular, took advantage of this offer. The restaurant part had carpeting and tables that were set with snow-white tablecloths and napkins, along with good flatware. The chairs were upholstered in a red plush material. The restaurant part was famous for their *Schweinshaxn* (roasted pork knuckle). Occasionally Father and Mother would take me there to eat. My favorite meal was the *Schweinshaxn* in dark beer sauce served with potato dumplings and red cabbage. When

I got older, I added their famous *Dunkle Weisen* (dark wheat) beer to my order.

Back at school I began to think about teachers who were either what we called "200 percenter" who were party members or, and at the other extreme, passively reluctant teachers who went along with the program in order to retain their positions.

We students knew who was and who was not one of them, but our only concern was whether they attacked that which we valued the most, Hitler. If they did, we held such actions against the teacher personally and reported them promptly to our HJ leaders.

It was Hitler, Goebbels, Goring, and the rest of Nazi leadership that influenced us most. We used to listen to their speeches on the radio, see them in newsreels and read what they said in the papers. Despite the discrepancies from one day to the next we generally believed what they said. Teachers had to be watched! It was our reasoning that, because they were our leaders, they naturally only wanted the best for our country and if anyone would lie to us it would have to be the foreigners.

To qualify for membership and receive my Hitler Youth dagger, I had to participate in war games and a day-and-a-half-long march, achieve a set of minimum standards on the playing field, and pass tests of my knowledge of Nazi doctrine, including the words of the Horst Wessel Song. After months of meetings, encampments, parade-ground drill, small-arms practice, semaphore instruction, and indoctrination, some of the member's enthusiasm dimmed.

I remained enthusiastic and attained leadership rank.

In addition to the Hitler Youth activities, students who completed their elementary education were required to help with the harvest each year.

The summer of 1934 was especially memorable for me.

It was the summer Anna and I participated in the harvest. She had already spent a summer on a farm outside of Berlin and would not stop talking about how wonderful her experience was. Anna's vision of the perfect life was to live on a farm in the true tradition of a German.

I was not so enthusiastic about the idea of farm life. It seemed to me to be a lot of hard work. I enjoyed living in Berlin with all of the shops, busses and the zoo. Our Hitler Youth instructors extolled the virtues of living the traditional life but it never really resonated with me. Regardless of my feelings, we all had to spend at least one summer on a farm so I was determined to make the best of it. I reasoned that since Anna and Guenther would be there, we could have some fun cooking over a fire and telling stories like we used to.

After saying our goodbyes to our parents, we met at our *Heim* and boarded a truck that would transport us to the farm.

Anna looked especially beautiful that day with her hair in pigtails.

There were eight others in our truck, two boys from our *Heim* and three boys and three girls from around the city. We quickly became friends and discovered how similar our experiences had been. Guenther sat beside a girl from North Berlin. She was very cute and very developed for her age. Guenther could not stop looking at her breasts. Anna and I noticed and smiled to each other. I could see that I would not have to worry about Guenther finding a friend.

A short while after we left Berlin for the countryside, it began to rain. Fortunately, the truck had a tarpaulin over the back. Even in the rain, it was a pleasant ride.

Most houses displayed the Nazi flag.

A sense of pride came over me as I began to think about what we were involved in. I kept thinking how lucky we were to be German and how fortunate we were to be living in those times. Anna and I talked about how we were part of something so wonderful, something so monumental, that it would change our nation. Everyone in the truck joined the conversation. We were so idealistic then, so filled with patriotism and purpose.

We all knew that what we believed in was right.

It could not be otherwise!

Hitler was right and the youth of Germany would create the next world order.

But first, we had to help with the harvest. We all sang as the truck made its way along the country roads.

The truck stopped between two long buildings. The driver told us the building on the left was for girls and the boys would occupy the one on the right. Behind the two buildings was a large building that looked like a dining facility. It was obvious that the government had spent some money creating this camp. While the farm was rather large, they had no need for these structures on their own. This was the case all across Germany.

The Nazis helped farms by providing labor, buildings and equipment. Our group went into our respective buildings to discover rows of bunk beds with a room containing common showers and latrines at the end of the building. We found some empty beds and stowed our gear in wall lockers that were between each bunk. Most of the other beds were taken but we were the only boys in the building. We figured they must still be out in the fields working.

As we were acquainting ourselves with the building, a man walked in introducing himself as Eric, supervisor of volunteers. He had a clipboard with a list of names and assignments. Guenther and I were to work with one of the teams bailing hay. He reviewed the schedule and the meal times and told us to walk around and familiarize ourselves with the camp. Our workday would start the next day. We walked out the back door of the building and ran into Anna and Helga, the girl that Guenther sat beside in the truck.

The girls were also assigned to our bailing team. We decided that our team would be the best team of all. We wandered around the camp until dinner time, talking about how we were helping to build a new Germany.

The dining facility was full when we arrived. There were several long tables with benches accommodating about one hundred boys and girls. Everyone seemed very friendly as we introduced ourselves. Behind the dining facility was a large fire ring with several rows of benches organized in a circle around the ring.

Every Saturday evening we would all gather to tell stories and sing songs. The work was hard on the farm but we were served good food and treated well. We all felt that we had done something special for our country.

I felt that all of us at the farm had the same views and believed the same things.

The Hitler Youth organization was extremely thorough in getting the message out to all members. I did not talk to anyone at the farm who did not believe that there was a Jewish problem.

None of us at the time were quite sure what to do about it though.

Hitler Youth leaders would periodically visit and when they did, work would stop while they delivered news and read excerpts from Hitler's and Dr. Goebbles' speeches.

The visiting leaders would facilitate discussion about speeches and praise our work on the farm. They would leave copies of all of the Hitler Youth and SS magazines for us to read.

I especially looked forward to the SS magazines.

I think most of us looked up to the SS and wanted to be like them someday. They embodied what the Arian race was all about. Many of the friends we made on the farm that summer went on to do great things for their country.

Joseph Marks, one of the boys from our *Heim*, worked for Dr. Goebbles and became a famous speech writer for many of the Nazi officials.

Guenther's friend Helga became the national leader of the *Bund Deutcher Mädel*. All of us knew that there was something special about us.

By the end of the summer, I had gained a better appreciation for farm work and an understanding of why it was so important for Germany to expand to the East in order to provide Germans the opportunity to be involved in agriculture.

Germany's population was growing and we needed more space.

The relationship between Anna and I deepened that summer. She was wonderful to be with. Even when our bailing team was working long days cutting hay with a scythe, bailing and tying, she never complained. She was always ready to help someone else. As it turned out, our team out-produced the other teams consistently for which we were awarded the Hitler Youth Excellence Badge.

Anna and I did find time to sneak off to be alone, as did Guenther and Helga. I was really pleased that Guenther had met a girl and got along so well.

He was always shy around girls.

One of the group leaders caught them naked in a large hay stack one evening. No one was concerned if we had sex, as it was considered part of the experience of growing up and we were all members of the Hitler Youth.

I came back to Berlin after that summer feeling older and more mature.

Campfires, cookouts, Indian games, and adventurous field trips all made the *Jungvolk* so attractive. Now that we were in the Hitler Youth, we participated in war games. A popular game called Roman chariot, emulated horses, and charioteers. We learned infantry tactics, camouflage, how to plot an enemy position with a map and compass. Those who showed proficiency won awards.

Guenther and I advanced to firing rifles and using gas masks. We would engage in a tug of war with helmets and gas masks to become accustomed to wearing them. We first used air guns and then moved on to bolt action .22s. We would develop our skill throwing wooden sticks shaped like the army's potato-masher grenade.

Beyond weapons and training, we were also taught to defy danger and to accept glory in the idea of dying heroically in battle. We would carry a recumbent comrade in a simulated night ceremonial funeral while the other members would hold wooden swords and shields blazoned with the ancient Germanic Sig-Rune "*S*" symbolic of victory. We marched to the field, a large area outside of town, with mounds of earth and excavated pits. The grass and underbrush were overgrown in between the pits, making it a perfect spot for war games!

We were organized in groups, red and blue. The objective was to remove the colored yarn from the wrist of the opposite without loosing your own. Once a member lost his yarn, he was expected to retire from the field.

Our leaders were constantly telling us that Germany was preparing for an unavoidable war, and we would be an integral part of it. Constant vigilance and discipline were practiced. We would take exhausting marches to historically significant sites such as, Schleswig in Denmark and sites near the Polish border.

I didn't realize it at the time but we were getting familiar with the very routes our army would take in the future. I remember in particular our hike to Schleswig. 233 kilometers to the North West, it was a formidable march. Fortunately, we were to be transported by truck to Flensburg, near the border.

Following the defeat of Germany in World War I, the Allied powers arranged a referendum in Northern and Central Schleswig. In Northern Schleswig seventy five percent voted for reunification with Denmark and twenty five percent voted for Germany. In Central Schleswig the results were reversed; eighty percent voted for Germany and just twenty percent for Denmark. On June 15, 1920, Northern Schleswig officially returned to Danish rule.

The countryside is lowlands with virtually no mountains, the highest elevation being the Bungsberg at only 168 meters. There are many lakes, especially in the eastern part. Strategically, Denmark was relatively unimportant to Germany, except as a staging area for operations in Norway. The country is small and relatively flat, ideal territory for German army operations.

Our job was to record the roads, rivers and towns of the area so our army could make invasion plans. Who would suspect a group of boys on a hike?

We sang and told stories the entire trip. We were free from parental supervision and with others who believed as we did. We were so excited to be part of something so wonderful. Our squad rode in the same truck and between songs, talked about what we would do in the future.

Rolf said with confidence, "I will be a lawyer and practice in Berlin. Maybe I will become a judge and serve our government in that way."

Guenther offered, "I am not sure what I will do. My parents want me to be a teacher, like them. Maybe I will be a ski instructor."

Hearing Guenther, everyone in the truck began to laugh.

Someone shouted, "Our country needs soldiers, not teachers!"

Rolf spoke up, "Yes but it also needs ski instructors to train our mountain forces."

Everyone became quiet. Guenther glanced at Rolf as if to say, *Thank you for saving me.*

Rolf was the undisputed leader of our squad. Everyone respected him and would do anything he asked. He was strong. No one would even think about challenging him.

We dismounted the trucks after pulling in to the park in the center on Flensburg and quickly formed up on the road, ready to march.

One of the older leaders addressed our group, "Today we will hike along the German-Danish and camp along the way. You will practice some of the skills you have learned. You will draw and take notes about what you see along the way, paying particular attention to roads, bridges, streams, two-story buildings that would make good observation posts, and marshy areas that tanks would have difficulty crossing. We will camp overnight where we will cook our food and sing songs. Are there any questions?"

We followed the group leaders doing exactly what was asked. During the evenings around the fire, our sketches and notes were collected and compared. Any discrepancies were discussed and corrected. After reviewing our notes, we sang songs while cooking sausage over the open fire. It was reminiscent of our days in the *Jungvolk*. After songs, the older leaders would read from Dr. Goebbels' or Hitler's speeches and we would discuss the topics. A popular topic was the Jew. There were different stories each night.

We each took our turn reading stories provided by our leaders. Rolf read a story that explained the Jewish book the Talmud.

Rolf read:

"In the Talmud it is written only the Jew is human. Gentile peoples are not called humans, but animals. Since the Jews see Gentiles as animals, they call us only Goy. The book says work is injurious and not to be done. Therefore we Jews don't work, but mostly engage in commerce. Gentiles are created to work. There is no lower occupation than farming. A Jew should neither plow the field nor plant grain. Commerce is far more bearable than tilling the soil. It is permitted for Jews to cheat Gentiles. All lies are good. It is forbidden for a Jew to cheat his brother. To cheat a Gentile is permitted. The Jew is permitted to swear falsely before a Gentile court. Such an oath is always to be seen as compelled. Even when a Jew swears by the name of God, he is allowed to tell a lie, and in his heart to reject the oath he has made."

The next night it was my turn to read. I read a story about how Jews torment animals:

"Two boys, Rudy and Otto, go to a Jewish slaughter house and hide themselves where they can watch the Jews killing a cow. The process of fixing the cow and the operation is described, involving callous brutality and gloating on the part of the Jewish butchers. Four Jews hold down the cow while its neck is being cut. The Jews stand there and laugh. At the end, Otto says, "Rudy, now I believe you. The Jews are the meanest persons in the world." Rudy answers, "Yes, the Jews are a murderous people. With the same brutality and lust for blood with which they kill animals they also kill human beings. Have you ever heard of ritual murders? On such occasions the Jews kill boys and girls, men and women."

Day after day we heard these stories. They were repeated in the classroom, at the Hitler Youth meetings and in the newspapers and on radio. They were defining who we were and what we believed.

By the end of 1934, Hitler was in absolute control of Germany, and his campaign against the Jews was in full swing. The Nazis claimed the Jews corrupted pure German culture with their foreign and mongrel influence. They portrayed the Jews as evil and cowardly, and Germans as hardworking, courageous, and honest. The Jews, the Nazis claimed, who were heavily represented in finance, commerce, the press, literature, theater, and the arts, had weakened Germany's economy and culture.

The massive government-supported propaganda machine created a racial anti-Semitism, which was different from the longstanding anti-Semitic tradition of the Christian churches. The Nazis tried various policies to encourage the Jews to immigrate.

An emigration policy which had not been able to keep pace with Hitler's peacetime acquisitions fell apart almost completely with the outbreak of war. Yet, with each wartime acquisition the Jewish problem took on larger and larger dimensions. The imminent collapse of Russia would bring another 4 million Jews under Nazi control.

If there were to be a solution to the Jewish problem, it would require a drastically new approach. Most of us did not suspect at the time what it would be.

The search for a solution to the Jewish problem had been set in motion by the anti-Semitic energies, which constituted the heart of Nazism. It was driven forward by the frustrations of every successive policy failure. A more extreme approach appeared to be the only alternative to the less-than-total solutions, which had proved unsatisfactory or un-workable. We were all engrossed in the discussion of the Jewish problem. While Anna and I continued to develop our relationship many exciting events were happening in Berlin.

Hitler opened the 1935 Automobile Show in Berlin on February 14. It was at this show that the Volkswagen, or People's Car, was introduced to the public. It was to be affordable, costing 900 marks, and available to everyone. Posters were displayed all around Berlin with a common slogan, "Every member of the Volk can have a Volkswagen." Although none of the automobiles were as yet available, it was possible to order a car and have the installment payments deducted from pay. Father signed up and had five marks deducted from each paycheck. Once he paid 75 percent of the purchase price he was to receive a voucher with an order number. As it turned out, Father never got the car since factories were eventually converted to war production.

It was on my fifteenth birthday that I met Anna after her meeting and walked her home, as usual. As I was about to continue down the street, she grasped my hand and said, "Kurt, I have a birthday present for you. Come with me."

We went up the stairs to her apartment and went in. Anna closed the door and said, "My parents are away for the evening."

She led me to the couch and we sat down on the soft cushions. She seemed to know exactly what to do to get me excited. This was my first time with a women and I never imagined how good it was. Afterwards, we sat on the couch, my head in her lap.

This was to become a weekly event.

Each week, the sex seemed to get better.

She said, "You know Kurt, every good German girl should marry an SS officer and have many children for the Fatherland. You are going to be an SS officer some day, aren't you?"

I told her that I had thought about the SS but I would be an architect.

"You can still be an architect and be in the SS Kurt," she said tersely.

Anna became my companion and very good friend. I felt as though I could tell her anything. I became more interested in the SS and she talked about someday living on a farm in the Eastern territories. She came home from the farm very enthused about that life style. The work was hard but very satisfying to her. She would say that farming represents the true German values and life style.

I would tell her, "How can hard work be anything other than hard work?"

I was interested in other activities, like sports.

Hitler was fond of boxing and it was adopted as the preferred sport of the Hitler Youth. Large-scale regional and national competitions were organized among our members. I tried it but was not very good at it.

Football was my favorite sport, along with skiing.

Rolf became a very good boxer and made it to the national championship in 1935, only to be defeated in the finals by a boy from Munich.

Guenther excelled in skiing. His parents would go annually to Garmisch-Partenkirchen. We all could ski but he was much better than Rolf and I. It seemed to come natural to him.

Not all members of the Hitler Youth were happy with the sports and drills. Some were overextended physically. I remember a boy from our school, who was a non-swimmer, drowned in the deep end of the pool.

Many of the sports and drills were developed to humiliate the participants. It is easy to see how we lost some of our self-respect and became depersonalized. We had to run and do calisthenics for hours. Most of us were in excellent physical shape.

The underlying theme of the Hitler Youth was superiority of the fittest. Individual and group sadism, physical and mental torture and peer-group hazing were encouraged. There were many tests of courage that we had to perform such as jumping from a five-meter board into the water, climbing up the sides of ravines and endless rope climbs.

We didn't realize it at the time but the main objective of the Hitler Youth was to develop our physical and military ability and to indoctrinate us with Nazi ideas.

We thought of ourselves as just ordinary kids growing up in extra ordinary times.

On June 29th Goebbels proclaimed, "We want no more Jews!"

He also denounced middle-class intellectuals who made absurd statements that Jews are human beings.

At the Nuremberg Party Congress on September 15, 1935, Hitler, announced three new laws that were to be cornerstones of German racist policies and the suppression of Jews and other non-Aryans. These decrees became known as the Nuremberg Laws. They were decrees which in Nazi Germany had the force of law forbidding contacts between Aryan Germans and Jews, especially marriage, and stripping Jews of German citizenship.

The first 1935 decree established the swastika as the official emblem of the German state.

The second decree established special conditions for German citizenship that excluded all Jews.

The third titled The Law for the Protection of German Blood and German Honor, prohibited marriage between German citizens and Jews. Marriages violating this law were voided and extra-marital relations prohibited. Jews were prohibited from hiring female Germans less than 45 years of age. Jews were also prohibited from flying the national flag.

The first three Nuremberg Laws were subsequently supplemented with thirteen further decrees, the last issued as late as 1943, as the Nazis constantly refined the suppression of non-Aryans. These laws affected millions of Germans, the exact number depending on precisely how a Jew was defined. That definition was published November 14, 1935.

The Nazis defined a Jew as anyone who had three or four racially full Jewish grandparents or belonged to a Jewish religious community or joined one after September 15 when the Nuremberg Laws came into force. Also regarded as Jews was anyone married to a Jew or married to the children of Jewish parents. This included illegitimate children of even the non-Jewish partner.

I do not remember any serious public objection to these laws.

The intent of these laws was to define a Jew so that the policies towards Jews and their property could be carried out without the confusion of who was a Jew and who was not.

The Nuremberg Laws had the unexpected result of causing confusion and heated debate over who was a full Jew. The Nazis then issued instructional charts to help distinguish Jews from *Mischlinge* and Aryans. The Laws by their general nature formalized the unofficial and particular measures taken against Jews up to 1935. The Nazi leaders made a point of stressing the consistency of this legislation with the Party program, which demanded that Jews should be deprived of their rights as citizens. After the Nuremberg Laws of 1935, a dozen supplemental Nazi decrees were issued that eventually outlawed the Jews completely, depriving them of their rights as human beings.The *Mischlinge* presented a problem for the Nazis. The word *Mischlinge* means "half-caste, mongrel or hybrid." In the 1920s, when French colonial soldiers had affairs with women in German territories they occupied, the children who resulted were called *Mischlinge*.

Hitler believed that the Jews brought these French blacks to Germany to destroy the White Race. The term became associated with any mixed race. Two years after seizing power, the Nazis implemented laws to separate *Mischlinge* from Aryans. In 1935, the Nuremberg Laws created two new racial categories: the half-Jew (Jewish *Mischlinge* first degree), and the quarter-Jew (Jewish *Mischlinge* second degree).

Accordingly to Hitler, they were the products of unholy unions and the sad products of the irresistibly spreading contamination of our sexual life. He said, "the vices of the parents are revealed in the sickness of the children. Blood sin and desecration of the race are original sin in this world and the end of humanity which surrenders to it."

The 1935 Nuremberg Laws defined the categories of *Mischlinge* according to the religion of a person's grandparents. Nazi scientists were unable to differentiate between Jewish and German blood. Left with no reliable scientific method for physically identifying *Mischlinge*, Nazi officials had to turn to church achieves or local court records of evidence of a person's race.

Most *Mischlinge* soon discovered that the Nazis took away their rights. The Nazis denied them citizenship in practice and they could not hold positions of authority. Many viewed themselves as Germans. Many tried to be considered as Aryans and labeled as normal. They knew that the Nazis scrutinized *Mischlinge* to determine whether the Aryan or Jewish side dominated. Consequently, most fought a constant battle to prove that their Aryan side had completely eclipsed their Jewish side. Their desire for acceptance took on a new twist when they entered the *Wehrmacht*. Many believed that the armed forces gave them an opportunity to prove their Aryan roots. Most believed their meritorious service would convince their comrades and society to accept them as normal. Hitler permitted many *Mischlinge* to serve in the military.

By this time Rolf, Guenther, and I, along with most of the young people of our age, were indoctrinated into the Nazi ideology and beliefs. We wanted nothing to do with Jews or with *Mischlinge*.

Parents who attempted to intervene were threatened. Organizations who attempted to offer different views were crushed.

I remember reading in the newspapers about the ideological dilemma of our time. On one hand the SS wanted to ship all Jews to Palestine. On the other hand, the SS was concerned about a strong Jewish state. Adolf Eichmann's brochure was the topic of discussion. In it he stated:

"The work of the Zionist World Organization carries with it a growing danger – a strong Jewish Palestine.

For all time world Jewry will remain an enemy of Germany; a strong Jewish Palestine could be an important factor in its struggle. But the danger did not end there. Zionism threatened to challenge German anti-Semitism on its own ground and this it would do as soon a Jewish state had been formed in Palestine and could take the German Jews under its protection."

Citizens were all told to keep an eye on Jews and on Jewish organizations. There was one thing that was noticeably absent on the streets of Berlin at the time and that was crime.

Our *Führer* treated us with tough love. Those who committed crimes were dealt with severely.

Our streets were at last safe!

While we were learning politics, we still found time for fun.

Anticipation and excitement of the Winter Olympics had grown steadily throughout 1935. The games were held in the villages of Garmisch and Partenkirchen in the Bavarian Alps.

The *Führer* opened the games on February 6, 1936. All events were followed in detail and reported in the newspapers and on radio. A military patrol competition was held. The International Olympic Committee refused admission of this sport into the Olympic Program, but the expressed desires of Adolf Hitler forced them to make this program a demonstration sport. Military patrol is considered the precursor to biathlon.

The games also included the cross-country relay events and the first time combined Alpine events for men and women were offered. Both events were won by Germans, Christl Cranz and Franz Pfnür.

We were all very proud of our athletes.

The next big event for us that year was Hitler's birthday on April 20th. As usual it included a huge parade that we marched in with a big rally at the Olympic Stadium and speeches by Goering and other party officials prior to Hitler's speech. The parade lasted for four hours with all of the Hitler Youth organizations from around the country represented. The SS led the parade in their chrome helmets and sharp black uniforms, goose-stepping with precision. I remember being very impressed by them.

The last time Guenther, Rolf and I were together was at the 1936 Summer Olympic Games.

Rolf was accepted to the Falkenburg School, a prestigious gymnasium located at Krössinsee. He was to leave for school after the games were over to study law. The school was considered the elite of the Order Castle Schools and only for the children of high Nazi party officials. Rolf's father had risen steadily in the party and had gained considerable influence by this time. We had special Hitler Youth seats, courtesy of Rolf's father, just under the special Nazi Official field boxes.

The vast Olympic stadium was completed on time and held 100,000 spectators. It was built in a modernist style. 150 other new Olympic buildings were completed on time for the event. Hitler saw the Olympics as an opportunity to show the racial superiority of German people. Along the streets of Berlin flew Olympic flags side by side with the Swastika. Parks and city squares were groomed and planted with flowers as the city spruced itself up for the world visitors.

The opening ceremony of the XI Olympic Games was held on Saturday, August 1, 1936, inside the Olympic Stadium, which was jammed to capacity. It was a cloudy day with occasional rain showers. Hundreds of Hitler Youth boys acted as guides and messengers. Hitler and his entourage, along with the Olympic officials, walked into the stadium right past our seats amid a chorus of three thousand Germans singing the National Anthem followed by the *Horst Wessel* anthem.

We were thrilled!

The magnificent Airship Hindenburg flew low over the stadium trailing the Olympic flag with its five rings representing the five participating continents.

Hitler's opening proclamation was followed by the *Olympic Hymn* written by German composer Richard Strauss for the Games. The climax of the opening ceremony then occurred with arrival of the Olympic torch. It had been carried all the way from Olympia, Greece, by some three thousand separate relay runners over a twelve-day period.

It was the first time in Olympic history this had been done.

Germany headed the gold medals results, despite the American Negro, Jesse Owens winning the 100 meter race.

We were all certain that he been given drugs to improve his performance.

There was no way that a Negro was better than the German athlete!

Film-maker Leni Riefenstahl was commissioned by the International Olympic Committee to film the Games. This marked the first live television coverage of a sports event in world history.

The Olympic Village itself received rave reviews from everyone who stayed there. The 130-acre village was constructed by the German Army under the direction of Captain Wolfgang Fuerstner. It was laid out in the shape of a map of Germany and contained 140 buildings including a post office and bank. Each of the athletes' houses contained 13 bedrooms, with two athletes per room. There were two stewards always on duty in each house who spoke the athletes' native language. Training facilities in the Village included a 400 meter oval track and a full size indoor swimming pool. Fuerstner's Olympic Village was the finest housing ever provided to Olympic athletes up to that time.

Overall, the Berlin Olympics were a big success for our country. Hundreds of international journalists acknowledged that Germany had put on the most lavish and biggest Olympics ever. Many thousands of tourists also left Germany with happy memories of the courtesy extended to them by the Nazis and the German people, as well as the fantastic facilities and precise efficiency of the whole event.

The Nazis had succeeded in getting what they most wanted from hosting the Olympics - respectability. We were very proud of what Hitler had accomplished! In school, we discussed now the world could see what Germany was capable of.

On December 1, 1936, Hitler decreed *The Law Concerning the Hitler Youth* which mandated that all young male and female Germans, excluding Jews, would be educated physically, intellectually and morally in the spirit of National Socialism though the Hitler Youth from the age of ten onward. This law also effectively ended the Catholic Youth Organization, Boy Scouts, and all other non-Nazi youth organizations.

Guenther and I believed that the Hitler Youth was the only youth organization that spoke our language. We believed that the older generation didn't understand what Hitler was trying to do. In the Hitler Youth, we had a voice that was listened to.

By this time I was sixteen years old and had done well in the Hitler Youth, achieving the rank of *Stammführer* (Unit Leader). Guenther had done well too. He was an *Obergefolgschaftsführer* (Senior Cadre Unit Leader). Rolf had achieved the rank of *Oberstammführer* (Senior Unit Leader) and as such, was in touch with the Nazi party officials.

My grades in school had been exceptional. The subjects were not difficult and actually became easier after the Nazis changed the curriculum. Rolf and Guenther had achieved good grades too.

During the winter of 1936, Anna, Guenther, and I spent a great deal of time together ice skating in *Geschichts* Park. Hitler Youth and BDM girls would migrate to the park after school and on weekends after a day of collecting beechnuts to be made into cooking oil. The park became ours exclusively and non-members were chased away. There was a pond that would freeze-over and we would scrape the snow from the ice until it was smooth.

Guenther and Anna were very good skaters.

I tried but fell a lot.

The parks department would stack fire wood and we would build bon fires to keep warm. We all brought sausage and cooked over the open fire, singing our songs and talking about what we would do after school. Since our apartment building was across the street from the park, Mother would permit our friends to use our bathroom. Everyone was very polite and respectful.

She would always offer coffee.

We enjoyed many wonderful days and nights in the park. I remember how nice it felt to associate with our own kind.

Chapter Eight
Order Castle School

After Hitler Youth activities on Sunday evenings Anna and I would often go to the movies. We liked movies with Tom Mix, Laurel and Hardy and Charlie Chaplin. I especially liked the newsreels about the Spanish Civil War. From the first and throughout the war, Italy and Germany aided the Spanish ruler Franco with an abundance of planes, tanks, and other material. Germany sent some 10,000 aviators and technicians. Italy sent large numbers of volunteers, probably about 70,000.

Germany used the war as a testing ground for faster tanks and aircraft that were just becoming available at the time.

Our contingent was organized into the Condor Legion that was equipped with the most modern airplanes and a specially trained staff. Many of the newest airplanes were tested in real combat situations, among them the Heinkel HE 111, and the Messerschmitt BF 109. The Legion was divided into bomber, fighter, reconnaissance, seaplane, communication, medical, and anti-aircraft battalions, and included an experimental flight group.

The chief of staff was Colonel Wolfram von Richthofen, a cousin of *The Red Baron*. I enjoyed watching our aviators in action. Their successes proved again the superiority of our armed forces. Anna agreed with me but liked the movies more than the newsreels. Anna and I also spent many evenings listening to the radio.

I can never forget the radio broadcast of May 7, 1937. The night before, the Hindenburg had arrived in Lakehurst Naval Air Station in America and caught fire, quickly becoming engulfed in flames. Of the 61 passengers and crew, 13 passengers and 22 crew members died along with one of the ground crew.

Sabotage was put forward as the cause of the fire. The likely saboteur was Eric Spehl, a rigger on the ship who died in the flames. Reports kept coming in on the radio as more information was uncovered by the Gestapo. It was discovered that Spehl's girlfriend was reportedly a communist with anti-Nazi connections. The fire's origin was near Gas Cell #4, Spehl's duty station and he was an amateur photographer, making him familiar with flashbulbs that could have served as an igniter. The Hindenburg was the pride of Germany and its greatest ambassador.

Results of the investigation were broadcast in detail for weeks after the disaster and we all listened, captivated by the accounts.

We were all affected by this attack on Germany.

It was clear that world Jewry and the Bolsheviks had declared war on Germany.

Mother was not sure. "How can Goebbles be so sure that Jews were behind this?" she would say.

Father responded, "Mother, I agree with you that not all Jews are bad but, it appears that the evidence is clear, many are."

One evening after dinner, while we were sitting in the parlor listening to the radio there was a knock on the door. Father opened the door and greeted a man in a long black leather coat who introduced himself an agent from the Reich Ministry of Education. He said he was there to talk about me. Suddenly, I was cold all over and negative thoughts came to my head.

What had I done and how did they find out? Had they found out about our secret bakery collections?

While we all sat at the kitchen table, mother served one of her special coffee blends, and we talked about the Hindenburg disaster for a while.

I could hardly wait for him to get to the reason for his visit.

The agent told us that Hans Wolfe, the Regional Hitler Youth Leader, had nominated me, to attend the new Order Castle School at *Vogelsang* located at Eifel in western Germany.

I had not seen Hans in years and wondered how he knew about me.

Maybe Rolf was at work again.

The agent announced, "Kurt's academic and physical fitness records had been provided by his school and he has been selected to attend."

Mother asked, "What does this school teach?"

The agent replied proudly, "It provides physical, spiritual, and military training for the future leaders of the Third Reich. The training your son will receive will channel him into a career that will place the reins of government into his hands. He will also study Architectural Engineering."

It sounded as though his answer was memorized from a book but it sounded exciting. I was going to have an opportunity to study in school much of what we discussed in the Hitler Youth.

Parents did not understand.

This was our future.

This was the future of Germany.

Father spoke up, "So, Kurt will be trained to be a military officer, is that correct?"

"Yes, he will be prepared to enter the elite of the SS," the agent answered.

Mother spoke up, "I am not sure this is the right school for Kurt. He has shown interest in architecture and…"

The agent cut her off in mid-sentence, "I don't think you understand. Your son has been selected to attend a school that most parents would kill to get their son into."

He paused.

"This school is the ideal of the *Führer* himself. We must all do our duty these days for the Fatherland and your son's duty is to serve his nation as he is directed. He understands that. Your duty is to support that decision."

Father quickly spoke, "Margaret, this will be an excellent opportunity for Kurt."

"Kurt, what do you think?"

I stood up saluting and replied, "I am honored to have been selected and I look forward to serving the *Führer*. I would like to go, Heil Hitler!"

For the first time, I saw fear on Mother's face.

The man stood up and said, "It is settled then."

He reached into his satchel and pulled out a train ticket, tossing it on the table.

"Your train leaves three days from now. Your school has already been notified and you are not expected back. Everything has been arranged."

He thanked mother for her hospitality and headed for the door.

As he went through the door he turned and looked at me saying, "Oh, by the way, your friend Guenther will be joining you, Heil Hitler!"

With that, he closed the door leaving us standing in the kitchen looking at each other.

Mother was the first to speak, "I don't like this. We had no choice. Everything has been decided and we are supposed to just accept everything they do and say."

I said, "But mother, I am seventeen years old and I want to go. I want to serve the Fatherland."

She replied, "Kurt, they have you brainwashed. I am really worried about you."

Father spoke, "Margaret, these are difficult times that require us to have some trust in our leaders. You have heard

Goebbles on the radio. Our enemies are everywhere. Look at what they did to our beloved Hindenburg."

As she turned to continue her work in the kitchen she whispered, "Its all propaganda I say."

"These imagined enemies. Who are they? Show them to us."

In his January 1938 speech, Hitler expounded at length on the importance of the Four Year Plan and its execution. In the press, it was constantly emphasized that Germany must stand on her own feet and must not depend on imports. Collecting took on even more importance than when we were in the *Jungvolk*. Everyone was urged to collect scrap metal, paper, bones, rags, and leftover food. A container was placed in the back of each apartment building to receive every tenant's kitchen refuse, which was collected daily and used to feed pigs in order to increase Germany's meat production. Heir Schmitz did not like this idea since he had to attend to it. He was constantly complaining that it smelled and was messy.

Bones collected by Hitler Youth groups were ground into bone meal and used for glue. Housewives were encouraged to use their own shopping bags and nets to cut down on paper. Father became involved with the collection effort, much to Mother's dismay. He would bring home empty tubes of mustard, mayonnaise and toothpaste, pressing them together. He also collected keys to sardine cans and re-distributed them to shopkeepers. Mother did not like all of the clutter but, it gave my father something to do and he felt as though he was contributing.

Our parents saw us off at the train station. Anna was there too. We promised to write often.

Guenther and I boarded the train and settled in for the trip to *Vogelsang*. The coach wheels bumped and thumped over the track. A fat old woman across the aisle from us slept noisily. Her immense double chin quivered visibly to every bump.

The buildings at *Vogelsang* were reminiscent of those of the 13th century and of the Order of the Teutonic Knights in East Prussia. They were constructed of the best materials in stone, marble, and virgin timber in a unique combination of medieval and National Socialist architectural concept. There were sports fields and a ceremonial center. The deep-dish amphitheater was like those of ancient Greece.

Vogelsang, whose design molded into the hills of Eifel, was an outstanding architectural achievement with a 165-foot medieval tower that served as a water tower for the school.

A popular activity was to climb the spiral steps to the top and try to hit fellow students with water balloons. One of the most memorable features was the courtyard, guarded by two massive stone fledgling eagles poised for flight at either end of the quadrangle.

Guenther and I shared a room with two other boys. Heinrich and Heydrich were from Frankfurt and had gone to the same school together like Guenther and me.

I wondered if that was just a coincidence or by design.

They were very polite, well mannered, and easy to get along with. Both had been leaders in the Hitler Youth and already had discipline.

Our room had four beds, four chests of drawers, and a built-in closet for each of our uniforms and coats. There were no locks on anything.

It was understood that any thievery, no matter how small, meant immediate expulsion. We never had a problem. Each room had its own bathroom. We were responsible for keeping our room and the bathroom clean and orderly.

Laundry was picked up every Tuesday morning. We were given laundry bags with our names and room numbers embroidered on them and were required to hang them on the hooks outside our door. Our clean laundry was delivered to our doorstep every Friday morning, neatly folded, and wrapped in oilpaper with our names and room numbers written on it. The latest copy of *Der Stürmer* (The Stormer),

Julius Streicher's anti-Semitic newspaper was placed on top. The current articles would often be the topic of discussion is class.

The longer we stayed at *Vogelsang*, the more special we began to feel. We felt very privileged to have been selected to attend. Guenther and I would discuss it sometimes when we were alone at night. We also wondered how Rolf was doing. Rolf wanted to be a lawyer and much of his school curriculum was about law. The plan was for him to continue on to law school after order castle.

After graduation from the Falkenburg School, Rolf went to law school at the University of Freiburg, one of the oldest universities in Germany. It has a long tradition of teaching the humanities, social sciences and natural sciences. The university was one of Germany's most prestigious and a leading research as well as teaching institution in Europe. Only the sons of Nazi officials attended. Rolf wrote us often about the campus and his fellow students.

Freiburg is a city in Baden-Württemberg on the western edge of the southern Black Forest in southwest Germany, where it is more commonly known by its full name, *Freiburg im Breisgau*. It straddles the Dreisam River, on the foothills of the Schlossberg, a hill topped by a castle, in the centre of the city of Graz, Austria. The city is surrounded by the Black Forest Mountains Rosskopf and Bromberg in the east, and in the south and west by the Schönberg, Tuniberg and the Kaiserstuhl.

Rolf was very lucky!

We considered ourselves very lucky too. *Vogelsang* was a very nice place to be.

Everything throughout the school was impeccably clean and orderly. A large staff of workers were constantly cleaning and polishing everything. We ate all of our meals at long tables in a room that seated one thousand. Each place was set with silver, white linen and china with our school logo on all the pieces. The tables looked white due to the array of a thousand immaculate place settings; each enveloped in its napkin, folded in the shape of a flower, while near each glass, in a crystal vase was a fresh-cut flower from the garden. On the wall were tapestries with images of our lineage, the knights and the kings of our past.

We were receiving lectures on racial questions and racial hygiene, history of the Iron Age, other early history topics, and research into family. Our typical daily schedule had us waking at 5:00 a.m. followed by calisthenics.

We had to be washed, dressed and have our living quarters cleaned by 7:10 a.m. for the raising of the flag.

Then there was coffee time at 7:20 a.m., followed by mathematics and other engineering related classes until 12:15 p.m. and announcements and mail delivery.

From 12:30 p.m. to 1:00 p.m. was the mid-day meal followed by a half hour of quiet time.

Every day up to 2:00 p.m. was the same.

After 2:00 p.m., the schedule would change.

Monday was field service day where we studied map reading, reporting and camouflage. Other days we would focus on light athletics or close order drill and preparation for honor guard duties, and military leadership.

Saturday morning was usually devoted to shooting weapons. Saturday afternoon was devoted to cleaning weapons and study hall.

Every day at 6:00 p.m., we would take the flag down. Evening meal was served from 6:30 p.m. to 7:30 p.m. After 7:30 p.m. was free time, films, or theater. Lights went out at 10:30 p.m. On Saturdays, we were allowed to stay up until midnight. Sunday we were usually off.

Integrated into our studies were the biological foundations of Jewry, the early history of the Jews and the institution of the Old Testament, and the history of the Jews. Additionally, we would study the middle ages and German history and heritage. We learned about how Germany's former colonies had been acquired despite opposition from Great Britain. We had to read aloud in class.

One day Guenther read, "German colonies were run in an exemplary manner and had greatly improved the natives standard of living and education. These colonies were stolen from Germany by the World Jewish Conspiracy."

Germany's independence from foreign suppliers was stressed. It was important not to be reliant on foreign suppliers for raw materials and vital supplies. We were told how Germany's scientists were discovering new formulas for synthetic rubber and fuel. We learned about Teutonic and Germanic tribes and the Nordic gods, such as Odin, Thor, and Loki.

The permanent guard at Vogelsang was supplied by the SS. Honor guards from various SS units were assigned to the school on a rotational basis. They were also involved with our honor guard training.

The SS soldiers set a fine example for us and the honor guard training was one on my favorite classes. I recall one candle light midnight ceremony lead by the SS guards. Our choir sang, "Who is to the banner sworn...in our *Volk* can never die" while we chanted, "The oath of the blood standard binds us." The education and training at Vogelsang was designed to stimulate our entire makeup, physically, mentally, and spiritually. We learned about the new German Order that we were to be part of. The words of Hitler were posted throughout the school as a reminder of our mission:

"My program for educating youth is hard. Weakness must be hammered away. In my castles of the Teutonic Order a youth will grow up before which the world will tremble. I want a brutal, domineering, fearless, cruel youth. Youth must be all that. It must bear pain. There must be nothing weak and gentle about it. The free, splendid beast of prey must once again flash from its eyes. That is how I will eradicate

thousands of years of human domestication. That is how I will create the New Order."

Our uniforms consisted of an open collar 4-button front tunic with pleated upper pockets, hidden sash lower pockets, and French cuffs. The uniforms were a brown, very similar to the body of the Nazi standard overcoat. Bloused brown breeches were the same shade as the tunics, and worn with black boots. The tunic collars were piped in golden yellow. The paired shoulder straps were plaited copper-colored cords on yellow underlay. A wide brown belt with a cross strap was worn with a white metal twin-claw open frame buckle. We wore the cuff title of the school, which was machine woven in aluminum thread on a tan cotton tape band. The lettering was in Gothic letterform. Completing the uniform was the visor cap with a political eagle affixed to the left side.

Guenther and I really liked the uniforms. I thought they made us stand out as elite students.

One day we were instructed to report to the auditorium. We were told that examinations for entrance into the SS Academy where to take place. Each of us was called into one of the small rooms beside the auditorium to be interviewed. The review officer carried on conversations with us designed to provide them with a picture of our general character, and to weed out any who were considered mentally deficient.

Since the SS concerned itself mostly with character; they were evaluating our will power, mental stamina, courage, loyalty, independence, and obedience. They were looking to discern our personality, behavior patterns, demeanor, and ability to cope.

Hitler would often comment that he wanted German youth, "slim, swift as greyhounds, tough as leather, and hard as Krupp steel."

These attributes were to serve the SS well in the days and weeks to come.

I was impressed to see a thick file sitting on the table with my name on it. There were apparently fitness reports from my service with the *Jungvolk* and the Hitler Youth along with my academic performance reports.

I had to perform some physical exercises and mathematical calculations, write an essay about the scourge of Jewry, and take dictation. This was all done very quickly. I guess the interviewers wanted to see if we could think on our feet.

Once the interviews were over, we were taken by bus to a house on the other side of town. There, we were led through the house and into the cellar, from the cellar, to the loft and back to the cellar again. Once in the cellar again, all the lights were turned off and we were asked questions about what we had seen in the house. We were given a compass and asked to point to the school. Guenther and I were totally unprepared for this and had to act and react quickly. The review officers were looking for the attributes we displayed while trying to make quick decisions in the confusing environment. They transported us all back to school and after they told us we would be informed about how we did by letter, left as abruptly as they came.

We went on with our studies and most forgot about the interviews. About sixty percent of us who started graduated.

We were very proud to be part of the elite!

Guenther and I came back home to Berlin to find bonfires lit in every neighborhood where Jews lived. On them were thrown prayer books, Torah scrolls and countless volumes of history and poetry. Jews were being chased, loathed and beaten. In the first twenty-four hours of our return home, ninety-one Jews were killed and more than thirty thousand were arrested and sent to concentration camps.

The night of November 9, 1938 holds a special memory for me. As Anna and I were walking to the cinema, members of the Berlin SS unit set fire to synagogues. If they thought fire would endanger nearby buildings, they smashed the synagogues as thoroughly as possible with hammers and axes. During that night thousands of homes and shops were broken into and ransacked. Tombstones in Jewish cemeteries were uprooted and graves violated.

Many people not in uniform joined in, crying, "Down with the Jews."

The destruction of the synagogues led the government to call that night the *Kristallnacht*, or night of the broken glass.

Chapter Nine
SS Academy

A letter from the SS Office was waiting for me when I got home from Anna's. I didn't notice it until Father cleared his throat and motioned to the table were the latter sat.

Rolf's father had delivered it personally.

I opened it and read the letter aloud, "The racial authenticity of your family has been verified, and you have been highly recommended for admission to the SS academy. It is with great pleasure that I inform you of your selection as a candidate in the SS, signed Heinrich Himmler, *Reich Führer* SS."

Father hugged me then shook my hand saying how proud he was of me.

Mother, her usual cautious self, said, "Are you sure this is what you want?"

I said that this was exactly what I wanted. I went back to Anna's to tell her the news. She was extremely happy, as were her parents.

After visiting with her parents, Anna and I decided to go to the zoo. Berlin had one of the finest zoos in Europe at the time. We especially liked to see the wandering bears that were led around on a leash by their trainers. They would perform tricks, standing on their back legs, dancing and turning around in circles. We would sit for hours watching the wandering bears and eating flavored crushed ice.

Anna and I talked about what we would do after I graduated from the SS academy. We would be married, of course, and depending on where I was stationed, Anna would join me. She was still very interested in living on a farm someday but, for now, we would see what the SS had in store for me.

Anna had been very active in the *Bund Deutcher Mädel*, achieving the rank of Group Leader. As such, she was responsible for the political instructions. She was always enthusiastic about the ideals of National Socialism. We would discuss the speeches from the radio and agreed wholeheartedly with our leaders.

Anna, Guenther, Rolf and me, like most of the youth of our age, believed that we were the future of Germany. We would often meet on our apartment building roof and tell ourselves how fortunate we were to be living in these days.

We knew we were special!

Guenther was happy when I told him about being accepted. I got the feeling that Rolf somehow had something to do with my acceptance. Guenther had also applied but had not yet received word. It was a week later when Guenther came to the apartment to tell us that he had been accepted too. His letter told him to report on the same day as me.

I again wondered if Rolf's hand was in this.

Rolf's father progressed in the party over the years. By then, he was the Assistant Reich Minister for Postal Affairs. Rolf's mother had become acquainted with Leni Riefenstahl, Hitler's film maker. Rolf's parents had become very influential.

I think it was Rolf's father who protected Guenther's parents. Even though Guenther's parents were known to be liberal, they kept their jobs at the school when many liberal teachers were replaced.

It did make a difference who one knew in Germany in those days.

In 1938, Hitler expanded Germany's borders by absorbing neighboring Austria and the Sudetenland (western portion of Czechoslovakia) with their large populations of ethnic Germans. As a result, Hitler Youth membership swelled to 8.7 million.

In September, the last peacetime Nuremberg rally took place. It had the theme *Gross Deutschland* (Greater Germany) and was the largest one ever held, with nearly 700,000 members of various Nazi Party organizations participating during the weeklong festivities. Rolf, Guenther, Anna and I attended.

On Saturday, September 10, over 80,000 Hitler Youths marched into the city stadium and performed military-style parade maneuvers, which they had been practicing for an entire year, ending with a grand finale in which they spelled out the name Adolf Hitler in the grandstand. After a tumultuous welcome, Hitler gave a speech, in which he spoke candidly about his own youth and painful adolescence and then ended by telling us:

"You, my youth, are our nation's most precious guarantee for a great future, and you are destined to be the leaders of a glorious new order under the supremacy of National Socialism. Never forget that one day you will rule the world!"

We all broke down in tears listening to Hitler's words.

He had become like a Father to us. Even more, he was our leader and our salvation!

I think it was that night when I decided that I would do anything for him.

Father, Mother, and Anna took me to the train station. Guenther's parents were there too to see him off.

It was a warm spring day. The smell of lilacs permeated the platform. Soldiers and baggage handlers were everywhere. The platform was loaded with parents and wives who came to see their sons and husbands off. Mother had tears in her eyes as she kissed me and told me to be careful.

Father told me how proud he was of me.

Soon it was time to board the train that would take us to SS basic training.

I kissed Anna and told her I would write as soon as possible. She agreed to do the same.

The conductor called, "all aboard,"

Guenther and I walked up the metal steps into the car. Our families stood beside each other on the platform and waived as the train pulled out of the station. I remember looking back and wondering if my life would change.

After a while, everyone settled into their seats. Some read books while others stared out the window at the passing buildings. The train picked up speed after we left the station. The steady click, click of the rails put many people to sleep. I looked over at Guenther who was sound asleep. Guenther could sleep anywhere, any time. I was too excited to fall asleep. I watched as we made our way out of Berlin and into the countryside.

Finally, the clicks of the rails were too much for me too, and I was a sleeping. I remember dreaming of our days in school and of camping over night.

It was so much fun.

I wondered if what we were going to would be anything like it or just plain hell. Rolf had said in a couple of his letters that the drill sergeants yelled a lot.

We were all awakened by the sound of the train whistle and slowing down as we pulled into the Lichterfelde Station.

The train had barely come to a stop when the doors opened and the drill instructors came aboard.

They immediately began shouting, "Get up, and get your things. Get out off of this train you lazy bums!"

Guenther was startled and for a moment did not know where he was.

He looked at me with a surprise and said, "I wonder what is in store for us Kurt?"

Rolf wrote that the drill instructors yelled because they wanted to toughen us up and really did not mean anything by it.

It sure seemed that they were serious.

I helped Guenther get oriented and find his things and we got off the train. Before we left we agreed that whatever was thrown at us we would handle. After all, we were Hitler Youth and had passed many challenge tests.

We both agreed that basic training would be a snap.

Once all of us were assembled on the platform, the drill instructors shouted for us to board one of the trucks that were parked beside the platform.

One of the drill sergeants yelled, "Get your lazy asses on the truck. You have had it easy up to now. That is all going to change. Your mothers are not here to wipe your noses anymore."

We climbed into the back of one of the trucks and sat down on the bench. The tarpaulin was removed, and we rode in the open. It was warm and the robins were singing. Spring had begun in earnest.

I was glad we could see.

The town was beautiful. It seemed like everyone had flowers planted in their yards and many were starting to bloom. Flags were flying on most of the houses and some of the people waved at our trucks.

After winding through the streets of Lichterfelde for about thirty minutes, we arrived at the Kaserne Barracks, the headquarters of the *Leibstandarte-SS* Adolf Hitler. This was the home of the famous Bodyguard Division and the SS basic training headquarters.

The truck pulled up to a two story brick building. The doorways were arches with "SS" carved into the keystones of each door.

Along the side of the building was a rock garden with a swastika made from painted rocks in the middle. Everything was neat and perfectly clean. The brass knobs on the doors were highly polished.

Guenther said, "I wonder who keeps this place so neat?"

We didn't know at the time that it would be us who would keep this place in order.

The drill sergeant jumped from the cab of the truck and began yelling, "I am Sergeant Kruger. Get out of that truck you lazy bums. What do you think this is a Sunday ride in the country? Go inside and find a bunk. Stow your gear in a locker and get out here on the street."

Guenther and I found a bunk bed. He wanted the top bunk and I took the bottom. We stowed our gear as instructed and went back outside to the street in front of the building.

The drill sergeant was yelling at someone when he spotted Guenther. Guenther had his hands in his pockets, a particular bad habit that he could never seem to break.

Sergeant Kruger ran over to Guenther and yelled, "Who told you that you could put your hands in your pockets? What do you think this is a picnic? Drop down and give me fifty pushups."

Guenther did the pushups while the drill sergeant was off yelling at someone else. Finished, Guenther stood up.

Sergeant Kruger ran back to us, turned to me, and yelled, "Why did you stand there and let him get up without permission? Aren't you a Hitler Youth Platoon Leader? You should have known better. Drop down and give me fifty pushups too."

Another lesson learned, I thought.

How did he know I was a platoon leader? I wondered.

After Sergeant Kruger was done with Guenther and me, he told us to line up with the other recruits who were standing in the middle of the street. There were forty of us in total, a platoon.

Kruger continued yelling, "You are all worthless!"

"None of you will complete basic training!"

He said we were all sissies and we should quit now and save him the trouble of kicking us out later.

After about thirty minutes of berating, we marched a couple of blocks to a large warehouse-type building to get our uniforms and field equipment. We received three uniforms; a camouflage, a grey and a black uniform. Sergeant Kruger told us to hang the black uniform in our locker and not to touch it until told to do so. He said we were not worthy to handle the black uniform of the SS. Back in our barracks, with our uniforms and equipment, we had a few free minutes to introduce ourselves, and to find out where everyone was from.

We all marched to dinner and had to line up in alphabetical order to enter the dinning hall. A corporal was at the door and we had to tell him our name, rank, and service number before we were permitted to enter. If he didn't like the way it sounded, he would make the person go to the back of the line.

Guenther and I got in on our first try and went through the food line.

There were long tables with benches on both sides. Each table was large enough for a platoon. Each platoon had an assigned table.

Once Guenther and I got our food, we found our platoon table. No one was permitted to sit down until everyone from the platoon was present. A couple of our platoon members were sent to the back so the rest of us stood by our seats with our trays until they got their food. Once we were all accounted for, the drill sergeant told us to sit and begin eating. He said that in the future, we could take anything we liked but we had to eat it all, nothing could be thrown away. I had bean soup, three boiled potatoes, a piece of bread, and a chocolate pastry. It was good. After dinner, we all marched back to our barracks where the drill sergeant instructed us in the proper way to make our beds and how our uniforms and equipment were to be stowed.

Everyone in the platoon worked diligently at getting everything in order.

Guenther was having some trouble with making his bed tight enough so that a coin would bounce when dropped in the middle.

Soon it was 10:00pm, and time for lights-out and sleep. It had been a long day and I was tired.

I lay on my bunk thinking about Mother, Father, Anna and about Rolf who had been through this a year earlier.

I wondered if Guenther and I would see Rolf again.

I felt a sense of pride, mixed with admiration and fear. After all, not everyone was selected to serve in the SS. We had brand new uniforms and I was very proud of my appearance.

Guenther, Rolf and I had come a long way since the days at the *Jungvolk Heim.*

It seemed like just yesterday.

So much has happened since then. Now, I was really going to serve the Fatherland. I was going to make my parents proud.

We sprang up in our beds when we heard the bell. A brass ship's bell hung from the open rafters at the end of the bay.

Sergeant Kruger was banging it with a hammer and yelling, "Get up you sleepy heads. What do you think this is summer camp? Your mothers are not here to pamper you now."

We quickly dressed in out Physical Training (PT) uniform and assembled in the street. It was 5:00am. We marched to the PT field and did some stretching exercises before beginning calisthenics. After pushups, setups, straddle hops, and knee bends, we ran three miles and came back to the field. More stretching, then we went back to the barracks for personal hygiene. This was our early morning routine, rain, or shine, for eight weeks. We marched to the dinning hall to get our morning ration of hot fresh bread and jelly. They always served hot black coffee from Italy.

After breakfast, we marched back to PT field to practice close-order drill. We were all used to drilling in the Hitler Youth however; we could do nothing right in the eyes of the drill instructors.

"So you're the Hitler boys!" one greeted us, regarding us suspiciously.

"And I'm to turn you chosen ones into fighters!" he said, shaking his head.

Somewhat intimidated, we huddled around the big table in the barracks and looked at him.

"I must train you for military service. Well, let's get started."

He placed the rifle on the table.

"Can anyone tell me what this is?" he asked.

Guenther spoke up. "It's a rifle."

The sergeant laughed so hard I thought he was going to hurt himself.

"A rifle says this member of the master race. It is a *Karabiner 98k* 7.92mm rifle and you chosen ones will get to know it well."

"Now we will watch this smart ass do pushups."

Guenther got very good at pushups.

We were to learn everything about the weapon and about other ones too. A great deal of out time was spent assembling and disassembling weapons. Once we demonstrated that we could perform these tasks sufficiently for the drill sergeants, we moved to the ranges and fired each weapon.

I enjoyed learning all about the weapons.

A highlight was returning from a training field all the way back to the barracks on foot. This was a 75-80 Kilometer trek that was expected to be completed in one day's time. This was the most exhausting physical ordeal I have ever experienced. While this was hard, not one man dropped out. The main reason for this test of endurance was to prove that one could live up to the expectations of his masculinity and be accepted by his group.

To be called a *Schlappschwanz*" (pussy) was seen as the worse blow to one's creation of identity, as it identified us with the feminine. We would rather have endured physical torture than be given this emasculating nickname.

We were also ordered to participate in the slaughtering of animals for the yearly harvest. Though Guenther found it sickening to chop the heads of chickens, twist the heads off pigeons with our bare hands, or clobber little rabbits behind the ears with a stick and then cut their throats, we did it without blinking an eye. After all, none of us wanted to be called a "pussy."

A certain kind of happiness thrived in our barrack. It was the happiness of comradeship. It was a pleasure to go for a cross-country run together in the morning, and then go naked into the communal hot showers together, to share parcels that one or another received from home, to share the responsibility for misdemeanors that one of your comrades had committed, to help and support one another in a thousand little ways.

During our fourth week, we moved into the classroom to learn about land navigation. Drill sergeants told us that the four teams who completed the course the fastest would be given a weekend off.

Guenther and I were looking forward to a weekend off. It had been non-stop since we arrived at Kasserine Barracks. We decided that if we were one of the successful teams we would take the train back to Berlin to see our families. I missed my parents and I especially missed Anna. But first, we had to be one of the first teams to finish. The classroom instruction lasted all day and was very thorough.

Guenther and I thought it was easy.

Drill Sergeant Kruger chose the composition of the teams.

After breakfast the next day we were instructed to form up on the street with our field gear where we would learn who was on which three-man team. Guenther and I were on the same team along with Louis, from Düsseldorf.

He was a likable person but quiet. His parents were high up in the Nazi Party but he never brought it up.

We all boarded trucks that dropped us at our start points. Each team had a different start point but had to finish at the same point. Each team was issued a compass, map, and instruction sheet, which gave the compass heading and distance to our points.

Our team was letter "K." Louis and Guenther decided that I should operate the compass and they would orient the map to the terrain and keep the pace. We were very confident that we would finish in the top. The first couple of points were easy to find.

Louis commented, "This is easier than I thought it would be. At this rate, we will be the first to finish."

Our team continued on, finding the trees with the colored dots that corresponded with the color on our instruction sheet. There was a five-digit number written on a small plaque under the colored dot. We had to write the number in a space beside the color on our instruction sheet to get credit for the leg of the course. The course took us down stream banks and through jagged brushes.

Louis and Guenther would take turns going ahead and lining up on the compass heading, based on my direction. We would all check the distance using our pace. All was going extremely well until we reached the sixth leg. We followed the direction listed on the sheet and paced the distance as before but could not find the tree with the colored dot.

During our classroom instruction we were told that if we thought we were close to the target but could not find it to have someone circle around, looking for the marker. I stood still while Guenther and Louis began circling in ever-increasing circles. Ten minutes went by with nothing.

I was starting to get worried.

I could see our free weekend slipping away.

After twenty minutes, I knew were we were in trouble. I don't know why but I decide to look up. When I did, I spotted a green dot and the number plaque we were looking for. All the other dots had been at eye level. This one was about ten feet up the tree.

Another lesson learned about assuming.

I called Guenther and Louis in and we proceeded on. Now that we knew to look more carefully, the course went smoothly. Each team had been given sandwiches and water. Since we had wasted so much time on point six, we decided to eat our sandwiches as we moved.

There were thirty points on our sheet and we had one more to go when we spotted our trucks parked in an open area along side a set of bleachers. There were several people sitting on the bleachers and several milling around one of the trucks.

I suddenly got a queasy feeling in my stomach.

I just knew that out problem at point six was going to cost us the free weekend. We found the last point close to the opening and went to the bleachers to report to Sergeant Kruger. He looked at his watch and our sheet.

He announced, "Team K is the fourth team to finish in proper order. They qualify for a weekend off. Congratulations."

Louis, Guenther, and I hugged each other and shook our heads in disbelief. We went over to the truck for coffee and to wait for the other teams to arrive. It took several hours for all of the teams to come in. A couple of the teams had to be retrieved by the drill instructors because they were totally lost.

I felt sorry for them.

Their weekend would be comprised of remedial land navigation training. I was happy though. I would be going to Berlin.

Guenther and I caught a ride to the train station with the mail truck. We were excited to be going home in the Grey uniform of the SS. I had telegrammed Anna that we were coming and asked her to meet us at the station. I asked her not to tell Father and Mother. I wanted to surprise them. The train ride from Lichterfelde to Berlin seemed a lot longer than when we first came. Neither of us could sleep. We were too excited about getting home.

As the train pulled into the station, I spotted Anna on the platform. She looked as pretty as ever in a pink-flowered dress. Her long blonde hair protruded from her hat. As the train came to a stop at the platform, the steam from the engine engulfed those waiting. Anna disappeared in the fog.

Suddenly, I had a chill come over me. I couldn't explain it. It was like something supernatural telling me that everyone would be engulfed. The fog cleared, with Anna smiling as she spotted us coming down the steps.

I hugged her as she said, "Kurt, you are freezing. Are you sick?"

"No, I just had a sudden chill. I am fine now and very happy to see you!"

Anna hugged Guenther and said, "You look healthy Guenther, and I am happy to see you."

We got caught-up on the things that had happened in Berlin while we were gone and I told her all about basic training.

We were not permitted to write or receive letters until our fifth week so I was out of touch.

I didn't realize how much I had missed Anna until I saw her. I knew then that we would be married some day. I made up my mind to ask her to marry me while I was home that weekend.

I wondered what Father and Mother would think. Father seemed to like her but Mother was not fond of Anna's political beliefs.

Guenther left us to buy something at the store and Anna and I continued down Lehrter Street to my parent's apartment.

Just before we reached the building, I stopped her and said," Anna, I want to ask you something."

She looked me in the eyes and said, "Kurt, I missed you very much and I want to be with you always."

"Anna, this isn't the proper place but, I love you and will your marry me?"

She replied, "Of course I will. I love you too."

We arrived at the front door to the apartment building hand-in-hand. Anna rang the bell to keep the surprise going.

Mother answered, "Anna, how can I help you?"

She released the door lock and we both went up the stairs. Anna knocked on the door while I stayed out of sight. Mother opened the door greeting Anna.

Then, I appeared. Mother was surprised to see me and began admonishing Anna for playing along. Father was sitting in the parlor listening to a speech by Goebbels.

Mother commented, "That's all he does now. He goes to work, comes home, and listens to propaganda. He is brainwashed too"

I said, "Mother, I see that your opinion of our government hasn't changed."

"What, in four weeks, you think my position would change?"

Father spotted us at the door and joined the reunion.

We all hugged and went into the kitchen for coffee. We sat at the kitchen table and caught up on events for several hours.

That evening, Mother cooked my favorite meal, served with some dark beer from Aschinger's. After dinner, we retired to the living room.

As soon as we were all seated I said, "Mother and Father, I have something to tell you. I have asked Anna to marry me and she has agreed."

Mother immediately commented, "Are you sure you are not jumping into something too soon?"

Father said, "We would be very happy to have Anna as part of the family and I hope she will give us and the Fatherland many children."

Anna blushed at his comment.

Mother gave Father her usual look of displeasure.

Anna and I decided to go to her parent's apartment to tell them. I felt confident that her parents would approve since they liked me and I was soon to be an SS officer. They believed, like Anna, that her duty was to marry an SS officer and have many children. I did ask her father if he would permit me to marry Anna.

This was a custom that was disappearing in the new Germany but I decided to make the gesture anyway.

Anna's father appreciated it and agreed. We all agreed that the wedding would be after I was commissioned. We would begin the application process now since it could take a while.

Even though my background was checked thoroughly before I was accepted into the SS, the Ancestral Heritage Bureau, which was charged with the study of the German people's racial origins, had to approve marriages. With our application for a marriage license, I was required to submit a photograph of Anna wearing a bathing suit. With his view of German-Nordic measurements in mind, Himmler himself often studied the photographs, paying special attention to the shape of the skull and forehead, the distance between the eyes, and the curvature of the nose.

If Himmler's verdict and the genealogical investigation concurred, a marriage license would be issued. Our respective family's background had to be checked for racial purity.

The SS could not have mixed blood!

I was learning more and more about the negative effect of mixed blood had on the people of Germany.

I was confident there would not be a problem but the paperwork had to be processed anyway. I walked to our apartment that night feeling good about life. I was going to be married and once I completed basic training, I was off to SS officer training.

Life was good, I thought.

Anna and I spent the next morning at the zoo, walking around, planning our life together. My train was to leave at 7:00 p.m. There was time to check into a hotel and spend time in bed. The registration clerk didn't question me in my grey SS uniform.

Who knew when we would see each other again?

It had been a wonderful weekend. Anna's parents had Mother, Father, and us to their apartment for an early dinner. All agreed that Anna would walk me to the train station. We just made small talk on the way. We didn't want to discuss when the next opportunity would be that we could see each other.

This weekend was a bonus that we had not planned for. I told her that I would write as much as I could and she promised to write every day.

We saw Guenther and his parents standing on the platform and strolled over to them. Anna told them of our marriage plans and everyone seemed genuinely happy. It was time for Guenther and me to board the train. We found our seats and waved out of the windows as the train slowly pulled out of the station.

As the train started moving, the steam once again engulfed the platform and the chill again came over me.

Guenther said, "Kurt, you look like you just saw a ghost. What is the matter?"

As the train pulled away from the station, I replied, "I don't know. I suddenly had a strange feeling come over me. I can't explain it. It happened when we pulled into the station too. It is like a look into the future and we all perish in the fog."

Guenther said, "You are just sorry to be going back. You had such a wonderful visit."

I replied, "Maybe you're right."

The next four weeks of basic training kept us busy with physical training, drills, weapons firing, classes, and political briefings. We learned military songs, and all joined in whenever we could. Basic training was the most severe challenge I have ever experienced. We were exhausted at the end of each day. We often fell asleep at dinner. Our marching and close order drill had improved significantly although the marching came easy to most of us. We had done a lot of marching in the Hitler Youth. Anna kept her word and wrote every day. I tried to write every night as time permitted. I looked forward to her letters.

In order to graduate, we had to do a twenty-five kilometer march at quick-face, with full equipment and radio set. This was followed by night exercises including an orientation race using sketches and a prismatic compass.

I wrote to Father, "We have to learn and train until we perfect all of the skills. The intensity of the training is tremendous and there is no rest for anyone."

He wrote back that this training would save casualties in the future. I didn't see it at the time but he was right.

Two days before graduation, Sergeant Kruger told us to get our black uniform out of our lockers. We would graduate in the black uniform of the SS. We pressed and adjusted our uniform and polished our dress boots to a high shine in preparation for the big day. Everyone in my platoon made it to graduation.

We were very proud of what we had accomplished together.

We really felt as though we were a team.

Relatives were invited to the graduation ceremony. Mother, Father, Anna, and her parents all planned to attend. I couldn't wait to show off in my sharp black SS uniform.

We woke early on graduation day, straightened the barracks for the last time, and practiced lining up and passing in review in the field behind our barracks. Then it was time to line up for the last time on our street with our drill sergeants. Each one came to us and wished us good luck. Then Sergeant Kruger announced the future assignments.

Guenther and I were off to Munich for the SS officer candidate induction ceremony that evening then to Bad Tolz for officer school.

There would be no time to go home to visit Anna and my parents. I would have to make the best of their visit.

All of the visitors were seated in the stands facing the parade field. Mother, Father, Anna, Anna's parents, and Guenther's parents sat together.

It was a warm summer day and there wasn't a cloud in the sky. The band played as we marched down the street and onto the parade field.

We took our positions behind our company banner, just as we had practiced. All of our movements were crisp. We were a sea of black on the parade field. Our chrome ceremonial helmets glistened in the sun. We were proud of how we looked and proud of what we had accomplished. The commandant and some VIPs from the army reviewed us and then spoke.

I thought the speeches would never end.

Speaker after speaker talked about how we were about to embark on a journey that would lead to glory for us and for Germany.

Amid all of the music and the fanfare, my thoughts kept coming back to Anna. I could not make her out in the stands but I knew she was there. I could sense her presence. We had not seen each other since the bonus weekend and I missed her very much. I missed my parents too, but in a different way. After the final speech, we marched, one company at a time, to the reviewing stand.

The commandant called each of our names and we left the formation, climbed the stairs to receive our graduation emblem, and then returned to the formation. Once we all received our emblems we marched past the reviewing stand and back to our barracks to collect our belongings and to say our last goodbyes to each other. Our class would be scattered all over Germany to various assignments. We didn't know if we would ever see each other again. We had trained and learned together, surviving the trials of basic training and becoming close. It is hard to describe the camaraderie that develops through mutual sacrifice.

Our guests were told to meet us at the dining hall where a luncheon had been prepared. We made our way to the hall to find our families and friends. Guenther and I introduced Anna and our parents to Sergeant Kruger and the other drill instructors.

Our train to Munich was scheduled to leave at 6:00 p.m. We didn't have much time.

After the lunch, we had a few hours to visit. Anna and I went off on our own after a little while.

We walked through the park, around the commons, and past the ceremonial cannon, which was fired when we raised and lowered the flag every day. She kept telling me how she couldn't wait to me married and to have my baby. We talked about a name for the baby and agreed that if it were a girl we would name her after Anna's mother, Bertha. If the baby were a boy, his name would be Rolf. Events in Europe were moving very fast and we did not know what the future would bring. We vowed that day that if something happened and we were separated, we would meet at Uncle Frederick's shop in Rothenburg. He knew and liked Anna and I knew he would take care of her if something happened to our parents.

We walked to the coffee shop at the train station where we had arranged to meet everyone else and visited until it was time for our train to leave.

The scene on the platform was impressive with all of the black uniforms. There were SS flags placed every fifteen or so feet all along the platform waving in the wind. There was a band playing the SS anthem.

Guenther and I said our goodbyes, hugged, and boarded the train. We had made it through basic training, now were off for Munich and the SS Induction Ceremony, after which, we would officially be members of the SS and officer candidates.

Chapter Ten
SS Officer School

To Heinrich Himmler, the SS was more than a group of party faithful committed to crushing the foes of the Third Reich. It was an exalted order of the Nordic men. A mystic brotherhood inspired by the tales of Teutonic knights and medieval legends. He saw the SS men as new aristocracy of the Third Reich.

At 10 p.m. November 9, 1938, the anniversary of the 1923 Munich putsch, as was the tradition, our class of new recruits, took our oath as a group at Munich's *Feldherrnhalle* (Field Marshall's Hall).

Torches symbolizing the martyrs of the putsch fifteen years earlier lighted the stage. Beneath the pillars of flame that lent a striking sacramental light to the proceedings, our group pledged obedience unto death. Adolf Hitler, himself, presided over the ceremony. Hitler consecrated the SS flag by holding one hand on the blood stained flag from the Munich putsch and one on the SS flag. Tears came to my eyes when, by the light of the torches, our class recited the oath in chorus:

I swear to thee, Adolf Hitler
as *Führer* and Chancellor of the German Reich,
Loyalty and Bravery.
I vow to thee and to the superiors
whom thou shalt appoint
Obedience unto Death.

So help me God.

If only Anna and my parents could be here to see this. I knew they would have been proud.

That night, we were free to explore Munich.

Dressed in our sharp black uniforms, Guenther and I went to the old city and to the Hofbrau House. This was the place were Hitler had declared that the revolution had begun. It became a must visit place when in Munich. We drank lots of beer, ate sausage, and sang the Horst Wiesel song with the rest of the patrons. People kept buying us beers. I can't remember getting back to hotel. Guenther said he had to help me. I do remember the headache the next morning.

After lots of coffee, we were off to Bad Tolz in the Bavaria Alps for officer training. I wrote to Anna during the train ride to Bad Tolz.

The atmosphere at Bad Tolz was very much like that at Vogelsang. We dined at a great round table, as in the King Arthur legend. We all engaged in fencings and chess. We were taught that the SS was to be the living embodiment of the Nazi doctrine of the superiority of Nordic blood, and of the Nazi conception of a master race.

I really began to experience a transformation at Bad Tolz. I was beginning to see what all of our teachers had been telling us about the Jews and the gypsies and the enemies of Germany.

All SS officer candidates were thoroughly examined and checked. I was asked for the political reputation record of my parents and the record of their ancestry as far back as 1750. I was asked for a record of hereditary health showing that no hereditary disease existed in my parents and in our family. Last, but perhaps most important, was a certification from the race commission. This examining commission was composed of SS leaders, anthropologists, and physicians. The very process of selection and acceptance gave us a sense of superiority. Only pureblooded Germans in good health could become a member. He must be of excellent character, had no criminal record, and be well versed in all

National Socialist doctrines. The members had to be ready and willing tools, prepared to carry out tasks of any nature, however distasteful. Absolute obedience was the necessary foundation stone of the SS.

Our obedience had to be unconditional. We were told it corresponded to the conviction that the National Socialist ideology must reign supreme. Every SS man was prepared, therefore, to carry out every order that was issued by the *Führer*. We were also taught a view of the past based on racial struggle and *Lebensraum* (Living Space).

The past provided a sense of continuity and showed me that the Jews and Slavs had always been the enemies of Germany. This meant that the need for living space and a solution to the Jewish question was deemed inevitable.

All of us incoming cadets received an etiquette manual that defined table manners and even contained instructions for closing a letter ("Heil Hitler! Yours sincerely, X"). Correct form was encouraged through cultural activities and lectures on Nazi ideology. The heart of the regiment at Bad Tolz was a mixture of athletics and field exercises meant to yield officers nobly conditioned to command.

The classroom challenges undertaken by Guenther and me in training ranged from playing war games in a sandbox to unraveling the meaning of Hitler's *Mein Kampf*. Ideology excited me less than military theory. Ideology was an important factor in the examinations that eliminated one candidate in three during the eleven-month course.

On one test, I had to expand on these words of Hitler, "The mixing of blood and the sinking of the racial standard contingent upon this is the sole cause for the demise of all cultures."

In the university-like hall decked with swastikas, our instructors lectured on Nazi philosophy. A goal of the officer school was to produce officers who were fit to fight on the run. Building on mobile tactics introduced late in World War I, General Hausser's techniques prepared us cadets for rapid assaults that would leave the enemy reeling.

This approach, according to Hausser's assistant, Colonel Felix Steiner, required a supple, adaptable type of soldier, athletic of bearing, capable of more than the average endurance.

To forge these soldier-athletes, the SS spared no expense.

The facilities at Bad Tolz included a stadium for football, track and field events, separate halls for boxing, gymnastics, and indoor ball games, and a heated swimming pool and sauna. The complex attracted outstanding talent. At one time, eight out of twelve coaches at Bad Tolz were national champions in their events.

Himmler, who was infatuated with aristocratic customs, sanctioned duels with sword or pistol, decreeing that every SS man has the right and duty to defend his honor by force of arms. Not wanting to loose anyone to duels to the death, Himmler instructed that every man involved was always permitted the opportunity to apologize and save face.

I don't remember of anyone actually being killed although there were some scars produced.

The athletic program emphasized group exercises, such as lofting the medicine ball or tumbling through a human hoop, as well as individual events, such as running and high hurdles. The school enhanced its reputation by competing successfully against teams representing the army and the *Luftwaffe*. We received instruction in the basic training devoted to handling weapons and clearing obstacles. After the basics, we learned the advanced skills required of a small-unit commander, including field communications, coordinating infantry and artillery fire, and landing assault craft on a hostile shore.

While most Germans of the day traveled on our superb system of urban trains, a fleet of drivers in private limousines chauffeured SS officers around to appointments. Guenther and I were impressed.

Himmler had made certain that we looked trim and elegant. The German firm Hugo Boss supplied our uniforms. In contrast to the scruffy brown tunics and pants of the army, we were decked out in black with silver collar flashes. On our hats, we wore a silver death's head, an ominous touch that symbolized "duty until death." Such finery served a dual purpose. It intimidated victims and was meant to add to the man's sex appeal, boosting the chances of one's success with the girls.

We had been there almost one year and Guenther and I had become accustomed to the routine at Bad Tolz. We where beginning to think of ourselves as very special. Anna's letters always supported our training. She wrote often about family and what was happening in Berlin. I wrote her a long letter.

The political situation in Germany was changing. We heard about the seizure of the German radio station *Sender Gleiwitz* in Gleiwitz Upper Silesia on August 31 by Polish troops and broadcast of an anti-German message.

On September 1, 1939, our army invaded Poland. The Polish army was defeated within weeks of the invasion. From East Prussia and Germany in the north and Silesia and Slovakia in the south, our units, with more than 2,000 tanks and over 1,000 planes, broke through Polish defenses along the border and advanced on Warsaw in a massive encirclement attack. After heavy shelling and bombing, Warsaw surrendered to the Germans on September 28, 1939. Britain and France, standing by their guarantee of Poland's border, had declared war on Germany on September 3, 1939. The Soviet Union invaded eastern Poland on September 17, 1939. We didn't realize it at that moment, but World War II had begun.

On September 21, 1939, Reinhard Heydrich, The Chief of the Reich Central Security Office, announced at a conference of SS commanders, that Jews were to be concentrated in big cities near major railroad lines. In these cities, they were forced into designated areas that later became the Jewish ghettos. This announcement was a general directive. A specific law creating ghettos was never announced.

As we studied this decree, it became clear that the goal of the German policy in 1939 was to facilitate the forced mass emigration and expulsion of Jews from all territories under German rule. Jews from the villages and towns were deported to the ghettos in the cities, which lead to overcrowding. Sanitary facilities were overtaxed, and with few medicines available, disease was rampant.

The unhealthy conditions justified the sealing of the ghettos as a preventive measure to save the population from the diseases said to be caused by the Jews. On October 1st, German troops moved into the Sudetenland and Hitler demanded the return of all lost German colonies. I remember all of us meeting in the grand hall to listen to the radio broadcast of our victorious army. We sang the National Anthem and drank toasts of Dom Perignon Champaign to our comrades.

The next day at our commissioning ceremony, Himmler presented a sword and scabbard to each member of our class of new Lieutenants proclaiming, "One principle must be absolute for the SS man. We must be honest, decent, loyal and comradely to members of our own blood and to no one else."

After our officer training, Guenther and I were assigned to the new *SS Verfugungs* Division. We were given three weeks furlough before we had to report for duty. We rode the train back to Berlin together, very proud to be wearing the black uniform of the SS. Everyone on the train looked at us with respect. I remember the old conductor stopping by our seats to tell us how he had served in World War I and how we would even the score with those who stabbed Germany in the back.

Anna met us at the train station.

She was so beautiful!

She stood out from everyone else of the platform. Her blond hair glistened in the sunlight that lighted the train station. After a long kiss, I told her I only had three weeks leave and we should get married as soon as possible. We went to her parent's apartment and consulted with them. Then, we all went to my parents do discuss our plans, with all parents present.

With everyone in agreement, we set the date and I phoned Rolf's father. He was able to clear all obstacles and we were married in the same church where I was baptized. While church marriages for SS men were not outlawed, they were not encouraged. I wanted to get married in the church for Mother.

Having important friends had its benefits in Germany in those days. Being an SS officer didn't hurt either. Anna looked beautiful in her white flowing gown. The bridesmaids wore white dresses with floral patterns and silk flowers in their hair. I was dressed in my black SS uniform. Uncle Frederick came back from Rothenburg for the wedding. Guenther was my best man but Rolf telegrammed that he was involved in some sort of very special project and could not come but would see me soon. After he graduated from law school he was assigned to Reich Central Security Office and worked with the Gestapo.

The ceremony included many of the members of our SS training class.

I was sorry that Rolf could not attend.

Anna and I went to Garmisch for our honeymoon. We didn't have much time and time seemed to fly by. We only had four days to spend in the beautiful mountains. We stayed at the Grand Hotel Sonnenbichl, overlooking the snow-capped Bavarian Alps. Set among baroque churches and picturesque houses decorated with wall frescoes, the hotel is four kilometers from Zugspitze, Germany's highest mountain.

I could see why Adolf Hitler liked the Garmisch area so much.

Anna and I were very happy.

Everything that we had dreamed of was coming true.

We had a wonderful honeymoon and didn't want to go back to Berlin, but Guenther and I had to report to our new unit. Anna decided to live with her parents until I was stationed somewhere where she could follow. I don't think she could have gotten along with Mother for an extended period.

When I meet Guenther on the train I discovered that he had matched-up with a girl from Anna's old *Heim* who attended the wedding. Apparently, they had a wild time while Anna and I were away on our honeymoon.

The *SS Verfugungs* division had just moved from the Pilsen area of Czechoslovakia into western Germany. Guenther and I reported in November and were assigned our duties. Guenther was assigned to a motorcycle company and I was assigned to a pioneer company.

We spent the next six months carrying out intensive training at company, battalion and regimental level. During April 1940 a number of sub-units were raised and added to our numbers.

I wrote to Anna that the increase in strength and the intensive training led us to believe that we would soon be in combat.

On May 10th, when the war in the West opened, we became part of it. We thrust into Holland by a rapid advance to break through a succession of defensive lines which the Dutch had set up along the rivers and the canals. My company led the way, clearing mines and obstacles.

Guenther's company was split up and assigned to seize intact the bridges across Holland's rivers before the Dutch could flood the land.

Our intensive training was put to good use as we succeeded with minor causalities. Anticipating an Allied attack in northern Belgium, we were placed on the flank of the Eighteenth Army with orders to hold until slower-moving units could come forward to relieve us. When the Allied attack did not materialize, we were ordered to thrust toward Antwerp with the principle task of guarding the flank of the force which was threatened by French Seventh Army.

We were ordered to capture the islands of *Walcheren* and *Beveland* and to interdict shipping in the *Westerchelde*.

The Allied defenders were well supported by heavy artillery fire from Antwerp as well as ships from the Royal Navy out at sea. It was a bitterly fought operation and our causalities were high. Finally, the superiority of the German soldier won out and we succeeded in capturing the islands and Antwerp. On June 1st, we marched to Bapaume in northern France and began resting as part of Army Group reserve.

We all appreciated the rest and took the opportunity to write. I had received many letters from Anna but had not had the opportunity to respond. She wrote about the bombing of Berlin on the night of August 25, 1940. The event was unnerving for most residents although there was little damage. I spent many hours writing how much I missed her.

We rested in Bapaume, refitting and training until January 1941 when Himmler's office issued orders that our division was to be renamed *SS Das Division Reich* (Motorized) and given a new role. The divisional infantry regiments were restructured and new units were added, to include a self propelled artillery battery and a motorcycle battalion. We conducted intensive training and improved co-operation between the several arms of service.

Guenther really enjoyed the motorcycle battalion training.

By the end of March the division was considered to be ready for active service in our new motorized role. Wild rumors circulated and bets where laid on were we would be assigned. On April 6th, we learned that the Division's destination was Romania.

I was preparing for the move when I received a telephone call from Rolf. He was at Pretzsch, a town on the Elbe River, northeast of Leipzig. There was a special unit forming there. He was very excited but wouldn't give any details over the phone.

He just kept saying repeatedly, "Kurt, you must come and be part of our new unit. We are to be part of the *Einsatzgruppen*.

"We are to perform special duties!"

"The *Führer* himself authorizes us!"

"Heydrich himself chose me!"

"Oh, and I have been promoted to Captain. You must come. I can arrange to have you transferred immediately."

I responded, "What about Guenther? Can he come too?"

Rolf replied, "Kurt, you know how Guenther is. He is a good soldier but has a soft heart. This job requires men as hard as steel. Kurt, I need people I can trust. I need you here."

I wondered why Rolf thought I could be as hard as steel.

I agreed to go although I had no idea what I was getting into.

I guess I couldn't say no to Rolf. When I told Guenther I was surprised by his reaction.

"Kurt, it's okay, I like it here. I want to be a motorcycle platoon leader. I have always liked motorcycles and this is my chance to ride them every day. If I go with you, I may miss this chance."

It only took two days after I spoke with Rolf to get my orders. Guenther saw me off at the train. It was difficult saying good-bye. We had been together since elementary school, having done everything together. Guenther and I had become adults and SS officers together. Wishing each other well, we promised to write often. As my train pulled away from the station, the steam enveloped Guenther and the feeling I had experienced in Berlin came over me again.

I was suddenly cold all over.

I had a strange feeling that I would never see Guenther again.

By the spring of 1941, the French had collapsed, and the British were limited to their own territory. The low-countries had capitulated and Germany held absolute dominion over the whole of the European mainland.

There was some substance to Hitler's argument that an invasion of Russia would not be a second front. He believed the Army was ready. The *Wehrmacht* stood victorious and hardly bloodied. Our soldiers were trained and equipped to perfection. The army was a balanced and coordinated fighting machine at the pinnacle of military achievement.

The German officer corps prided itself on its doctrine, a unity of training and thought that allowed junior officers to exercise their initiative because they understood their commander's intentions and they knew how their peers in adjacent units would react to the same situation. A feeling of invincibility permeated the army and the national leadership.

We sensed it too.

I didn't meet anyone who thought that our armies could be beaten.

The Red Army of 1941 was in serious disorder. Although its strategy was now defensive, its official operational concepts remained the offensive, deep-operational theory. The Soviets had neglected the development of detailed defensive concepts and procedures. Purges by Stalin had produced a severe shortage of trained commanders and staff officers able to implement official concepts. The army contained a few qualified leaders from the Japanese and Finnish campaigns but lacked both the experience and the self-confidence of our veteran officer corps.

Beating the Russians would be easy, we all believed.

Chapter Eleven
The Mission

Rolf met me at the Pretzsch train station with another Captain he introduced as Erwin. I saluted Rolf and him. Rolf saluted back and hugged me.

"Kurt, it is good to see you. I am so sorry I could not attend your wedding. I hope my parents were able to assist. How is Anna? How is Guenther? It has been over a year since we have seen each other."

As usual, he asked many questions in one sentence.

After bringing him up to date, I asked him what this assignment was all about.

Erwin spoke up, "This assignment would be concluded by December at the latest and would be putting down resistance behind the troop lines, protecting and pacifying the rear army area."

I asked, "Resistance from whom? The only fighting that is going on now is in North Africa."

Rolf replied, "Kurt, we are about to be part of a campaign that will assure total victory for Germany. This campaign will also finally get rid of Bolshevism and the Jewish conspiracy."

Surprised, I said, "Rolf, what are you taking about? We have a treaty with Russia."

Rolf went on, "Kurt, I don't know everything that is involved but, our Colonel, Otto Ohlendorf told us he was at a meeting where Reinhard Heydrich, head of the Reich

Security Main Office, who briefed the leadership of Kurt's new unit on the mission. He would not give us many details. He would just say that we were about to make history and those involved would have to be tough men who could carry out orders."

The commanders of the *Einsatzgruppen* and the commanders of the sub-units of the *Einsatzgruppen* were chosen by Himmler and Heydrich from a list compiled by the RSHA. Most of the handpicked leaders were lawyers or police officers.

I often wondered if Rolf had been chosen because of his family's connections. His father had become an acquaintance of Heydrich.

A few members were physicians or educators and most had earned doctoral degrees. A reserve battalion of the regular *Ordnungspolizei* (Order Police) completed the Pretzsch roster. Erwin had come from the Order Police and had a criminology degree. We had people from many backgrounds at Pretzsch. They included economists, architects, engineers, teachers, police officers, and low and medium ranking officers of the *Gestapo* (Security Police).

Some of them were passed on by their home units because they were considered too wild. Hans Wolfe was there too. I wondered how he got there.

He was a very strange fellow.

The Waffen-SS, the small but growing SS army, contributed enlisted men who comprised the support staff of drivers, translators, radio operators, cooks, clerks, etc. Our numbers totaled about 3,000.

The three-week course at Pretzsch in June 1941 consisted of familiar lectures on honor and duty and the subhuman nature of the people we would be asked to round up. We conducted some military exercises that were more like games of hide and seek.

We also received lectures on how people would hide by digging holes and covering them with straw and how some would build false walls and hide behind them. We learned how to locate these hiding places. We were also taught that when searching a building that appeared empty to make noise as though we were leaving and to leave someone in the building to listen. Often, the people hiding would think that we were all gone and make noise or expose themselves. We were taught that the Bolshevik Jews would stop at nothing to undermine Germany and our troops.

We went to the range and fired our weapons, everyone qualifying.

By then, most of us were expert marksmen.

We were supposed to take part in physical training but after we received inoculations, everyone one of us came down with fever and weakness.

The instructors had to cancel the physical training and any intensive military exercises. There were a number of briefings about the aims and activities of the *Einsatzgruppen* in the Nazi-occupied territories of the Soviet Union.

At a briefing, which took place shortly before June 22, 1941, high-level *SS* and Police chiefs attended.

As Heydrich was unable to attend he sent a memorandum specifying our mission:

"All the following are to be executed:

Officials of the Commintern, together with professional Communist politicians in general, top and medium level officials and radical lower level officials of the Party, Central committee and district and sub-district committees. In addition, peoples commissars, Jews in Party and State employment, and other radical elements, saboteurs, propagandists, snipers, assassins, inciters, etc., insofar as they are, of special importance for the further economic reconstruction of the Occupied Territories. The principal targets of execution by the Einsatzgruppen will be political functionaries, Jews mistakenly released from POW camps, Jewish sadists and avengers, and Jews in general."

We received instructions about the *T-4 Euthanasia Program*. Established in the fall of 1939 in order to maintain the purity of the Aryan race, the program systematically killed children and adults born with physical deformities or suffering from mental illness. It put much emphasis on the survival of the fittest and argued that genetic selection should be practiced deliberately. This included the breeding of a racial elite and the extermination of racially inferior or damaging groups. Slavs, Gypsies, and Africans were considered racially inferior to our race of German Aryans. We were taught that our race was weakened by what our instructors called the Jewish cancer.

It wasn't until June 20, 1941 that we learned the exact details of what our mission entailed.

Colonel Ohlendorf called together his group of 500 and told us that the Reich was preparing a surprise attack against the Soviet Union. The operation was named Operation Barbarossa and was scheduled to begin in two days. As the *Wehrmacht* invaded Russia from the west, we would follow.

After Colonel Ohlendorf's briefing, we got together with our groups. Rolf assigned me as the logistics officer for our group because of my engineering training, he said. I was to be responsible for all food, ammunition, cold weather heating stoves, medium-size tents, portable field desks and chairs, spare parts for vehicles and numerous other items for living in the field.

I had an NCO, Sergeant Kruger, our old drill sergeant, and twelve other men to assist, including three cooks. We had four Opel Blitz 3-ton cargo trucks and a motorcycle with sidecar. I was to ride in the sidecar. I wondered if Guenther was riding in a sidecar. I was sure he would rather be riding his own motorcycle.

The rest of Rolf's command was organized in four sub-groups of approximately twenty men per group. The size of the sub-groups would vary, depending on the mission. There were several occasions when all four groups joined. The plan was for the units to move out with their basic load of supplies with us following close behind with the rest of the supplies. Each group was similarly organized. Daily rations and re-supply of ammunition and other goods would come from the *Wehrmacht* units we followed or from the local economy.

I was responsible for coordinating with *Wehrmacht* supply officers. I rather liked this assignment. I always found logistics interesting. It was my best class in SS officer training.

I wondered if Rolf somehow knew that.

I would ask him when I had a chance.

I went off to arrange supplies while the other officers and NCOs reviewed reports from the Gestapo on the locations of partisans and Jews. Beside myself, there were eight other lieutenants and eight sergeants, one each for each operations squad. The rest of the squads were made up of a mix of soldiers from the order police, security services, and Waffen-SS. The operations squads had interpreters, telephone operators and radio operators also. All of the officers in our group were graduates of the SS school.

I wrote to Anna about how excited I was to be with Rolf and part of an elite organization.

After midnight on June 21st, the Berlin-Moscow express train cleared and checked without any deviation from normal practice. It passed over the border and on to Brest-Litovsk without a hitch. To the north, nothing disturbed the calm of the East Prussian frontier. Southwards, in Army Group South's attack area the Russians manned their fully illuminated posts. Shortly after 0300 hours on the morning of June 22, 1941, 30 specially selected *Luftwaffe* bomber crews crossed the Soviet frontier. In groups of three, these bombers struck

10 major Soviet air bases precisely at 0315 hours, the time when a brief artillery bombardment signaled the start of the ground war.

As soon as the sun rose, the *Luftwaffe* followed up this attack with a force of 500 bombers, 270 dive bombers, and 480 fighters to hit 66 Soviet airfields in the forward areas. The Red Air Force lost over 1,200 aircraft in the first morning of the war. Throughout the next few days, the *Luftwaffe* had undisputed air supremacy, and all Soviet troop and rail movements received relentless bombardment.

The initial ground advance met little resistance in most areas. Some border posts were overrun almost before the Soviet border guards could assemble. In addition to the advantage of surprise, our army had secured an overwhelming superiority of numbers and firepower at the points selected for their armored penetration. We had two hundred and twenty divisions from the Barents Sea in the north to the Black Sea in the south, a distance of some two thousand miles. Twenty of our divisions were armored.

Our plan envisioned a rapid separation and annihilation of the Russian forces and the conquest of the main industrial areas in west Russia. The intent was to seize the wheat fields and the coal and iron mines of the Ukraine.

Finally, we would invade the Caucasus region with its oil wells and pipelines and its access to Iran and India. Our government felt, if successful, we could continue the war indefinitely against any coalition of foes.

Our army surprised border garrisons that offered only confused resistance, advancing thirty miles into Soviet-occupied Polish territory on the first day. We received reports that Polish citizens applauded our advancing troops. They were very happy because under the Russians, they were not permitted to conduct church services and felt liberated.

This report made us feel that our cause was just.

A large portion of the *Wehrmacht* regarded the Russians as bumbling and potentially treacherous sub humans.

By all accounts, our invasion of the Soviet Union was a major success as the Russians were completely surprised. Many of the Soviet Forces were crushed in the initial attacks. Sixteen hours after the opening of Operation Barbarossa, the German Army in the east had virtually unhinged two Soviet Fronts, the Northwestern, and the Western. At their junction, the Soviet 11th Army had been battered to pieces. The left flank of the Russian Eighth Army and the right flank of the Third Army had been similarly devastated. North of the Kaunas, German armor was over the Dubissa River and south of the city, German tanks were astride the Nieman. On the left flank of the Western Front of the Soviet 4th Army was in no position to offer and effective defense. The Russian Front commanders struggled desperately to maintain the cohesion of their forces.

The German operations in the south were dazzlingly successful. All of the objectives Hitler had outlined were achieved. The Pripet Marshes were cleared. The Dnieper bend was occupied. The Donetz basin and the industrial complex of the Ukraine were denied to the enemy, through either dispersal or seizure. Above all, the mass of the Red Army in the south was battered to pieces in a battle that cost the Russians a million causalities.

The reports of Russian atrocities against civilians were coming in. Civilians who were suspected of not supporting the Bolsheviks were hung in the town squares and from the trees along the roads. Many of their bodies were mutilated.

It appeared that all we had been taught about sub human nature of the people in the east were true.

One of the greatest problems for our forces was the guerilla bands operating in their rear areas. Men and women sniped at our troops, swooped down on our outposts, wrecked trains, and hurled homemade grenades at of tanks. Guerilla bands were constantly on the watch for our paratroops who were dropped to eliminate Russian pockets of resistance. The Russians even used children for there murderous tasks.

We heard about one little girl who hid a grenade under her skirt. When some of our soldiers approached her, she exploded it killing her and our soldiers. Another little girl went daily to wash clothes near a stream. There she listened with earphones for instructions that were relayed to local guerrillas. Peasant girls would pass through our lines with messages to Red army units.

These activities had to be brought under control if we were going to secure the area. This would be our job.

We knew the Jews were sympathetic to the Bolsheviks and we knew they did not like us. Our mission was clear. We had to secure the areas won by our heroic army if there was going to be any chance of re-settling the territory with Germans.

It was becoming very clear what had to be done.

Chapter Twelve
East from Pretzsch

The *Einsatzgruppe* A task force started out from East Prussia, and its units rapidly spread out across Lithuania, Latvia, and Estonia. *Einsatzgruppe* B had Warsaw as its starting point. Some of its units passed through Vilna and Grodno on the way to Minsk, where they arrived on July 5, 1941. Other units belonging to *Einsatzgruppe* B passed through Brest-Litovsk, Slonim, Baranovichi, and Minsk, and from there proceeded to southern Belorussia: Mogilev, Bobruisk, and Gomel, advancing as far as Briansk, Kursk, Orel, and Tula. *Einsatzgruppe* C made its way from Upper Silesia to the western Ukraine, by way of Krakow. Two of its units, *Einsatzkommandos* 5 and 6, went to Lvov, where they organized a pogrom against the Jews with the participation of Ukrainian nationalists.

We were part of *Einsatzgruppen D*, attached to the Eleventh Army for logistical support and would operate in southwestern Ukraine (Bessarabia), southern Ukraine, the Crimea, and the Caucasus. We were the smallest of the four task forces. Colonel Ohlendorf divided *Einsatzgruppen D* into five sub-units. Rolf commanded sub-unit B, Erwin and I were assigned to Rolf's group of 90 men.

We were a fully motorized unit with automatic rifles. I was surprised at this since the *Wehrmacht* itself was only partly motorized in 1941. We were given the best of equipment and new boots and uniforms. Officers were issued the

Mauser Model 1910 and *Walther* P-38 pistols. Enlisted men were issued the Mauser Kar 98b rifle. Both officers and enlisted men were issued the Bergmann 9mm Model 35/I machine pistols. Machine guns would control the perimeters and hand grenades would flush victims from their hideouts.

There would be no need for larger weapons because as I learned our mission was not combat, it was to be execution.

On June 24th at 0700, our group moved out. We advanced through Bratislava and northern Transylvania and reached Piatra-Neamt, near Bessarabia on July 5, where we went into action.

My squad, with our supplies, was delayed, as usual. We couldn't move as fast as the others.

Rolf and the rest of the group had already been in the city for several hours. We were told of Joseph Stalin's order of July 3, 1941, calling on the entire Soviet civilian population to conduct a campaign of terror, sabotage, and guerrilla warfare against the Germans. We knew that Jews were especially active in this campaign. This news added to our contempt for these people!

I reported to Rolf upon arrival. He was in the middle of a discussion with the local Romanian army commander.

Apparently, Romanian soldiers carried out considerable excesses repeatedly against Jews during the past couple of days and nights. The number of Jews killed could not be established, but might have been several hundred. On the evening of July 6, Rumanian military authorities rounded up some 400 Jews of all ages, including men and women, in order to shoot them in retaliation for attacks on Romanian military personnel. Rolf said he understood the commander's wish and would not stand in their way. Rolf asked me to lend the Romanian our shovels so they could dig graves for the Jews. We decided to set up camp in the city and organize ourselves for future operations.

I guess at this point, it still had not sunk in that we were going to kill a lot of men, women, and children.

So far, the Romanians had done the killing, not us. We found many people more than ready to conduct *pogroms* (a form of riot directed against a particular group) against the local Jews and who they thought were partisans. I was to learn that old grudges lasted a long time in this region and some of the arguments were several generations old.

We billeted for the night in some abandoned houses. Once we were all settled in, we built a fire and passed around the Schnapps. The night ended with songs and laughter. It reminded me of our Hitler Youth camping trips. We felt relatively safe and comfortable. Most of us wrote home.

I wrote to Anna about how excited I was to be part of a special unit serving the Fatherland. I told her our army needed us to keep the rear areas safe and Germany needed us to make room for German settlers who would occupy this land after the war.

I had not yet seen the horrors of war or smelled death yet.

My letter was of happy times and of idealism. Images of Berlin whirled through my head. Images of Anna made my heart pound. That night was for sentimental thoughts. I wrote that I believed more now than ever that the battle against the sub humans, who had been whipped into a state of frenzy by the Jews, was not only necessary but came in the nick of time. Our *Führer* has saved Europe from certain chaos. I told her that those at home must always keep in mind what could have happened if these hordes had overrun our Fatherland. The horror of it is unthinkable. I went to bed thinking about Anna, Father and Mother and especially about Guenther.

I wondered how he was making out.

We knew that the 2nd SS Division crossed the frontier as part of Panzer Group 2 in Field Marshal von Bock's Army Group Center.

Guenther was probably in one of the lead motorcycle grenadier units.

I was beginning to feel a bit guilty. We were billeted in comfort. We hadn't been shot at or had to shoot anyone.

This was about to change though.

The next morning, all of the officers met Rolf to discuss future operations. He said that he had received orders from task force headquarters that we were to work closely with the Romanian army to round up all the Jews and Bolsheviks in the greater Piatra-Neamt area and liquidate them. It was explained to Rolf that the reason for this was evidence of a coordinated sabotage ring trained by the Russians to attack our army. This was certainly a plausible explanation, although the order seemed a bit severe to us at the time.

The order didn't say anything about women or children, just men.

Rolf assigned each operations squad leader a sector and they went off to find the Romanians soldiers and the Jews. Rolf decided that I would also be responsible for the reports that were to be sent back to *Einsatzgruppen D* headquarters at the end of each day's activities. He re-assigned several clerks from the other squads to mine.

While the other squads were out looking for Jews, I made contact with the closest *Wehrmacht* unit and arranged to pick up some supplies. I left on my motorcycle with two empty trucks and set out to find the *Wehrmacht* unit. The army was moving so fast that finding them turned out to be more difficult that I expected.

After several hours, I caught up and secured the supplies. By the time the supplies were loaded and I returned to Piatra-Neamt, it was evening. I went to the command post to report to Rolf.

The clerk told me he went to the synagogue located at the town center. I went there to discover the building packed with men, women and children. There must have been 600 people packed inside the building. I found Rolf talking with the local Romanian commander. The commander was insisting on setting the church on fire and burning all inhabitants. Rolf would not permit it and tensions were getting higher.

Finally, Rolf and the Romanian army commander agreed to take the Jews out of town and dispose of them. The plan was to select some of the men inside the synagogue to dig a grave while the others waited inside. The men were selected and loaded up on a truck. Once again, I provided the shovels.

It took most of the night for the large pit to be dug. Rolf asked me to find quick lime for the grave. I went to the local farm store and loaded all of the bags that were there and had them transported to the gravesite. Finally, at just after sunrise, the grave was completed. The Jews from the synagogue were loaded on our trucks, with some additional ones supplied by the Romanian army, and transported to the gravesite.

The trucks stopped about one hundred meters short of the grave and the Jews were ordered to dismount. There they were ordered to remove all of their clothing and stack it neatly on piles. My team would later gather it all and inspect it for usable items. I drove out to the gravesite looking for Rolf. I spotted him on the edge of the pit and went up to him.

I said, "Rolf, I thought the order you read us didn't say anything about women and children."

Rolf replied, "While you were out after supplies, I received a new order from headquarters. In fact the order came from Heydrich himself. We are now to eliminate all Jewish men, women, and children. They have been conspiring with the Bolsheviks against Germany. They must be eliminated so the areas are safe for German re-population. As long as they are here, good Germans will not be able to safely farm this country."

Rolf read an announcement that Hitler had made on July 16, "Germany would never withdraw from its newly won territories in the east. Instead, I would create there a

Garden of Eden, taking all necessary measures to accomplish this."

"I know that is what we have been taught," I said to Rolf. "But who do the children harm?" I asked.

Rolf answered, "Kurt, the children will grow up hating us for eliminating their parents and we will have to kill them anyway. We may as well do it now.

"We must do our duty, these are our orders!"

"I am not saying I entirely like this either, but what choice do we have and the *Führer* is talking about us. We are making history!"

By this time, about twenty naked Jews were directed to lay face down at the bottom of the pit. Our soldiers looked around at Rolf as if to ask for instructions. Rolf removed the pistol from his belt and walked along the rim of the pit shooting each person in the back of the head as he went. Then he told Erwin to continue with his squad. Rolf told the squad leaders to rotate the duties until the job was done. Other members of the squads spread a layer of the quick lime I had found between the layers of bodies. This went on most of the day until there were no more people to shoot.

The Romanians covered the pit and I got my shovels back. There were some bags of quick lime left and we loaded them on a truck. The final count was 299 men, 100 women, and 216 children. That is what I put into my first daily report.

When we were all done, I went to find Rolf. He was at his billet, a small house just off the town square. He asked me in and offered me some liquor. He was already drinking. I never drank liquor before but decided to start. We both got drunk that night as we talked about how things had changed so much since our days in the *Jungvolk*.

This was the beginning of many nights of drinking until we would pass out or until we couldn't think straight anymore.

The next morning we left Piatra-Neamt and went to Kishinew and more round-ups and pits with 451 killed there. Tighina was next and another 700 dead. By now, some of the men were starting to show the signs of stress. Some were asking to be transferred to other units. A great deal of Rolf's time was being spent counseling the men. Rolf kept telling everyone how they were doing their duty for Germany and how they were heroes. I wondered what Rolf was really feeling.

I was beginning to feel strange. Maybe hardened is the right word.

We were still in Tighina on August 7th when we had an unexpected visit from Colonel Ohlendorf. He had us all stand in formation while he promoted Rolf to Major. Then I was called to the front and promoted to First Lieutenant.

The promotion order read, "For outstanding support of critical operations. Your service brings great credit to yourself, your unit and to the Fatherland. Signed; Adolf Hitler."

I was very happy but didn't think I had done that much. Apparently, RSHA headquarters were so impressed with the thoroughness of the reports I was sending them, they adopted my format as the standard. There were some additional promotions and after we gathered in the village town hall to celebrate.

There was plenty of wine, cheese, and caviar. Colonel Ohlendorf had brought the alcohol and food with him. He was very bright and very confident for a young officer. A lawyer in civilian life, he could carry on a conversation about almost anything. I was sure he would get in to politics after the war. He would probably be a cabinet minister.

After we celebrated for a while, I noticed that Colonel Ohlendorf and Rolf went for a walk. Rolf told me later that the Colonel was becoming concerned about the effects the shootings were having on the men. He instructed Rolf to organize the shootings so there were multiple men shooting at the same target. He believed this would lessen the strain on the men especially when it came to the women and children. He also told Rolf that some other groups were beginning to experiment with other methods of getting rid of the undesirables.

Some units experimented with using quicklime. We were already using the quicklime in the trenches between the layers of bodies. When it rained, water mixed with the quicklime, forming Calcium Hydroxide. This is similar to a process that was used with farm animals at one time. This process involves the placing of a carcass into a sealed chamber, which then puts the carcass in a mixture of lye and water, which breaks chemical bonds keeping the body intact. This eventually turns the body into a coffee-like liquid, and the only solid remains are bone hulls, which could be crushed between one's fingertips. This seems as if it could be an ecologically friendly way of getting rid of remains when compared with cremation. It was thought that if the victims were made to lie down on top of each other, quicklime could be spread over the bodies and water added. Colonel Ohlendorf said this method proved too grotesque, since the victims were still alive when the water was added. The method turned out to be harder on the men then shooting and was discontinued.

After trying to dynamite the victims and burn those alive in their homes and barns proved unproductive, the RSHA began to look for alternative methods of execution. Colonel Ohlendorf asked Rolf if he had any ideas. Rolf told him that he and I had discussed some alternatives, involving the use of vehicle exhaust gas. The Colonel was very interested and sent someone to find me.

I was enjoying the caviar, Russian of course and wine with some of my men when I was summoned.

I found Rolf and the Colonel sitting on a small park bench in the town square. Ohlendorf asked me to describe my ideas. I told him I had read about the use of Carbon Monoxide on children born with physical deformities. My idea was to pipe the exhaust gas into the compartment of a sealed van where the occupants would suffocate. I explained that in this way our men would not have to be directly involved in the killing. We could find labor to unload the vans and bury the dead. There would only be a small group of people to dispose of after they covered in the holes. The prisoners would do all of the work and our men would drive the vans.

Colonel Ohlendorf was very interested in my concept. He instructed me to detail it, along with any sketches, and send the information to Colonel Paul Blobel the commander of Einsatzgruppen *B*. Berlin had charged him with the main responsibility for coming up with a new extermination technique. Working with him on the project was Hans Wolfe.

Somehow, this did not surprise me.

I sent my ideas on to Colonel Blobel the next day and found that in a short time gas vans were being produced and distributed to some Einsatzgruppen units. Blobel took full credit for the idea, never even mentioning my name. I was upset at the time but, in hindsight, that probably saved my life.

The allies hanged Blobel.

Rolf gave me the nickname of "Gas Meister." The men had no idea what he was talking about. They thought it meant I passed gas. Rolf would laugh every time he used the nickname, knowing that it still irritated me that Blobel took all the credit.

The gas vans were eventually replaced by the gas chambers at the concentration camps and we were eventually out of the extermination business.

I was tasked to visit Colonel Blobel's headquarters to examine the vans. While I was away, our unit moved.

Chapter Thirteen
More Killing

I caught up with our unit in a small village about fifty kilometers from Odessa, a Black Sea port in the southwestern Ukraine.

Hearing of the approach of our unit, the Jews of the village had gone into hiding. When we reached the village, Erwin's squad entered. The only person who his men saw in the street was a woman with a baby in her arms. She refused to tell them where the Jews were hidden. Erwin snatched the baby from her, gripped it by the legs, and smashed its head against a door.

The women gave away the hiding place.

Erwin then shoot her.

I went up to him and said, "Erwin, do you think that was really necessary? I mean the baby."

He replied, "These sub humans must be eradicated like rats. Look at them, they live in filth, they spread disease."

Erwin's eyes were wild looking. He looked at me as if he didn't know me.

I was going to tell him they live like that because they are hiding from us. I decided not to talk to him anymore and to find Rolf and report in. I found Rolf meeting with the other officers on the outskirts of the village.

As soon as he spotted me he shouted, "Kurt, come over here. It is good to have you back. How is your mother? How is Anna?"

Before I could answer any of his questions, he stopped me and said with enthusiasm, "Come here and listen to this. Odessa has a population of nearly 600,000 of which roughly, 180,000 were Jews. The Gestapo estimates that between 80,000 and 90,000 remain. We are going to need the Romanian army to help us here. What a job this is going to be.

"Can you imagine, 90,000 Jews?"

Rolf was as excited as when we used to go camping at the farm outside of Berlin when we were children. I wasn't gone very long but I could see a change in Rolf, in Erwin and in many of the other officers.

It was as if they were so into the work that nothing else mattered.

I wondered if we were all in some type of shock. Our group alone had been involved with the killing of thousands of men, women, and children. The ones who couldn't take it were transferred to other SS units or Wehrmacht units. No one thought poorly of them.

I think deep inside, we all wondered if we could continue.

It was about this time that my hands began shaking. The only way I got them to stop was to drink.

Everyone drank constantly. Alcohol was never in short supply.

Rolf spoke again, "I am going to meet with Colonial Ohlendorf and the local Romanian army commander. Kurt, set up camp in the village. I will see you tonight and you will tell me all about your visit home. By the way, while you were gone, we received 5 of your gas vans. We used them one time but had to give them to Blobel's unit."

We never saw the gas vans again!

I found Sergeant Kruger, who had done an excellent job in my absence, and told him of the plan to set up camp in the village.

He knew what to do.

Gathering up some of the men, he was off to scout out the best houses for billets. We carried several tents and tent heaters in our truck but did not have to use them. We always found empty houses wherever we went. The downside of using the houses was the lice.

They were everywhere!

These people were filthy!

It was August 1941 and the temperature was beginning to get cool in the evenings. I wondered if we would have an early winter. We were not issued winter clothes when we left Pretzsch and I knew from talking with the Wehrmacht supply folks that they had none either. The war in the east was supposed to be over by Christmas and based on the reports from the front and our advances, our troops had made remarkable progress.

I had to travel further to coordinate with the Wehrmacht units for supplies as they traveled further east. For the most part, we had procured our own food from the local economy. Therefore, my visits to the supply trains were less necessary and were confined to ammunition, oil, fuel, etc.

I lead the rest of the squad into the village to meet Sergeant Kruger when we saw about twenty old men surrounded by the operations squad led by Lieutenant Trapp. Trapp was shouting at them while some of his men were striking the old men with the butts of their rifles.

I told the motorcycle driver to stop and I went over to Lieutenant Trapp and asked, "What are you doing Trapp?"

He responded, "They know where there are more Jews hiding and they are going to tell or be beaten to death right here."

I asked, "Did you ask them or just begin beating them first?"

Trapp looked at me with the same look that Erwin had and said, "Lieutenant Schultheiss, this is my operation, you need to go about your business and leave us alone."

"Go to your supplies, where shooting is not required."

It was obvious to me that there was no reasoning with him so I got back in the sidecar and went to locate

Sergeant Kruger. I would bring this and the incident with Erwin up with Rolf tonight.

As I drove off, I heard shots from Lieutenant Trapp's location. I didn't look back although I knew I would be issuing shovels again.

I had not shot anyone yet, Trapp was right.

It sounded like Trapp resented that.

I wondered if the others did too.

I wondered if Rolf gave me my assignment to protect me from having to shoot.

The killings were beginning to become routine. The more it went on, the more brutal the killings became. It was as if we were blaming the victims for our fate. Rolf did offer the opportunity to anyone who did not want to participate in the killings to step out. Of the members who remained, no one did, of course.

Stepping out would be an admission of weakness, or *Schlappschwanz*.

I had been thinking about our mission here ever since I went back to Berlin. Were these people truly as bad as we had been taught?

That group of old men did not look threatening. Certainly, the women and the baby that Erwin disposed of earlier did not appear to be a threat to Germany. However, what schemes could those old men have been plotting?

What did that woman know?

She did know the hiding places of other Jews and what did they know?

The child would have probably grown up hating Germans.

Who would raise a Jew child?

Maybe the child was better off.

I couldn't get these thoughts out of my head. Alcohol was the only thing that helped. Drinks with breakfast were common place now.

We found Sergeant Kruger in the village near a store. He had the cooks working on the dinner meal. The others were setting up the store as a supply room. A man from Lieutenant Trapp's squad came by for shovels. There were only four left. The other squads had come earlier for the rest.

All of the buildings were made of dried mud with thatched roofs. The floors were dirt. Some of the buildings had a stove in the center of the room.

The operations squads had rounded up all of the residents of the village and marched them off into the woods about 1,000 meters away. I pitched in, helping the men unload supplies. Sergeant Kruger didn't like it when I helped the men.

He would always say, "Officers are not to do manual labor. It is not right."

I would tell him that I would never do it again, until the next time.

He would give me an exasperated look.

Sergeant Kruger and I had a good relationship. I liked and trusted him. He was from Hamburg. Before the war, he worked as a municipal police officer. At forty-one he was older than the rest of the men. They looked to him as their father.

He was a good drill sergeant too.

Of course I was twenty-one and I think he looked at me as one of his children.

We could hear shooting coming from the direction of the woods.

The village residents were not coming back.

It was about 6:00pm when Rolf arrived from his meeting with the Romanian commander. About that time, all of the squads gathered for dinner. Rolf announced that there would be an officer's meeting at 7:00pm.

I approached Rolf and said, "Rolf, I would like to talk with you about a couple of things."

He said, "Yes, yes, right after the meeting." Rolf seemed distracted. We all had a wonderful dinner of chicken and boiled potatoes. The cooks had found the local chicken coop. They served a strong red wine. I don't know where Sergeant Kruger found the wine but it was good.

At 7:00pm we assembled in Rolf's command post. All the operations squad officers handed me their reports, which I would fashion into the official report to task force headquarters. Rolf signed all the reports that were submitted. Rolf told us about his meeting with the Romanian commander and Colonial Ohlendorf.

Rolf said, "The Gestapo is finally convinced there are still 80,000 to 90,000 Jews in Odessa. Colonial Ohlendorf's orders from Heydrich are to eliminate all of them. Obviously, we cannot accomplish this job ourselves. Therefore, we have solicited the help of the Romanians who are eager to help. Colonial Ohlendorf is assuming direct command of this action. His staff is working on a detailed plan that assigns specific sectors to us, and outlines the procedures by which we will follow. His staff will issue an operations order within the next few days. Men, we have a few days to rest without any action and to prepare for this order. As I get more information, I will brief you."

The meeting was over and everyone went back to his billet. I remained to talk with Rolf.

"Rolf, I want to talk to you about a couple of things that happened today. I say Erwin smash the head of a baby and then shoot the mother. Then I saw Trapp and his men beating some old men. They both had a wild look on their face. What is happening to them?"

Rolf offered me some liquor and said, "Kurt, you know that our job here is hard. Most people do not know how hard. Erwin and Trapp were doing what they need to do to accomplish our mission. I am watching all of the officers for signs of strain and I can assure you that I will give them some rest if I see a problem. We all have a few days rest now. Kurt, what we do here is important work. You know that our people cannot populate this country until all of the vermin are eradicated."

"Lebensraum Kurt! Don't you remember? We do this for the Fatherland Kurt."

"Yes I remember but, the women and children?"

"Rolf, another thing, did you assign me as logistics officer so I would not have to shoot?"

Rolf emptied his glass and refilled it saying, "Kurt, we have known each other for over fifteen years. You, Guenther and I grew up together. Have I not tried to take care of you both? I knew that Guenther could not do this work. He is too sensitive. You are sensitive too but will do your duty. I can trust you to take care of details. You are doing a fine job as the logistics officer. Let us just leave it at that, shall we? Some units have your gas vans, do they not?"

"Another thing," Rolf explained, "Soon, we will not have to worry about killing these people. We will put them on trains bound for camps where they will be dealt with accordingly. Plans are in the works for many large camps to be built and you can be proud that your gas van idea was the beginning of the next phase of the final solution for the Jews."

"You will see. Soon, we will be out of this business."

"Now come on, tell me about Berlin. What was it like?"

I told him about the air raid drills and the black out at night.

I told him I stopped to see his parents but no one was home. I left the letter he asked me to give to his parents.

We were both drunk again.

We were never out of alcohol.

I was out of bed early the next morning, awakened by the roosters nearby. The streets were eerie with no civilians. There were just soldiers on the streets, walking around in the morning fog.

Everyone else was dead.

The feeling I had experienced at the train station came over me again.

I started wondering if I was starting to go crazy.

The tally on the report I sent to headquarters yesterday was 178 men, 188 women, and 98 children. This was the total population of the village. They were all buried in the woods but the job was not done.

We had to process their belongings to ship to headquarters then back to Germany. Their money had to be counted and their clothing had to be gone over for serviceability. Items that were not serviceable were burned. This was a poor village so not much of their clothing was usable. Our men went house-to-house looking for any items that could be useful. Everything was bought back to my squad, organized and packed for shipment to headquarters. Mostly, the men found lamps and some farming tools. These tools would be useful to the Germans who would some day settle this land.

It would usually take us a day or two after the operations squads disposed of the Jews to finish our work. Often, while the operations squad soldiers were sitting around drinking or playing cards, my men were sorting and packing. We worked all day re-organizing the supplies. The rest of the unit cleaned their weapons, polished their boots, washed their clothes, talked about home, and did other soldier things. Once the items to be shipped were crated and marked, they were loaded on trucks and driven to the nearest train bound for Berlin.

We had just sat down for dinner when Rolf called for all of the officers to assemble. Apparently, that morning a bomb exploded in Romanian military headquarters in Odessa. The blast killed 67 people, including the Romanian military commandant, 16 other Romanian officers, and four German naval officers. Using the incident as an excuse, Romanian army units assembled 19,000 Jews in a public square in the harbor area and shot many of them. They doused others with gasoline and burned them alive.

At least 20,000 other Jews were assembled at the local jail and then taken to the village of Dalnik. There, the Romanians shot some of the Jews and locked others into warehouses that they then set ablaze. Romanian troops shot and killed any Jews trying to escape the fire. Many Jews scattered into the countryside and we were to help find them. For now, all available manpower was to be used in rounding up the Jews. Just when we thought there would be some rest, we were back to work.

The Romanians were already working on establishing two ghettos, Dalnik and Slobodka, on the edge of the city. All of the Jews found were to be deposited in one of these two ghettos. Rolf told us that headquarters was not pleased with the methods used by the Romanians since so many Jews were now scattered throughout the countryside.

The Romanians were crude and had no discipline. Unfortunately, we needed them. We did not have the manpower to accomplish the mission.

Tonight, we would rest, each of us in our own way. I received a letter from Anna today. She says Mother is fine but the bombings are getting more frequent. I wrote to tell her how much I miss her and to be careful. It wouldn't do any good to suggest that she and Mother leave Berlin. They would never even think of it.

Rolf relaxed with the bottle again.

I was really starting to worry about him.

He drank a lot, although, we all did.

I would go to bed early. I knew tomorrow would be a long and trying day. I had received a letter from Guenther that morning. I decided to read it before turning in for the night.

His unit's first advance was east of the Bug River across the Pripet Marsh. He said it was slow-going due to the knee-deep mud. Away from the marsh, the soil was predominately sandy, scoured, and ruined vehicle engines. Rivers often overflowed and caused widespread flooding.

The further east they traveled, the more prominent the conditions became. Guenther said that day after day and week after week they passed through endless fields of sunflowers or cornfields from horizon to horizon. It was typical for his unit to travel 70 kilometers and then to finish the day with a firefight against a Red Army rear guard. The boredom was only broken when sniper fire came from the cornfields.

Guenther said he was surprised by the lack of adult men and women in the villages they came across. We had already been briefed that the withdrawing Red Army rounded up most of the adult civilians, men and women. They were then formed into makeshift worker's battalions and then sent into attacks to make up weight and numbers. It did not matter that the civilians were untrained. Most were sent into battle without arms. They were expected to pick up the arms of those who had fallen. Meanwhile, Guenther wrote, Army Group Center, advancing north of the Pripet Marshes, had completed one large encirclement around Bialystok in the first week and another around Minsk in the second. The two pockets, which had been cleaned out by July 11th, yielded 290,000 prisoners of war.

I promised myself to write back to Guenther telling him to be careful. I would describe the nature of our work as rear security. I told tell him that Rolf had been promoted to Major, he had appointed me as logistics officer, and that I was now a First Lieutenant. I wouldn't say anything in my letter about the killings.

Maybe I was ashamed.

Guenther was at the forefront of the attack of Russia and I was stuck rounding up men, women, and children and processing their belongings. It didn't seem to be the thing we were trained for.

I never wrote the letter to him.

In a couple of days I received another letter from Anna. They were experiencing heavy bombing. Fires could be seen all over the city. Men, women, and children all helped put the fires out and clear the rubble. She wrote that our Heim was destroyed, along with the park that Rolf, Guenther, and I used to play in.

Many people where leaving the city, going to small villages in Bavaria were they thought it would be safer. Anna was thinking about asking Mother and her parents to leave with her. I knew that would be hopeless. Mother would never leave Berlin. She considered Berlin her home and she was not about to leave it.

Anna was a very considerate person.

I was starting to worry about her and Mother.

Our army was making great strides in capturing Russian territory and men. It seemed that nothing could stop us from defeating the Bolsheviks by winter.

Things were going well in our group too.

We were finding Jews in every village and hamlet. While some escaped into the forest, it was a relatively simple task to round them up, make them dig large trenches and make them kneel at the edge to be shot.

They were like sheep.

Most of them walked to their death as though they where in a trance.

Our men were averaging about 350 deaths per day, every day of the week since we began the campaign.

These constant deaths were taking a toll on the men who were doing most of the killing. Although they had plenty of alcohol, it seemed that they required more and more to help them deal with all of the death. I wasn't assigned to a death group but the continual processing of the belongings was starting to work on me too. A couple of the men went to Rolf and asked to be transferred to other units. Rolf accommodated their requests without any negative remarks in their records. In fact, I don't remember anyone who was reprimanded for asking to be transferred.

At first, some of the men would taunt anyone who expressed any reservations about shooting. After a while, the taunting went away and everyone settled into a kind of a business-like demeanor. It was as if we all moved about our work automatically. Jews and sympathizers were found and herded into the local church or village square. Some of their men were selected to dig trenches on the outskirts of the town. Once the trenches were completed, the Jews were marched or transported to a holding area near the trench. They were made to remove all of their clothing and stack it neatly. Any jewelry or other items were placed in burlap sacks for sorting later. The Jews were led, in small groups, to the trenches and directed to lie on top of the ones who had gone before them into the trench. Some of the ones in the trench were still alive. Several of our shooters would walk along the trench shooting them in the back of the neck. When the trench was almost full, the men who had dug the trenches took their place on the bodies.

After the Jews were shot, our soldiers would spread quick lime over the bodies and close the trench with dirt. The day's work would be done and our men would head back to camp for some food and alcohol. While all of this was going on, my group would load the belongings on our trucks to go back to our camp for processing and packaging. Any clothing of value had to be separated, packaged, marked, and shipped to the Reich Minister's office. Reports had to be made on the numbers killed and of the items shipped.

This was our daily routine and we were getting very good at it.

Jews were not our only victims. In one village, a number of boy scouts from twelve to sixteen years old were collected in the marketplace against the wall and shot. We received intelligence reports that the boy scouts were being used by the Russians as spies. A priest who rushed to administer the Last Sacrament was shot too.

One day we were ordered to prepare pits for an expected shipment of undesirables. I coordinated with the army for the use of some of their political prisoners. Since we had given our gas vans to Blobel, we had them dig pits in a nearby forest. We were instructed by Reich Headquarters to meet a train and to transport the men, women, and children to the pits.

I led the convoy of trucks to the local train station and was shocked by what I saw. The cattle cars were crowded with mentally and physically disabled. We delivered the victims to the forest. Rolf was there to greet the trucks. I went over to him and started to protest.

He was obviously drinking and cut me off, "Kurt, we have our orders."

There was no use in trying to talk with Rolf when he was like that.

The first victim was a woman about thirty years old. She had blonde hair and pretty blue eyes. She just stared straight ahead, never looking around or making eye contact. Rolf personally shot her with a *Genickschuss,* a shot in the neck from behind at the point where the spinal cord enters the skull. She was instantaneously killed and fell into the pit. Our shooters filled the pits with 2,363 bodies that day.

To eliminate witnesses, Rolf had the political prisoners who dug the pits shot and our soldiers spread the quick lime and covered the holes with dirt.

I wondered how I was going to explain to the army why their prisoners would not be returning.

We were under strict orders not to tell anyone what we were doing, not even the army. I think many in the army suspected what we were up to but decided that it was better not to ask. They had their hands full with the Russians and didn't need anything else to worry about.

I discovered later that some of the army leadership knew what we were doing and were disturbed by our actions. It was not the victim's suffering that disturbed the military leadership. They were hardly concerned with the victims. Rather, they were concerned with arousing resistance and with the effect of the killings on the character and morale of the soldiers and that of the German nation.

I looked at the pamphlet we had received from headquarters. It advised us to be careful as we dealt with the female civilians. The pamphlet described how the Red Army had infected all of the women remaining in the villages with syphilis in order to infect us and slow us down.

I thought to myself, *if this is true, this proves what we have been told about these people. These people are truly sub-human. This was a re-affirmation of our cause.*

I wondered if the Red Army had actually gone to that length.

I made a note to order more prophylactics from the *Wehrmacht* supply.

As the October 1941 chill turned into the cold of November, we came under pressure from headquarters to accelerate our efforts in order to make room for an influx of SS and German civil administration personnel. We were told that the towns of the occupied East needed to be cleared. There was to be a future SS base built near the village we occupied. Our colleagues needed the highest standard of overall living conditions in order to maintain peak performance. They could not be exposed to the filthy people who lived here.

There was only one solution to this problem. All of the inhabitants would have to be removed and the town made clean. Construction on the new base was to begin in the early spring, after the ground had softened. We had all winter to prepare the area. Surveyors and construction engineers began to arrive and it soon became apparent that we were going to have a housing shortage. I wrote in my report to headquarters that the village was a jumble of a few good stone buildings, quite a few serviceable wooden houses and a good many dilapidated log shacks that would have to be demolished. The influx of refugees from the surrounding countryside was causing overpopulation.

At the evening Staff Meeting Rolf told us, "Our men deserve, from the first day they arrive, decent accommodations, enough to eat and to be able to live in a style that embodies German culture and the prestige appropriate to it. We have too many mouths to feed here."

He assigned me to insure that the town and surrounding area was suitable for the arrival of our soldiers. I was surprised by this assignment since I had been mostly involved with logistically concerns and reports to date. Rolf asked me to remain behind after the meeting.

Rolf began, "Kurt, I have been getting complaints from some of the others group leaders that you are never assigned to, what everyone calls, our real work. I had no choice but to assign this mission to you. Plus, your organizational skills will come in handy here."

I responded, "Rolf, you know that I will do my best."

Rolf went on, "I have to go to Odessa and meet with Ohlendorf. You will be in charge while I am gone. Use Erwin to take care of the Jews, he is good at it and enjoys the work."

We drank a toast to the successful completion of my mission.

The next day I got with Erwin and the other group leaders to organize our efforts. Erwin estimated that there were approximately five thousand Jews in the village and the surrounding area. We agreed that the first order of business was to reduce this number.

Erwin registered the entire Jewish population, noting age, gender and profession. He issued passes and separate accommodations for all the skilled workers. The remaining population was herded into the section of the town with the dilapidated log shacks. My men had strung barbed wire around the area and we posted guards to insure that no one left the enclosure. I sent another team door-to-door to expropriate any useful property and furnishings to equip the buildings to be used by our SS comrades and the construction engineers.

Of course, it all had to be fumigated!

These filthy people!

The manual work would be done by the healthy Jews of the log shacks, at least, those who survived the winter.

Erwin had about fifty of the Jews from the enclosure working at digging a large pit on the outskirts of the village. After the hole was finished, the workers were made to jump into the pit. Most were still alive when I arrived at the site.

Erwin's men were standing around the parameter and using the Jews in the pit for target practice.

I was amazed that not one of the men in the pit said a word. It was as if they had accepted their fate.

When I went over to Erwin one of his men handed me a machine gun. Erwin said, "Kurt, it is your turn to do your duty for the Fatherland. Show our men that no officer shirks their responsibility.

Erwin's men had stopped firing and were all looking at me.

I knew that I had no choice but to fire.

I shot the Jews until I ran out of ammunition and then Erwin's men started firing again killing the rest of the Jews in the pit. I don't know how many I killed, maybe twenty or so.

After the firing stopped, Erwin saluted me and handed me a flask of whiskey. Erwin said confidently, "The first time is the hardest. Then, it becomes easy and even fun."

I said, "I have never looked at what we are doing as fun."

Erwin responded, "Kurt, we are doing our duty for our nation. I can not think of a job that brings so much joy. We get rid of these vermin and have fun in doing so."

As we were talking, our men had ordered the Jews standing in the forest near the pit to strip and to place all of their belongings on the piles that separated jewelry, clothes and other items. Erwin ordered the naked Jews who had been watching into the pit while I drank the entire contents of the flask. It seemed that every one of them looked at me as they made their way into the pit. In the crowd were women, men, children, and mothers with children in their arms.

It is hard to describe the wailing and crying.

Some Jews were jumping without an order. The ones who resisted were beaten and pushed down the slope of the pit. Some mothers jumped in while holding their children. Some were throwing their children in first and jumping on top in an effort to shield them.

As Erwin and I were watching the activities, a woman crawled up to Erwin's feet and began begging. He seemed to enjoy watching her beg. After a few minutes, he pulled out his pistol and shot her in the head. Her blood splattered over his boots.

Erwin looked at me and said, "See Kurt, these people are vermin. Look how they crawl! Shoot them Kurt. Shoot these things that poison Germany!"

I took out my pistol and shot two of the women who were crawling in the mud towards Erwin. The rest turned and went into the pit.

The action continued until darkness began to fall. There were no more Jews to process. There were only ten old men who had been spared to cover the hole. They would be shot and their bodies burned. Erwin left the last details to one of the group leaders and we rode back to the village together.

Dinner was ready when we arrived. We had fresh coffee and a fine dinner of pork with a kilo of bread each. We all passed around wine that had been confiscated. We received news that Japan had conducted a surprise attack on the American's Pacific Fleet at Pearl Harbor in Hawaii on December 7th. We all wondered how the American could have been taken by surprise.

Agreeing that the America would surely not enter the war in Europe now, we toasted Hitler and each other. We were certain the Americans would be busy in the Pacific.

The more I drank, the more I began to accept the events of the day. With the Americans most likely out of the war and our successes with the Russians, I knew we would be victorious. I drank constantly from that day forth though.

This was a harsh environment that required harsh methods, I kept telling myself.

We had to make this area suitable for Germans.

It was a cold Russian winter and our new clothes offered comfort from the cold. We were receiving reports that the war was beginning to go badly for our army. The Russians had turned the tide at Stalingrad and stopped our forces short of Moscow. My confidence in a total victory over the Russians was beginning to fade with every report. We all felt that at least here, we were making a difference.

I began to wonder why these people offered little resistance. I think that generally, many factors made Jewish resistance both difficult and dangerous. At first, most Jews believed they would be re-settled to a productive life. Many Jewish leaders believed that by working for the Germans they could survive and limit the suffering of other Jews. As fear and terror became everyday truths for most Jews, standards of daily reality shifted dramatically. One reality that could not be overlooked was the power of the German army.

Our superiority posed a major obstacle to the resistance of mostly unarmed civilians from the very beginning of the Nazi takeover of Germany. At the outbreak of war in September 1939, Poland was overrun in a few weeks. France, attacked on May 10, 1940, fell only six weeks later. Clearly, if two powerful nations with standing armies could not resist the onslaught of the Germans, the possibilities of success were narrow for mostly unarmed civilians who had limited access to weapons. We had also created and used the idea of collective responsibility to thwart resistance.

In Dolhyhnov, near the old Lithuanian capital of Vilna, the entire ghetto population was killed after two young boys escaped and refused to return. In the ghetto of Bialystok, Poland, the SS shot 120 Jews on the street after Abraham Melamed shot a German policeman. The SS then threatened to destroy the whole ghetto if Melamed did not surrender. Three days later, he turned himself in to avoid retaliation in the ghetto.

He was then shot, of course.

The speed, secrecy, and deception that were used to carry out deportations and killings were intended to impede resistance. Millions of victims rounded up either prior to mass shootings in occupied Soviet territory or for deportation to killing centers where they were gassed, often did not know where they were being sent.

Rumors of death camps were widespread, but Nazi deception and the human tendency to deny bad news in the face of possible harm or death took over, as most Jews could not believe the stories. The German or collaborating police forces generally ordered their victims to pack some of their belongings, thus reinforcing the belief among victims that they were being resettled in labor camps.

The Wannsee Conference was held on January 20, 1942, in a villa owned by the *SS-Nordhav* Foundation in the attractive Berlin lakeside suburb of Wannsee. It was presided over by SS-Lieutenant General Reinhard Heydrich, Chief of the Security Police and Security Service.

Heydrich summoned fourteen men representing the governmental and military branches most involved in implementing the practical aspects of the "Final Solution." *Reichsmarschall* Hermann Goring had charged him with arranging all practical matters concerning the implementation of the Final Solution of the Jewish question. One of Heydrich's foremost intentions was to make sure that all these men understood perfectly what duties and responsibilities their office was expected to fulfill. In the years leading up to World War II, the phrase "Final Solution of the Jewish Problem" had taken on a series of increasingly ominous meanings in the Nazi vocabulary. The various implications had included voluntary emigration, confinement to ghettos in cities and referred specifically to the murder of all European Jews.

Heydrich wanted to be certain there was no confusion among the group. The atmosphere of the meeting was one filled of cooperation and agreement.

At the time of this meeting, *Reichsführer* -SS Heinrich Himmler had already stopped emigration and the Führer had approved a new solution. The Jews were to be evacuated to the East.

Heydrich's order stated, "These actions are nevertheless to be seen only as temporary relief but they are providing the practical experience that is of great significance for the coming final solution of the Jewish question."

Heydrich continued by listing the number of Jews killed in each country and observed, "Approximately eleven million Jews will be involved."

He further stated in his order, "In large, single-sex labor columns, Jews fit to work will work their way eastward constructing roads. Doubtless, the large majority will be eliminated by natural causes. Any final remnant that survives will doubtless consist of the most resistant elements. They will have to be dealt with appropriately because otherwise, by natural selection, they would form the germ cell of a new Jewish revival." In other words, none would be allowed to survive."

Chapter Fourteen
A New Mission

It was February 10, 1942 when Rolf called all of the officers together. He read the news about the Americans who where fully engaged with the Japanese in the Philippines. It looked like they would have to completely evacuate the islands. He also told us that our priority had changed. We were to concentrate on fighting Soviet partisans. *Generalfeldmarschall* Wilhelm Keitel had ordered decrees allowing the seizure of property and the execution without trial of all persons suspected of compromising German security in the occupied zones.

This was not new to us!

Now the rest of the army was about to adopt the techniques that we used on the Jews.

We were to form counterinsurgency teams that could be rushed rapidly to an area of suspected partisan activity. We were still to report our activities to RSHA in Berlin, but we were to take orders from the local army commander. I obtained some smaller, more agile vehicles and arranged for heavier machine guns to be issued with plenty of ammunition and extra clothing. We moved back to Odessa to await further orders.

While we were waiting in Odessa, Rolf was promoted to Lieutenant Colonel and I was promoted to Captain. Guenther's letters were less frequent and their tone was less positive. I could tell he was having a bad time of it. One evening, Rolf called me to his office. He had been crying. That was the only time I ever saw Rolf cry. I thought something had happened to one of his parents.

"Kurt, I have very bad news. Guenther has been killed in action."

I was shocked. I could not speak. Words would not come out of my mouth.

I finally said, "How? How did it happen?"

"From what I can tell from the report, he was leading a motorcycle patrol on the outskirts of Stalingrad with the 6th Army, when his patrol was overrun by advancing Russian tanks. Guenther rode his motorcycle in, around, and between the tanks allowing the other members of the patrol to escape. They were able to report the location of the tanks to the *Luftwaffe* who slowed the advance."

"He was a hero!"

"Guenther acted like the heroes at the Battle of Langemarck."

"They are going to posthumously award him the Knight's Cross and present it to his parents."

I wondered how his parents were going to take it.

In his letters, Guenther had written about the many seasons and faces of the war. He had become a prolific writer and was thinking of writing novels after the war.

He wrote, "Rain, mud, cold, snow, heat, and dust formed a recurring theme of the entire war for me and many of the soldiers. Many of us slept day and night in the same uniform, on a plank bed, wrapped in a wool blanket. In the rainy season, the mud was so think that it is a chore just to move. In winter the bitter cold and snow slows everything down."

He wrote, "No soldier could escape the unpleasant business of living rough, of coping with a harsh environment under conditions of extreme physical and mental exhaustion. The real enemy was the weather, the effects of living in the open, and the stresses and strains endemic to a group forced into proximity with an often-unfamiliar natural environment."

Guenther described how throughout long hours of boredom and loneliness, deprivation and hardship, horror and agony, they soon became familiar with many of the myriad faces of war. Fear was the real enemy of most soldiers. The fear of death or of cowardice was on his mind. The fear of the conflict within the spirit or, a simple fear of showing fear could surface at any time.

I wondered if he had written these things to anyone else.

Rolf and I opened a bottle of cognac he was saving for a special occasion and toasted Guenther, drinking the entire bottle. We spent most of the night talking about how much fun we had together in the *Jungvolk*.

When I got back to my quarters, I wrote to Anna about Guenther and about what I felt we had become. Our appearance had somehow become metallic. We accepted pain as a natural occurrence, we were hard, and functional, we had become machines. We witnessed and created horror every day and somehow it had become commonplace. I saw the inhumane and didn't even blink an eye. We were like characters in a play, acting out our parts with absolute precision. However, I saw not an end to the play, no curtain, only death.

I posted the letter, later wishing that I had not sent it.

What was she going to think?

We weren't subject to the censor's pen like our comrades in the army. I guess high command thought we were too committed to the cause to write any disparaging remarks.

I wondered *if a man reaches a point where all of the horror piles up and affects his judgment.*

I was very conflicted at that time.

We were told what we were doing was the right thing for our people. I had seen how these sub-humans lived and how they acted. Surely, they had to be exterminated or they would pollute decent society. These hordes had invaded the west before and left destruction in their wake.

Surely, it was our generation's destiny to conquer these people before they could infect our lands. Furthermore, the children had to be killed. If not, they would grow up and take the place of their infectious parents. I had been told these things since I was a child. Surely, it must be true.

While some of Colonel Ohlendorf's units were tasked to fight the partisans, we sat in Odessa until March 15, 1942 when Rolf called the officers together again. The news bulletin reported that the American General MacArthur and his family and staff had run away from Corregidor in the Philippines. Rolf told us our priority had once again changed. We were to retrace the route we had taken from Dalnik westward. No one could believe what our new mission was to be. Not even Erwin, who was probably the coldest person I had ever come in contact with.

As we began to develop our plans I received a telegram that Father had a heart attack and was very sick. The doctor said he didn't expect him to last very long and I should try to get home if I could. I went to Rolf and asked him for emergency leave. I caught the next transport to the local train and made my way back to Berlin.

When I arrived, at the Berlin train station, it was night and the entire city was blacked out. I walked the six blocks from the training station to my parent's apartment and noticed air raid warden stations had been placed at most intersections. I rang the door and was met by Heir Schmitz. He commented that I looked very grown up. I took that to mean that I looked like I had aged beyond my years.

I certainly felt like I had.

Anna was sitting with Mother in the kitchen when I opened the door. They both got up and hugged me.

Mother said. "Your father doesn't have much time, he is asking for you."

I thought he was sleeping when I entered the room but he opened his eyes and said, "Kurt, it is you. I am glad you are here. Come close, I want to tell you something. Kurt,

I am proud of what you have made of yourself. You are a hero"

He grasped my hand and squeezed it. Before I could say anything, he left go and he was gone.

If only he knew what I had made of my self. Although I hadn't actually shot anyone, our unit had murdered women and children. I didn't know how many all of the groups had killed by now and I didn't want him to know any of it.

Father had passed away thinking that I was a hero.

I guess that's okay.

Mother took his passing hard. I stayed with her for a couple of nights until after the funeral. I didn't realize that Anna stopped in to see Mother and Father every day, without fail. She would bring cakes, sit, and chat. While Father and she would chat for hours about politics, Anna and Mother maintained a polite relationship.

Anna and I only had one night alone before I had to leave to rejoin my unit. Anna promised to check on Mother, even though Mother said it was not necessary. We went out for some dinner at Aschinger's and spent the rest of the evening in the apartment catching up on things. Although we were sworn to secrecy, I told Anna about what we were doing. She was supportive.

We slept together and decided to try to have a baby.

She was more anti-Semitic then me and said, "Kurt, I am so proud of what you are doing for Germany. You, Rolf, and the others are the true heroes of the Fatherland. Most people will probably never know the sacrifices you boys have made. I am so proud to be your wife."

She walked me to the station the next morning and waved as the train pulled out.

I will never forget her face that day. She was so lively, so bubbly.

She kept waving until I could no longer see her on the platform.

Back in Odessa with the unit I learned the full magnitude of our new mission.

We were to find whomever we could to open the pits where we had buried all of the victims, burn their bodies and scatter the ashes over the countryside, leaving no trace of the killings. Rolf told us the order came from Himmler himself.

Apparently, the advancing Russian army had found some of the mass graves in other sectors and went wild. They fought with no regard for themselves. All evidence must be eliminated before the Russians found it. We could not give them a reason to fight harder. We were to have the full support of the retreating army. We all knew that meant that we were on our own.

We were all stunned!

We asked ourselves how it had all gone wrong. If only our army had winter uniforms, things would have been different. We were certain that had the *Führer* been aware of the uniform situation, he would have fixed the problem immediately. We were also certain that traitors within the army kept the facts from him.

After the shock of the new assignment had settled in, we took out the map that I had plotted the location of all the graves on. I was very thorough and had pinpointed every action and every gravesite. I never thought the map would be used to dig up graves. I assumed future use of my map would be for German settlers to use so they would not cultivate the sites for farming.

With this new mission, I had to find shovels, many shovels, and something that could be used as masks for our men. I had already discovered that by applying a mixture of cedar leaf oil, nutmeg oil, thymol and turpentine oil to cotton masks, the smell of death was covered. Since the army was in retreat, I could not count on them for much logistical support. They would have their hands full just staying out of range of the Russian gunners. We would have to scrounge and Sergeant Kruger was the master of scrounging.

We looked over the map and planned our route, trying to estimate how long each site would take. I recommended that we place provisions and supplies along the route, tasking the Romanian army with guarding them. Since we could not completely trust them, we planned to leave a few SS troops to keep an eye of the Romanians.

At that point, they still would not dare to attack a German soldier, especially an SS soldier, for fear of swift reprisals. They had seen what we were capable of. Rolf liked the idea and sent a message to Colonel Ohlendorf asking for support. Erwin was in charge of rounding up the labor to uncover the pits, burn the corpses, and spread the ashes.

First Lieutenant Mueller asked, "What about the extra dirt?"

We all looked at him as if he was crazy.

"What extra dirt?" Rolf asked.

Mueller explained, "When we remove all of those bodies, there won't be enough dirt to fill in the holes."

No one had the answer.

We agreed to cross that bridge when we came to it. It was eventually decided to take dirt from the village gardens. Somehow, we thought that this wouldn't look conspicuous.

For now, the most important thing was to get rid of the bodies and witnesses. If the Russians found large unfilled holes they would have to wonder about it. They could guess what they wanted but would have no proof.

It took us a couple of days to obtain supplies, organize ourselves, and get the Romanians working on provision stockpiles.

Rolf divided us into five groups of approximately fifteen soldiers each. There would be four groups directly responsible for the bodies and my group was again responsible for logistics. Rolf assigned each of the groups specific gravesites. We had drawn up a master plan that had us all meet at the supply locations every several days.

The first group went back to Dalnik. The Romanians had shot about 15,000 Jews and buried them in shallow graves. We all agreed that the Romanians did very sloppy work.

None of their gravesites was indicated on a map. Our soldiers had to search the forest with the Romanians to try to locate the sites. Fortunately, the graves were only a couple of months old and not difficult to spot.

The biggest problem for our group in Dalnik was not so much locating the graves but finding people to handle the bodies. The Romanians had killed all of the Jews and Russian sympathizers. There just wasn't anyone left who could be put to work.

The Romanian army flatly refused to handle the bodies. Rolf went to meet with the Romanian army commander to try to convince him to help. He would not even consider it. He kept saying something about their religion.

It was baffling.

They killed all of those people but would not dig them up because of religion.

Since they were still our friends at the time, we were frustrated. We needed them for security and to watch our provisions. Rolf had to re-assign the other groups to help. We had to get this done!

The Russian army was about fifty kilometers away when we finally started burning the bodies. Complicating matters even further was the number of attacks by the partisans. Rolf had to split up two groups to provide security. My group was pressed into service to help with security. We had more soldiers providing security than taking care of the bodies.

According to my calculations, we had, either directly or indirectly, been involved with killing 76,530 undesirables. The task of digging up all of those bodies and burning them while trying to stay ahead of the Russians was daunting. Based on the speed of the Russian advance, I had my doubts that it could be done.

Our army was fighting heroically, delaying the Russians as best as they could. The situation in Dalnik had slowed us down considerably.

I received a letter from Mother. Anna had given birth on December 31st to a healthy boy and she would write as soon as she could. Mother rarely wrote to me directly. Anna always included messages from Father and Mother in her letters. Mother's tone was serious and I worried about everyone.

Events had overtaken us and things were not quite working out as we had planned.

I could not help but wonder why our fortunes had turned.

Surely, we were on the right side of this war! I had written most of the details of what we had done in my letters to Anna but decided not to discuss what we were doing with the dead bodies. My main concern was that Anna, Mother, and Little Rolf leave Berlin as soon as possible. We were still trying to organize the efforts in the Odessa area when Rolf called us together.

He said somberly, "Gentlemen, I am sure you have already figured out that we cannot possibly accomplish our mission if we have to stay in Odessa and deal with the Romanians. After all, the Romanians were the ones who killed the Odessa Jews. RSHA has decided that we will bypass Odessa and let the Romanians answer to the Russians for their deeds."

I think we all wondered; *would the Russians believe that we had nothing to do with the Odessa killings? That was unlikely.*

Most of us still believed that the war was not lost. We thought our armies would hold the Russians at the original borders allowing Hitler to negotiate a peace with Stalin. We had to erase the evidence of our direct involvement if negotiations were to have a chance.

By January 1943 the reports from the front overshadowed all other news. They were grim and getting worse with every report. Rolf received a letter from someone he knew who was fighting with the Sixth Army. They had no ammunition, no winter clothes, no food, and no medical supplies. On January 31st, they surrendered.

We were shocked by the news. Adding to the bad news, we learned that the Americans and the British where beginning to make progress in the Pacific. We began to wonder if they would enter the war in Europe after all.

As the winter of 1943 got worse, a feeling of gloom was beginning to settle over us. For the first time, fear was starting to overtake us. In the back of our minds was the nagging thought of what the Red Army would do if they caught up to us. For most of us, the war was intensely personal. Many of us feared death but more than the fear of death was the fear of cowardice. We heard stories about the Russian attacks on our soldiers at Stalingrad. They could fight like wild animals, biting and chewing if they had no other weapons.

How can these beasts be allowed to win?

What would happen to our families, should the sub-humans reach our Fatherland?

I was worried about Anna and Mother.

What would the beasts do to them if they captured Berlin?

We had all become obsessed with death. Who could blame us? Death lurked everywhere. It was around the bushes and behind the trees. Bands of partisans roamed in our area, mostly on horseback, attacking small units at night. We had to keep a close look out. Most of us slept very lightly. The stress and the lack of sleep were having a toll on us.

We drank even more to help us cope.

I felt as though I awoke each day into a dream world. Surely what I was experiencing was not real.

I wondered how Anna would manage with little Rolf in Rothenburg. Hopefully, they we be safe there.

We read reports about the formation of the 12th SS-Panzer Division Hitler *Jugend*. Amid a dwindling supply of manpower, the division was formed. A recruitment drive began, drawing principally on 17-year-old volunteers, but younger members 16 and under eagerly joined. During July and

August 1943, 10,000 recruits arrived at the training camp in Beverloo, Belgium. By this time, the Americans had just about completed the capture of Sicily.

To fill out the Hitler Youth Division with enough experienced soldiers and officers, Waffen-SS survivors from the Russian Front, including members of the elite *Leibstandarte-SS* Adolf Hitler, were brought in. Fifty officers from the *Wehrmacht*, who were former Hitler Youth leaders, were also reassigned to the division. The remaining shortage of squad and section leaders was filled with Hitler Youth members who had demonstrated leadership aptitude during Hitler Youth Para-military training exercises.

The division was placed under of the command of 34-year-old Major General Fritz Witt, who had also been a Hitler Youth, dating back before 1933. Among his young troops, morale was high. Traditional, stiff German codes of conduct between officers and soldiers were replaced by more informal relationships in which young soldiers were often given the reasons behind orders.

Unnecessary drills, such as goose-step marching were eliminated. Lessons learned on the Russian Front were applied during training to emphasize realistic battlefield conditions, including the use of live ammunition. By the spring of 1944, training was complete. They were ready for assignment to protect the Fatherland. The Americans were progressing North in Italy and we wondered if we would encounter them.

We had our own problems to worry about though.

We went to Tiraspol where Erwin had found some unwilling workers to take care of 464 buried there plus the twenty five laborers. Next, it was Tighina and the 700 buried in the forest about twenty kilometers from the town. There we stacked the bodies like cord wood, doused them with petrol, and burned them. We found that the airspaces created by stacking the bodies made the fire hotter and burn faster. We adopted this technique as we continued from site to site.

The work was really taking a toll on the men. As we re-visited the villages and gravesites, many of the men were having trouble sleeping. Transfers meant going to the front to fight the Russians.

No one opted for a transfer.

We all just drank more.

Some of the men were acting even wilder then before, shooting anyone in the villages that made eye contact with them. Rolf could not control it anymore.

I found myself joining in the random shooting.

It started to give me pleasure.

Finally, by September of 1944, we were back at the village of Bratislava, were we had started. We disposed of the 1,000 bodies and wondered what was next for us. I asked Rolf if he knew of our fate. He said the only thing he heard was that we would be re-assigned back to our original units or to other units after *Einsatzgruppen* was disbanded.

I had a lot to do, finalizing reports to be sent to the RSHA and arranging for our dispersal.

I wondered if headquarters had a plan to destroy all of those reports we sent them should it look as though the allies would overrun them.

Those reports would get us all hanged!

Most of our group was re-assigned to the SS Tofenken division and placed in one of the concentration camps as guards. I guess RSHA thought the experience handling the Jews was needed in the camps. Some of us were transferred back to the units we came from. I was ordered back to the 2nd SS division. They were fighting the Russians at Kreme-chug, near the Dnieper River. Rolf was assigned to the RSHA headquarters in Berlin. I am sure his father was able to arrange it.

Rolf arranged for us to have some drinks the night before we were to leave for our units. We were far enough from the Russians to relax some.

Everyone got drunk.

I think we all had the feeling that night that most of us would probably not survive the war. We all sat around discussing what a good job we had done for the Fatherland and wondered what our new assignments would be like. No one wanted to talk about the killing. Everyone talked in terms of the sacrifices we made for Germany and our families.

I had three days leave before we had to report to our next duty station. I decided to ride the train back to Berlin with Rolf. We wondered what would become of us and of Germany. The reports from the Russian front were not good.

I asked Rolf, "What will you do if the Russians beat us?"

"Kurt, if the Russians beat us, they will decide what I will do. More than likely, they will hang me."

Chapter Fiveteen
Back to Berlin

I thought about Guenther on that train ride back to Berlin.

It was strange.

As much as I missed Anna and Mother, and I wanted to see my son, I couldn't get Guenther out of my head. I had telegrammed Anna to meet me at the station. I had no way of knowing if she received the message.

It was about 10:00 a.m. when the train entered the outskirts of Berlin. We could see considerable damage. Everywhere we looked, we saw bomb craters and smoke from burning buildings. It was a surreal scene. There were very few youth in the city.

As the Allies stepped up their bombing campaign, the Government began evacuating children from Berlin into *Kinderlandverschickung* (KLV), Hitler Youth camps, located mainly in the rural regions of East Prussia, the Warthegau section of Poland, Upper Silesia, and Slovakia. From 1940 to 1945, over 2.8 million German children were sent to these camps. There were separate KLV camps for boys and girls. About 5,000 camps were eventually in operation, varying greatly in sizes from the smallest, which had 18 children to the largest that held 1,200.

Each camp was run by a Nazi approved teacher and a Hitler Youth squad leader. The camps replaced big city grammar schools, most of which were closed due to the bombing.

Reluctant parents were forced to send their children away to the camps. Life inside the boys' camp was harsh, featuring a routine of roll calls, Para-military field exercises, hikes, marches, recitation of Nazi slogans and propaganda, along with endless singing of Hitler Youth songs and Nazi anthems. Schoolwork was neglected while supreme emphasis was placed on the boys learning to automatically snap-to attention at any time of the day or night and to obey all orders unconditionally. They were the new Hitler Youth.

Our train stopped about two miles from the station in the middle of an open field.

I kept thinking that we were sitting ducks.

Slowly, we started to move and enter the grounds of the station. There were sandbags along the sides of the platform and around the station buildings. Civilians and soldiers were everywhere, scurrying around like ants in a colony.

It was total chaos.

Baggage was scattered around the platform. Some of it was damaged as if it was tossed from the trains onto the wooden deck. Station workers moved among the people, gathering the baggage and piling it on the side of the main building.

I wondered who owned all of that mess.

People were pushing to get through the sea of bodies. It seemed like everyone was trying to get a train out of the city. Police officers were asking everyone for transit and identification papers. A sense of paranoia came over everyone.

How would Anna find us in this confusion, if she received my telegram?

Smiling uneasily, Rolf said, "This is not the Berlin of our youth is it Kurt?"

I nodded blankly.

"Rolf, what went wrong?"

He did not respond. He spotted Anna at the side of the platform and pointed her out to me. As the train stopped, the crowd surged forward to our train. Everyone was trying to position themselves near the steps to board the train.

The conductor looked tentative as he opened the door and folded the steps down.

He yelled, "Now make way. Let everyone off before you try to board."

The people by the door stepped aside when they saw Rolf and I come to the door. I guess the black SS uniform still demanded some respect in Berlin. Rolf and I made our way over to Anna.

I was sorry I had asked her to meet me at the station.

We hugged and looked for a way off the platform and to a taxi. I had not told her our group was disbanded and I was re-assigned. That could wait. I wanted to know about her and Little Rolf. She had left him with Mother.

"It has not been easy, with the air raids and all," she said as she smiled at Rolf and me.

"It must not have been easy for you two either. I am very sorry about Guenther. I went to the award ceremony with his parents. They did not take if very well."

Rolf replied, "He was like a brother to us. He died for the Fatherland. What more could one ask for these days?"

In unison we said, "Heil Hitler!"

We passed by a bombsite were several home guards were attempting to shift rubble. There wasn't much of the building left. It looked as though the fire had consumed the structure. Anna told us a new type of bomb had hit the house. It created great heat and suction rather than a blast and tore people's lungs apart.

Everywhere we looked was damage. There were abandoned cars along the streets. People left them where they stopped after running out of petrol. Small children went from car to car looking for anything of value.

I said to Anna, "You must leave Berlin! This is only going to get worse. You and Little Rolf have to get to Rothenburg.

There are no military targets within miles of the place. You will be safe there with Uncle Frederick."

Anna looked into my eyes and said, "Kurt, your Mother will not leave Berlin. My parents are leaving next week for the Swiss border. Mother's sister has a farm there"

"I will talk with my mother, but you must promise me that you and Little Rolf will leave Berlin when I do."

Rolf added, "Kurt is right Anna. This is only going to get worse and the day may come when you can't leave."

"All right Kurt, I will go to Rothenburg."

"Good, I will telegram Uncle Frederick to expect you."

Posters were all over the city with the same message, "Our walls break but not our hearts."

I suspected they were the work of Dr. Goebbles. The air raids were highly concentrated, targeting areas with government buildings, the center of the city, and districts with highest density of civilian population. Fortunately, none of our apartment buildings were touched, at least not yet.

As usual, Mother was busy in the kitchen, smoking a cigarette and drinking coffee when Anna and I arrived.

She had aged.

I could tell that the air raids were taking a toll.

We all sat down at the kitchen table. Mother poured some coffee and we discussed the situation in Berlin. I pleaded with her to accompany Anna to Rothenburg. She would have none of it.

"Kurt, Berlin is my home. I am not leaving it for anyone. The Nazis could not drive me out and neither will the Russians. Soon the war will be over and things will go back to normal. You will see."

I said, "Mother, I don't think you understand what could happen here. If the Russians keep advancing, they will enter the city. They are ruthless, ignorant, and disgusting people. There is no telling what they will do."

"Kurt, my family has always lived here and I am not leaving."

I told her that we had decided that Anna and Little Rolf would go to Rothenburg and find Uncle Frederick.

I hoped Mother would go too but it didn't look as though she would.

I helped Anna pack and played with Little Rolf. He was a healthy, blond-haired, blue-eyed baby who could be on a poster advertising the new race. He looked like the perfect Nordic baby and Anna and I were extremely proud.

We had to drape black cloth over the windows at night. Berlin was under a complete blackout. Fires could be seen everywhere. Firefighters raced from fire to fire desperately trying to put them out so they could not be used as beacons by the Allied bombers.

The front was nerve racking, but the constant bombings were too much. I had to get out of Berlin. I made one last appeal to Mother to leave, knowing that she wouldn't. That cold chill came over me again as I kissed Mother goodbye. Somehow, I knew I would never see her again.

Anna, Little Rolf and I went to the train station and into the chaos. People were shoving and trying to pull others off of the trains. They still moved aside when they saw my uniform though.

As Anna was boarding the train I placed a Luger in her hand and said, "Just in case."

She looked at me and said, "I know."

I got them on the train to Rothenburg and waited until it pulled out. I didn't know when I would see them again.

I was off to join Das Reich again.

Chapter Sixteen
Back to SS Das Reich

I joined the 3rd self-propelled artillery battery of Das Reich as their logistics officer. They were already withdrawing to the Dnieper River when I reported to Colonial Eicke. The Russians, having already crossed the river, compounded the difficulties of withdrawing. They established bridgeheads on the west bank and were busily engaged in reinforcing them.

The only bridge across the Vorskla, a river barrier west of the Dnieper River, was a single bridge, near Kremechug. This complication not only affected us, it affected the entire German Eighth Army.

We received orders from division headquarters to hold the area around the Vorskla Bridge at all costs until it could be blown. At 2:00 p.m. on February 15, 1944 we learned that the bridge was about to be destroyed and were ordered to cross the bridge. At 5:00 p.m., we watched as a Russian anti-tank gun hit one of our self-propelled guns. Then headquarters told us to hold the bridge until sufficient explosives and a demolition team could be brought up.

We formed our battery in a half circle on the eastern bank of the river. The Russians had worked their way through the gardens and houses of the village. Once they came within range, our gunners brought fire on them. We fought back and forth for over an hour until our demolition team arrived. We moved across the bridge while they placed charges. When the Russians saw our vehicles move across the bridge, they surged forward and their lead troops were blown up with the bridge.

My main job at the time was the re-supply of ammunition and medical supplies. This was difficult since all units were running short. We were able to secure some foodstuffs through the supply system although most of our food had to be scavenged from the local population. After all, we needed food more then them.

With the news that the Allies had landed in Normandy, we went on first stage alert. On June 7th, civilian vehicles were requisitioned and the first parties set out for the invasion area leaving the tracked vehicles to be loaded on trains.

Our tanks were assembled at Motauban to load on railway flat cars but had to wait four days for trains. The marshalling yard was then bombed. When the trains did reached Loire on June 11th, we found only a single-track span in use at Port Boulet. It wasn't until June 23rd that the last of the division's rail elements reached the battlefield.

As soon as we began to move north the Resistance attacked us. At every step along the way, we were ambushed and shot at. Our soldiers began to detest the Resistance fighters who never wore uniforms and could not be identified as the enemy until they started shooting. These attacks continued and then on June 8th the Resistance tried to liberate the town of Tulle from our occupying garrison.

In the battle that followed, the Resistance came close to capturing all of our troops, but before they could quite finish the job, our soldiers arrived to the rescue. Our troops made short work of the undisciplined and poorly armed Resistance fighters, who were soon in full retreat. When we had secured the town, we found that the Resistance had killed and mutilated some of our garrison troops who had surrendered. This was reminiscent of my *Einsatzgruppen* experience. Reprisals were called for. We rounded up all the men that we could find and after questioning them briefly, selected 120 of them to be hung from lampposts as a warning to the Resistance and anyone thinking of helping them.

There was no proof that these 120 men were actually members of the Resistance, but that did not matter, it would set an example. After 99 had been hung, we ran out of rope and so the remainders were deported to Germany as slave laborers.

On June 9th, we were asked to help drive the Resistance away from another town garrison that they were attacking. This town was called Guéret and Major Helmut Kämpfe commanded the group that went to their assistance. After driving to the town, he found that he was not needed and so they decided to return to his new headquarters at Limoges. Major Kampfe decided to drive on ahead of his men and about 10 miles from Limoges he met a truck carrying some Resistance fighters who kidnapped him. The Resistance men managed to avoid Kämpfe's men and took him to their local headquarters at Cheissoux. From there he was moved that night to Breuilaufa by way of Limoges. While he was being driven through Limoges, Kämpfe managed to throw his personal papers out of the vehicle as a clue to his whereabouts. They were found and handed in to his commanding officer, Colonial Stadler. The Resistance killed Major Kämpfe either on the night of the June 9th or early on the morning of June 10th.

During the day of June 9th the Resistance kidnapped Lieutenant Colonel Karl Gerlach and his driver and taken to Oradour-sur-Glane. Gerlach managed to escape, but not his driver and he eventually managed to make his way back to Limoges to report to Colonial Stadler what had happened.

On the morning of June 10th, Major Adolf Diekmann traveled from his headquarters at St. Junien to attend a meeting called by Stadler in Limoges and on arrival said that he had news of an unnamed captured German officer being held at Oradour-sur-Glane. This man he now assumed to be Kämpfe and requested permission to go and rescue him.

Stadler agreed and added that if Kämpfe were not to be found Diekmann should take 30 or more hostages and hold them prisoner in order to force the Resistance to release him. Colonial Stadler assigned me to accompany Major Diekmann to assist with any logistics issues. We left for Oradour via St. Junien after we had spoken to Gerlach in order to hear his story first hand.

On June 10th, we entered and then surrounded the small town of *Oradour-sur-Glane,* near the city of Limoges. At first, Major Diekmann told the Mayor that there was to be an identity check and that everyone must go to the fairground while this took place. After rounding up all the inhabitants that we could find, Diekmann changed the story from that of an identity check, to one of searching for hidden arms and explosives. He then said that while they searched for the arms the women and children must wait in the church and the men in nearby barns.

The women and children were marched off to the church, the children being encouraged by our soldiers to sing as they went. After they had left, the men were divided into six groups and led off to different barns in the town under armed guard. When the townspeople were all safely shut away we began to kill them.

A large gas bomb, made out of smoke-screen grenades and intended to asphyxiate the occupants, was placed in the church, but it did not work properly when it went off and so we had to use machine guns and hand grenades to kill the women and children. After we had shot all the occupants of the church, some of the soldiers piled wood on the bodies, many of which were still alive and set it on fire. This was reminiscent of what our *Einsatzgruppe* did with the un-earthed corpses.

At the same time that the gas bomb exploded in the church, our men fired their machine guns into the men crowded in the barns. They deliberately fired low, so that many of the men were badly wounded but not killed. The soldiers then piled wood and straw on the bodies and set it on fire. Many of the men burned to death, unable to move because of their injuries. Six men did manage to escape from the barn, but one of them was seen and shot dead, the other 5 all wounded, got away under cover of darkness.

While these killings were taking place, the soldiers searched the town for any people who had evaded the initial roundup and killed them where they found them. One old invalid man was burned to death in his bed and a baby was baked to death in the local bakery oven. Other people were killed and their bodies thrown down a well. People who attempted to enter the town to see what was going on were shot dead.

After killing all the townspeople that could be found, we set the whole town on fire and early the next day, laden with valuables taken from the houses, we left.

Back in St. Junien, I began to catalog and organize the liberated items and to prepare it for transport back to Germany. Most of us didn't think of the items as being stolen. We believed that anything that could be used to help our cause was to be confiscated. These people did not realize that they would be much better under German rule than their pre-war situation. Many of us wondered why the French resisted so much.

August 23, 1944 proved to be one of the decisive days of the entire war. With the Russian tanks on the Prut River and more racing south for the Focsani gap in Romania, the fate of the entire German Army Group South was uncertain. What changed the fortune of Germany's entire southeastern theater was the coup carried out that day in Bucharest, when King Michael had the Antonescu brothers arrested and Romania ceased to fight alongside Germany.

Romanian troops were instructed to cease firing on the Red Army and King Michael surrendered unconditionally to the Allies. The Romanian defection turned Germany's military defeat into a catastrophe, which it felt far beyond the limits of a single Army Group. The remainder of two Romanian armies fighting with Army Group South Ukraine laid down their arms.

The Sixth German Army was being slowly strangled at Kishinev and was inside an encirclement ring. The whole of southern Bessarabia, the Danube delta, and the passes through the Carpathian Mountains lay wide open to the Red Army. Ahead of the Soviet armies lay the route to Bulgaria and Yugoslavia, and the collapse of our entire defensive system in the southeastern theater.

The Chief of our General Staff, General Guderian, went on a tour of the Eastern army headquarters. What he learned from them and from his own observations was so alarming that he decided to make one last appeal to Hitler. This time he appealed for both more troops and for permission to make a pre-emptive withdrawal, which would allow a thinly defended buffer of land to take the first shock of the Russian attack. Intelligence reports indicated that the Russians had accumulated such strength that it was no longer within the power of the *Wehrmacht* to stop them in their tracks. Our only hope was to duck at the last moment, then to fight a flexible battle across western Poland until exhaustion and the spring thaw would take the impetus out of the Russian advance.

When Guderian presented Hitler with the revised estimates of Russian strength, Hitler lost his temper and declared that they were completely idiotic and pure bluff. Hitler went on to order General Gehlen, who had drawn up the estimates, to be committed to an insane asylum. This Guderian managed to deflect, but he achieved little else.

At the close of the interview, Hitler told him, "The Eastern Front has never before possessed such a strong reserve as now."

On September 28, 1944 the division opened an attack to recapture seven hills in the Dnieper bend, which the Russians had captured. That same day the American First Army captured Calais France. Initially successful, our attacks drained strength from the division. Throughout the weeks that followed, our front lines were pulled farther and farther westward.

Army Group South was forced to give up Kiev on November 5th. This enabled the Russians to strike into the western Ukraine. They were now into territory and villages that our *Einsatzgruppe* had visited.

I wondered if they discovered any of our gravesites.

By December 10th, the battalions of Das Reich had almost bled to death. It was acknowledged that the division was no longer capable of carrying out the demands of a full strength division and orders were issued to create a battle group from units still fit for action. This group would stay on the Eastern Front while the remaining divisional elements returned to Germany. They were ordered to report to the Toulouse area in southern France. I received orders reassigning me there to help re-constitute the division.

Once again, *I wondered if Rolf had something to do with my transfer.*

On that fateful day, France and Russia signed a treaty of alliance in Moscow. December 16th through the 18th brought some good news as our forces had punched through the American lines to Bastogne in Belgium.

The success gave us some hope.

Nearly 9,000 replacements came in during our time in the Toulouse area. They were assigned to the depleted regiments. My job was to insure that all the new soldiers were fitted with uniforms, equipment, and weapons. The new men soon adopted the spirit of our elite Division and were ready for deployment.

The level of partisan operations had begun to increase, indicating that the events in France were reaching a crisis point. From May onwards there was a rise in the number of attacks on our soldiers. From May to June 1945, more than one hundred men of the Division were murdered or had been kidnapped and nearly as many had been wounded.

Soviet operations in late fall and early winter of 1944-1945, had cut away at the German strategic flanks and reached the Baltic coast and the Budapest region. The *Wehrmacht* forces sent to meet the crisis on the flanks were barely able to stem the Soviet surge. In less then two months, German defenses in Poland and East Prussia were disintegrated, and the Soviet forces advanced up to 700 kilometers to the west, to within 60 kilometers of Berlin. In the process, German Army Groups A and Center were decimated. After reinforcements were sent to the Oder front to defend Berlin, in February and March, the Soviets again struck the flanks, battering Army Group Vistula and consuming Army Group South, Germany's last strategic reserve.

By March 26, 1945 the Russians had crossed and established footholds on the west bank of the Oder River. At Hitler's insistence, on March 27th, the 9th German Army launched a four-division counterattack from *Frankfurt-am-Oder* northward toward Kustrin. The 20th and 25th Panzer-Grenadier Divisions, the *Führer* Escort Division, and the ad hoc Panzer Division *Munchenberg* caught the Soviets by surprise and advanced to the outskirts of Kustrin. The attack, however, rapidly lost momentum, and our forces were decimated in open terrain.

By mid-April, Soviet forces had reached the Oder-Neisse River line on a broad front from Stettin in the north to Gorlitz on the Czech border.

At 0730 on April 14, 1945, reinforced Russian rifle battalions began reconnaissance-in-force actions on main attack axes to Berlin. In other sectors, first-echelon regiments joined the attack. In two days of combat, some of the forces succeeded in wedging up to five kilometers deep into our defenses. The Soviet air offensive began on the evening of April 15th and the artillery complemented the air effort on April 16 with a furious 30-minute bombardment.

It took two days for the First Belorussian Front forces to penetrate the Seelow Heights defenses and achieve its initial objectives. Taking place around the town Seelow, about 60 miles east of Berlin, this fighting was some of the most intense of the war.

On April 20th, while the Russian Marshall Zhukov's forces continued their advance, long-range artillery rained the first artillery fire on Berlin.

I was really worried about Mother.

The following day, intermixed units penetrated into Berlin's suburbs and began days of difficult urban combat. As Allied forces linked up along the Elbe River, Soviet forces penetrated German defenses on the western bank of the Oder River and pinned down the Third Panzer Army, depriving it of the opportunity to deliver a counterblow from the north against Soviet forces encircling Berlin. This was the long-anticipated attack, which Hitler hoped in vain would save Berlin.

Now, even Hitler realized that the war was lost, although he continued to issue hopeless orders for the Ninth Army to the east and the Twelfth Army to the west and the already pinned down Third Army to break through to the capital. Lacking any effective command and control structure, the remnants of the *Wehrmacht* fought on in block-to-block battles and with fanatic resistance. On April 29th, Russian troops began the symbolic struggle for the Reichstag.

By April 30th, the Soviet forces had cut the defending German forces into four isolated pieces and began smashing them in piecemeal fashion.

That same day Hitler committed suicide.

We all cried when we heard the news. It was hard to believe that our Father was dead.

Surely, traitors had gotten to him.

Soviet forces captured the Reichstag building on May 1st and on the evening of May 2nd, German resistance had finally ceased and the Berlin garrison surrendered.

Chapter Seventeen
Collapse

As the war was ending, Germany was collapsing and chaos was everywhere. The immediate goal of every soldier was to escape the *Kettenhunde* (the guard dogs of the military police) or the roving courts martial of the SS. Few who were tried by the mobile SS courts survived. They were under strict orders to look out for deserters. Anyone who could not produce proper papers was hanged and left on the rope as a reminder to any potential deserters.

Burning oil trucks and automobiles lay on the sides of the roads. Everything, it seemed, was on fire.

Discipline fell apart.

No one saluted officers or afforded proper courtesy.

Everyone was out for themselves.

We heard a rumor about an organization that was helping SS officers get out of the country. We heard that a group of former SS officers went to Argentina and set up a Nazi fugitive network code-named ODESSA, (an acronym for *Organisation der ehemaligen SS-Angehörigen*, "Organization of the former SS members"), with ties in Germany, Switzerland, Italy, and the Vatican, operating out of Buenos Aires. ODESSA allegedly helped Adolf Eichmann, Josef Mengele, Erich Priebke, Erwin, Hans Wolfe and many others find postwar refuge. They were providing false documents and transit to South America or to China.

The situation was desperate everywhere!

I received a telegram from Rolf, who was still in Berlin. It was the last message I was to receive from him.He and some of the other *Einsatzgruppen* officers were leaving Berlin and heading west. They did not want to be captured by the Russians. He said that the Russians had reached the eastern suburbs of Berlin and while the SS forces defending the city were fighting valiantly, it was only a matter of time until they captured the city.

Rolf's parents had decided to leave for Berchtesgaden in the Bavarian Alps. There was rumor that some members of the government would move the government there and fight in the mountains.

I kept thinking about my mother.

If only she was not so stubborn she could be in Rothenburg with Anna and Little Rolf.

I had not heard from Anna in months and *I wondered how she was doing.*

Coming within sight of the River Meus, *the Das Reich* Division was halted, and then slowly smashed by fierce Allied counter-attacks. Pulled out of the offensive, we were transferred into Germany to again refit, and then to take part in the last German offensive of the war in Hungary to attempt to break the siege around Budapest. This offensive also ground to a halt, and Das Reich spent the rest of the war more-or-less fighting in parts from Dresden, to Prague, to Vienna. In the end, most of us managed to escape to the West to surrender to the Americans.

Ultimately there was nowhere else to go and the various Das Reich units, which were now widely distributed in the field, were forced to surrender one by one. Those elements in Czechoslovakia were lucky enough to surrender to the Americans. The Russians were capturing much of the country.

I found my way to the Der *Führer* Regiment under Lieutenant Colonial Otto Weidinger, where we surrendered on April 20, 1945 with what dignity we had left in regimental march formation just outside Pilzen in Czechoslovakia. On May 9, 1945 all hostilities in Europe officially terminated as our surrender became effective.

By this time, I was a physical wreck. I had lost considerable weight and my hands wouldn't stop shaking.

The officers and enlisted soldiers were separated near the village. Each of us was questioned thoroughly. The Allies were looking for anyone who was involved in mass-killings or torture. I told my interrogator that I had been temporarily assigned to the eastern front as a logistics officer with *Einsatzgruppen D*.

I was transported in the back of a crowded truck to the prison at Nuremberg. I didn't know anyone in the cells around me. We were taken from our cells daily an interrogated by American officers. They would continually ask about mass-killings and torture. I continued to maintain that I knew nothing of such things.

After about three weeks, I began to hear gun shots coming from the prison courtyard. I could only imagine that the interrogators had found someone guilty of the things they were looking for. I never did know for sure what the gun shots were all about.

I was appointed a defense attorney, Major Parker, who would visit me every morning before the interrogations. He accompanied me during the sessions. Major Parker was a likable fellow and spoke perfect German. He told me that he was raised in Munich and moved to the United States with his family before the war.

Slowly I started to regain my health. The food was adequate and I was permitted to exercise daily in the courtyard. My hands still shook though.

It took a month before I was called before a tribunal of American officers. One read a document charging me with compliancy in the murder of over 70,000 people.

I sat there, without emotion, as the places we visited and the deeds we conducted were read. After a short while, I realized that they were reading from my reports. I remember

Rolf saying that our reports would probably get us all hanged.

After the charges were read the senior officer asked me to plead guilty or not guilty. I almost said guilty but thought, *these people didn't understand why it was necessary to do what we did.*

I said, "No, I am not guilty as charged."

My defense attorney told me that I stood a good chance of getting several years in prison, instead of being hanged. It appears that the court had Rolf's personal records, which stated repeatedly that I had never killed anyone. I had only been concerned with supplies and shipping captured goods back to Germany. The records even recorded the times when I protested to Rolf about Erwin's actions. As it turned out, those records saved my life. The records contained no account of me actually shooting anyone.

Rolf had saved my life.

Ironically, I was sentenced to five years in the Landsberg prison. I remembered visiting there in 1938 when delegations of the Hitler Youth organizations from all over Germany staged loyalty marches to Landsberg. In Landsberg, the boys of the Hitler Youth delegations were given tours of the Hitler Cell's in the prison, were handed a copy of Mein Kampfe, and participated in loyalty demonstrations in the central square of Landsberg which was decked out with acres of swastika flags and Hitler Youth banners.

Chapter Eighteen
After the War

The prison housed 110 persons convicted during the Nuremberg trials, 1,416 war criminals from the Dachau trials, and 18 from the Shanghai, China trials.

I was permitted to write a letter to Anna and tell her of my situation. As time went on, I was permitted to receive mail from her and write from prison, although all mail was read by American intelligence officers. I would not be allowed any visitors while in prison. It was through her censored letters that I found out what was happening in the world.

Communication was very difficult during the several months after the war ended. Masses of people were on the move. Many people were starving and thieves were dealt with severely.

I was in prison for about four months when Anna wrote to tell me that Mother was killed by the Russians. Heir Schmitz wrote to Uncle Frederick that the Russians wanted to use our apartment building to billet their troops. They ordered all of the occupants to leave. When Mother refused to leave and began berating a Russian officer, he shot her.

She was defiant to the end!

I took the news of her death very hard. I wondered what else the sub-humans would do to our people. It was only later that I found out that the Russians had destroyed Berlin.

Anna wrote about the results of the Nuremburg Trials. Colonial Ohlendorf and all of the senior *Einsatzgruppen* were executed, as was Rolf. Many of our members had vanished with no trace. I knew this had to be the work of ODESSA.

I had prepared myself for the news of his death but, it was still hard.

Rolf had been a true friend and leader.

Even at the very end he took care of his friends. From our days in the *Jungvolk*, he took care of his squad. Rolf represented what being a German soldier was all about.

As the years went by, I thought a lot about Rolf and Guenther and what we tried to do for Germany. The bad memories faded.

Anna and I continued to write weekly, planning what we would do after I was released. We discussed moving back to Berlin and even moving to America. The Russians now occupied our old neighborhood.

We ruled out Berlin.

Our decision was made for us when Uncle Frederick got sick and made Anna promise to keep the shop running in Rothenburg. He had provided to us in his will the shop and a considerable sum of money. He died one year before I was released.

Little Rolf was getting bigger and helping in the shop. He kept asking about me. Anna was always the epitome of the Third Reich Woman. She believed, as I did, that what we did was right. She told Rolf that I was being punished for trying to save Germany.

Later, he would come to a different conclusion.

Life at Landsberg prison wasn't that bad. The portion of the complex that I was in was minimum security on the opposite side of the complex from the cell where Adolf Hitler wrote Mein Kampf. My American guards were never far away but gave me plenty of space. The food was actually good by most standards of the time.

I wasn't too bad off.

I could roam around the grounds, and as the years went by I tended a garden and worked on wood crafts.

I especially liked to grow daisies.

Slowly, my hands stopped shaking.

As time passed in prison, I slowly began to force the horror of the war to the back of my mind.

I decided that what ever else had happened. I was going to put the war behind me and try to live the rest of my life in peace.

Finally, in the spring of 1950, the day came to be released. I was thirty years old but I felt like I was fifty. I hadn't seen Anna in over six years. I wrote her not to come to the prison. I didn't want Rolf to see me come out of that place. I processed out and used the money they gave me to buy a train ticket to Nuremburg and then to Rothenburg.

Anna and Rolf were at the station. She looked as beautiful as always. The long flowing blond hair and blue eyes is what I had kept in my mind all of those years. There were streaks of grey in my hair.

Rolf didn't know how to act. I was a stranger to him. He was eight years old and didn't know me.

We all got reacquainted and ran the shop, growing vegetables and herbs and minding our own business.

I considered myself lucky, since most of the men I served with in the *Einsatzgruppen* were either dead or on the run in South America.

In the middle ages, Rothenburg was Germany's second-largest city, with a population of 6,000. The population hadn't changed much since then. The old town is situated atop a sharp, steep bend in the Tauber River. The walls followed the cliffs on the inside of the bend, while on the opposite side there is an inner and an outer wall, separated in some places by a now-dry moat. Numerous tall towers dot both the inner and outer walls, many of them being decorated by a clock and beautiful archway.

I could see why Uncle Frederick liked the city so much.

As it turned out, the United States Army Air Corps bombed the city railway yards, of limited military value, during the waning days of the war, which resulted in damage also to the historic old city walls. The local military commander

Major Thömmes gave up the town, thereby saving it from total destruction by artillery. About 40 percent of the town was destroyed, although not the truly old historic part, where Uncle Fredrick's shop was located, and in the center.

After the war, the residents of the city quickly repaired the bombing damage. By the time I arrived there, there was no evidence of damage.

We had a very happy life in Rothenburg. The business and the inheritance from Uncle Frederick allowed us to live comfortably. We had enough money to go on holiday to Italy and Greece every year. The memories of the war faded with time and with the help of the West, Germany prospered. Rothenberg was about 5 kilometers from the East German border. We never went any further East because I knew that if the Russians ever captured me, I would disappear.

The *Einsatzgruppen* members captured by the Russians disappeared. They were taken to Russia and never returned. I suspect they were all shot or even worse, worked to death in the Russian Gulag system. Even if they were looking, we doubted if they would look so close to the border. And, after all, I was on record for serving my time in prison and the Russians and the Americans were busy with the Cold War.

I kept telling myself, *there was no time to look for old Nazis!*

Uncle Frederick had thought ahead and willed the shop to Anna, using her maiden name. So, my name didn't appear on any documents. After I was released from prison, we formed a corporation which owned the business. If anyone was looking, they would have to peel back several layers to find me. My name was in the *Einsatzgruppen* records but one had to look hard to make the connection. Schultheiss was a common name in Germany and Anna's maiden name, Berger, was even more common.

Rolf was about sixteen years old when he began asking questions about what I had done during the war. I told him that I was part of the rear guard, looking for partisans and saboteurs. I decided to tell him everything we had done.

At first he seemed very proud of me. Anna had told him that I was a national hero. We didn't talk too much about the war. We were all busy with our lives and the business. Rolf expressed an interest in accounting so we sent him to Nuremburg University.

He met a girl while in his third year at university and came home one day to tell us that he was getting married. His future wife, Gisela, was an ardent anti-Nazi and was very cool towards Anna and me. I suspect that Rolf told her that I was some sort of war hero.

After university, Rolf got a job in Nuremburg as an accountant. They would visit but, after a while, Gisela would stay home and Rolf would come alone.

The bright spot of our relationship came when they had a child. Anna and I were looking forward to a grandchild that we could spoil. Rolf would bring Leni and spend the weekend with us until she was about six years old. Then, he would bring her and leave, returning on Sunday to take her back home.

Gisela stopped coming at all and Rolf would talk less. We could tell that Gisela was having an effect on Rolf.

Leni would play in the sandbox I constructed for her in the back yard while Anna attended her herb garden.

One of the saddest days of my life came when Anna passed away. She didn't wake from her sleep. A heart attack said the doctor. He was convinced she felt no pain. She was my life-long friend and companion. We had survived the war and had enjoyed a good life together.

Everyone was gone now!

Rolf and I where becoming estranged.

Only Leni looked up to me and enjoyed coming to visit. As she was growing up, I tried to instill patience and understanding of other people. I told her we must be tolerant of other's views and religions. The older I got, the more I came to examine and question the things we had done during the war.

Maybe it is the destiny of old soldiers to wish that war did not happen again and to question the part they had played in their war.

I remembered the suffering, especially of the children.

Was Rolf right?

Would they just grow up and hate us for killing their parents?

Did they too have to be killed?

Was that the way it had to be?

When Leni was about sixteen, she asked me what I had done during the war. Determined not to make the same mistake as I had made with Rolf, I simply told her of my involvement with the 2nd SS Division. I purposely didn't mention anything about the *Einsatzgruppen*.

Very few people knew of our group and less knew what we had done. Our actions where somehow blurred with the greater army's actions in the eastern territories. The casual reader of history would have attributed our actions to the army. One had to dig deeper to find us. We were all sworn to secrecy and most of the former officers were dead. Most of the people we encountered in those villages were dead too. I decided not to tell Leni about our group. There were records, but most Germans just wanted to forget the past.

Chapter Nineteen
Tormented

I poured another glass of scotch. It was dark outside by now. All of the tourists had left and the streets were deserted. Old Franz, who helped me in the shop, closed and went home. It was only me in the room with a glass of scotch, my thoughts of the past, and Anna's Luger.

We had become professional killers. Mass murder had become routine. Normality itself had become exceedingly abnormal.

I recounted how every dead Jew gave up not only his life but also his watch, fountain pen, jewelry, clothing, shoes, gold teeth and fillings. Not unlike collecting scrap metal or paper in the *Jungvolk*; did this not have to be done for the nation?

No possessions were too extensive or too meager to be overlooked. Everything from houses, factories and automobiles down to the last pair of shoes was stripped from the Jew. Like the election returns, the reports of our actions poured into headquarters.

Our duty was to follow our army through Bessarabia and the Crimean peninsula, carrying out the orders of our Father and master, Adolf Hitler.

The Jew's partisan activities posed a continuous danger for the German occupation troops. Moreover, they could some day attack Germany proper, and self-preservation dictated their destruction before they began an aggressive march on Berlin.

A permanent security had to be achieved. For that reason, the children were people who would grow up and surely being the children of parents who had been killed, they would constitute a danger no smaller than that of the parents.

If our military offensive against Russia was ultimately a failure, surely our action against the Jew was not.

Were these things not true?

I kept thinking *could we all have been so wrong?*

Where Rolf and his parents wrong?

Even Father came to believe we were heroes.

Guenther was the true hero. He died in battle!

Were we all wrong?

Did we just not see what was happening to us and our generation?

Hitler had turned the economy around and created jobs. I had seen with my own eyes how the Jews and Bolsheviks in the Ukraine lived. They were sub-human, weren't they?

They lived with lice and filth.

If what we were taught was a lie, then our entire generation fell for it. Only my mother thought the Nazis were wrong. She never wavered, even to the end. Hers was the only voice of dissent I heard and I had rejected it.

We were cheered in the streets and told by everyone that we represented the new Germany, the Third Reich, and a Reich that would live a thousand years!

How could so many people have been wrong?

That seemed so long ago and now, we were all killers to the new Germany.

How things had changed, or had they?

The children of the new Germany are taught to reject the past and to reject us. Yet, the Neo-Nazi and other similar movements continue to gain strength.

I have been tormented by these questions since the war. A gnawing sense of waste, of lives squandered, of youth lost take over my thoughts. Yet, I still felt the sense of duty and honor learned in the Hitler Youth and in the SS.

In the fire I saw images of death and destruction along side images of ceremonies, parades, and campfires.

The images blended.

In an almost mystical way that someone who had not experienced it could never understand, the war formed men.

It formed me.

It was the great test, a hard but valuable school that also taught the true worth of people. In creating our intense loyalty to the German national community, the Nazis also laid the foundations for an equally fervent hatred and distain for those who did not belong.

These were the things, the ideas that created us.

We fought against Asiatic barbarism, against Jewish-Bolshevik conspiracy, and in defense of German culture.

We fought for Nazism and everything that it stood for.

Armed with ideological instruction, racial indoctrination, and a sense of absolute obedience to the *Führer*, we were highly motivated. We rounded up and killed Jews, Bolsheviks, Gypsies, and others, believing that we were performing our duty for the German people and for Adolf Hitler.

Amid the despair of our retreat, affection for those of us enduring the same horrors created a sense of unity and pride. We felt an intensity that rose to a level rarely achieved by mere friendship. Loyalty, mutual obligation, a willingness to sacrifice, pride and a sense of duty constituted comradeship for those of us who had grown up in the Hitler Youth and served in the SS.

The spirit of comradeship bound us together. A sense of belonging was created. To the intense pleasure in belonging was added the sense of participating in a shared belief that we were doing the right thing for our nation and for Hitler. The very intensity of our suffering welded us together in a community without parallel in civilian life.

Every soldier knew very well what fear and terror confronted his comrades, because he felt them himself, and all understood that it was essential to share this burden with friends rather than bear it alone. One simply could not leave a comrade to face the uncertainties and horrors of battle alone.

If only I could get Leni to understand these things.

If only I could get her to know what it was like then.

I picked up the gun and once again placed it to my temple. Just then, there was a knock at the door. I couldn't face anyone.

It was over!

I closed my eyes and started to squeeze the trigger.

"Papa, it's Leni," she called from outside.

"Let's talk. I want to hear your story Papa..."

Her voice startled me!

As the sound of the gunshot reverberated around the room, shadows of award ceremonies, camp fires, and thousands of Jewish faces danced in the flames of the fire.

Epilogue

Clearly, the *Einsatzgruppen* record is one of brutality and devastation. Beginning with the *Jungvolk* and later in public school, the youth who would become its members were taught to view Jews, Slavs, Partisans, and Bolsheviks as threats to the German people. They viewed these people as sub-human and through indoctrination and training developed a special motivation to conduct violence. This special motivation not only enabled them to kill, it enabled them to carry out cruel and bestial acts on their victims. The Nazi propaganda the *Einsatzgruppen* members had been exposed to clearly coached that the Jews, Slavs, Partisans, and Bolsheviks would bring destruction to the German way of life and to the Aryan race, if not eliminated. Advanced through a process, which began with singing songs around a campfire, and ending with violent and horrific acts, many German youth would do anything for Hitler.

In addition to their training, many issues faced the German soldiers as they moved into the eastern countries. The primitive living conditions of the average peasant and the seemingly endless numbers of non-European races impressed upon the Germans their own sense of cultural and ethnic superiority. The German boys, turned SS officers, were psychologically unprepared for what awaited them in the villages and towns of Russia and Poland. One day they may hear, that all of the sub-humans must be relocated further east, especially Jews. Later they were told that the Jews must be eradicated, eliminated from potentially poisoning the pure German blood supply. They were deemed a biological threat to the German people. They were also told that not all Russians were Communists, and that the German crusade was established to free the Russians from Bolshevism. At the same time, Russians were condemned for supporting the Bolsheviks while they were told the Jews supported and assisted the powers in Moscow.

We can see how the *Einsatzgruppen* grew out of a Germany that was economically crippled by World War I reparations, global depression and a national sense that the Jew was significantly to blame for their problems. Fostered by the ideals of National Socialism, the naivety of youth, the sense of pride and accomplishment that military service gave them, some German youth became fully indoctrinated into the beliefs of Adolph Hitler. They accepted Hitler's anti-Semitism by placing his desire to remove the Jews in the context of a wider theory of the struggle between races for living space. They accepted Hitler's view that the Jews, lacking a state of their own, were parasites trying to destroy those states, which had been established by superior races. They accepted that Bolshevism was a threat to the survival of Germany and to Europe. They believed their duty was to eliminate the threats. When one believes so strongly in his cause that he will do anything, then he truly develops a special motivation.

The attitude of the *Einsatzgruppen* can be summed up in a quote from *SS* General Otto Ohlendorf, commander of *Einsatzgruppen D*, during the Nuremburg Trials:

"The men, women, deeply excavated antitank ditches. Then they were shot, kneeling or standing, and the corpses thrown into the ditch. I never permitted the shooting by individuals in group D, but ordered that several of the men should shoot at

the same time in order to avoid direct personal responsibility."

Ohlendorf, like most of the *Einsatzgruppen*, expressed no remorse for his actions and was more concerned about the moral strain on those carrying out the executions than those actually being executed.

He went to the gallows believing he had done his duty for his country. He, like most of the *Einsatzgruppen*, had a developed a special motivation to carry out their work.

We will probably never know how many former Hitler Youth, like Kurt, were struggling with what they had done.

Perhaps, they still believe.

If there is a lesson in this story, perhaps it is that when people believe so completely and so strongly in a cause, they will stop at nothing to achieve their goals. We must be always vigilant of extremist and those who would profess to make the next new world.

Made in the USA
Charleston, SC
06 October 2012